THE STARLIGHT WITCH

WITCHES OF NEW YORK
BOOK 1

KIM RICHARDSON

KR PUBLISHING

The Starlight Witch, Witches of New York, Book One
Copyright © 2022 by Kim Richardson
Cover designer: Karen Dimmick/ArcaneCovers.com

www.kimrichardsonbooks.com

THE STARLIGHT WITCH

WITCHES OF NEW YORK

BOOK 1

KIM RICHARDSON

KR PUBLISHING

CHAPTER 1

I stood in the doorway, staring at my husband's naked body with his prominent, hard manhood. The voluptuous pretty brunette who climbed off him had guilt etching her face like she'd been caught stealing from the homeless. With her full cheeks and flawless skin, she appeared to be in her twenties, around half my age, with perky breasts and a tight body. She had no evidence of cellulite on her, either, but don't worry. It'll come.

"Leana? What? What are you doing here? You're back early," stuttered my husband. He covered his penis with the bedsheet made of Egyptian cotton, the ones I'd bought, not that it mattered. And not like I hadn't seen his tiny jolly stick for the last fifteen years. He wasn't much to look at, just a lanky body, balding head, and creeping beer gut.

Yet none of those things would've mattered if he had been kind.

We'd married young, both of us in our mid-twenties, and our marriage had never been perfect. From the beginning, I saw signs of his temper and narcissistic ways, but I chose to ignore them, thinking that's what good wives did. She soldiers on, right?

The last two years had been rocky, and this past year was a total mistake. I should have called it quits years ago, but I'd been lazy. Part of me had been afraid of finding myself single again at forty-one, after all these years of being with someone—even if that someone was all wrong for me.

But not anymore.

I'd been faithful. At the very least, Martin could have done the same until we'd both declared it officially over.

This past year, I'd had my suspicions that he was cheating: the late phone calls, leaving the room to speak on the phone with his so-called boss, and the late-night office hours, when he never came home until the early morning.

I couldn't blame only him for the marriage falling apart. First of all, he was human. I was a witch. That there should have been my red flag from the beginning. I couldn't be totally honest with him about who I was. He could never understand me or the paranormal world I worked in. Without honesty, the marriage was doomed to fail from the beginning, and that was on me.

Yet it was fun to see him squirm a little.

I crossed my arms over my chest, playing it out. "So, this is the child you've been banging?"

The brunette made a face. "I'm not a *child*. I'm twenty-three."

I raised my brows. "The response of a child."

"You're a bitch," snapped the naked brunette. "You're not even that good-looking. You're all old and saggy. You probably smell. Everyone knows old people smell."

"Shut up, Crystal," hissed my husband. His green eyes met mine, and he blew out a breath. "We haven't had sex in over a year. What did you expect? All men have needs."

I snorted. "Really? You're going to try and guilt me for your cheating?" I broke into a laugh I couldn't hold back. And once it started, I couldn't stop. All the emotions from the last year and the years before started pouring out of me until I was holding on to the doorframe for support.

"What's so funny?" growled my soon-to-be ex-husband.

I wiped my eyes. "You. This. This whole thing is like a bad joke. Or is it a *good* joke? I don't even know." I looked at the brunette, who was purposely keeping her body uncovered with a defiant look in her eye.

She might have a better, younger rack than me, but that was nothing to the wisdom built of my life experiences.

"I hope you like to clean, do laundry, and cook," I told her. "Don't expect him to lift a finger either. Oh, he might for the first few months, but then he'll stop. Then he'll get angry with you if you ask for some help. Reverse psychology at its finest. Best be prepared."

Crystal gave me an insolent smile. "I don't do housewife."

I gave a short laugh. "Good luck with that. You might want to start looking for your pacifier."

"You were always such a bitch," said my husband. He leaned back, leaving the sheet where it was and giving us a view of his man twinkie again. "You always thought you were better than me. No wonder I went looking elsewhere. And you got fat."

My smile fell as Crystal gave a fake laugh. "That's what happens when you're old," said the slut in my bed.

Forty-one wasn't old, not by any standards. In fact, I felt like I'd finally figured out who I was and what I wanted with my life. I felt comfortable in my skin for the first time, accepting all my flaws and owning them.

After many years of hard work and dedication to my craft, I was finally coming into my own as a witch, harnessing my magic and understanding it. But my magic wasn't connected to Earth's elemental magic like the White witches, nor was its power channeled by borrowing it from demons as it was with most Dark witches. No, my power lay else-where. Granted, it was more potent at night, which stood out among witches. But that didn't mean I couldn't draw on it now.

It would be weak. But I only needed a little.

I'd never told Martin what I was. He had no clue.

I'd never had much of a reason to. Not until this very moment.

"You know, Martin," I said, smiling. "I never told you this, but I'm a witch." I tapped into my will and channeled the energy that went way beyond the boundaries of the earth. It was faint, but I felt a ribbon of power churning in my core. I held it there.

Both Martin and Crystal started to laugh as expected.

"And as humans, you can't see magic, just like you can't see the paranormal around you."

"She's fucking crazy." Martin laughed harder, and Crystal joined him.

"I'd like to give you this parting gift," I told them after their laughter had subsided.

Martin watched me with clear amusement. "What?"

I flicked a finger, and a slip of brilliant white light sprang from my hand and crossed the room to hover above his penis.

I matched his smile, pulled on my magic, and said, "This—"

My husband let out a girlish wail of pain and terror as he stared at his penis, the tip bent at a ninety-degree angle like a broken candle. *Whoops.*

Crystal flew off the bed like she thought his broken penis was contagious, her eyes wide as she backed into the wall.

As the wailing heightened in pitch, I strolled into the walk-in closet, grabbed my carry-on bag, stuffed it with as many clothes as possible, and made my way out.

"What did you do to me? You crazy bitch! You fucking whore!" howled my husband.

When I reached the bedroom's doorway, I turned around, seeing my husband red-faced with tears streaming down his cheeks. It was a good look on him.

I shot him a finger gun. "Keep it up. What? Too soon?" I couldn't help myself. He was kinda asking for it.

"You bitch," he wheezed, tears flowing freely down his face as he stared at his man-twig, which had nearly doubled in size and had taken on a purple color, kind of like an eggplant. Was that supposed to happen? Who knows.

"She broke his penis!" cried Crystal to someone on the other end of her cell phone. "She's a witch! And she broke it!"

Yeah, no one was going to believe that. The witch part, I mean.

I pulled my attention back to my husband. "Consider this a divorce."

"You're dead!" he howled as I walked out and left the apartment. Maybe I'd gone too far. Conjuring magic before humans was forbidden. But it was too late for that. Plus, I doubted anyone would believe them if they blabbed.

A strange weight lifted from my shoulders as I hit Greenwich Avenue and turned north, the cool September air soothing my hot cheeks. My stomach rumbled, reminding me I had forgotten to eat dinner. After the events of the past hour, dinner could wait, but wine couldn't. I needed a glass of wine.

I didn't feel any loss or even regret. Was that bad? Was I evil? Possibly. But he had pissed me off.

"God, why didn't I do this a long time ago?"

I paused at the street corner, waiting for the pedestrian light, and pulled the letter I'd received this morning by registered mail from my pocket. I'd read it a dozen times, but I wanted to reread it. Just to ensure I wasn't about to make a fool of myself. My eyes rolled over the letter as I read.

Dear Leana Fairchild,

I am pleased to extend an offer of employment on behalf of the Twilight Hotel. To officially acknowledge your acceptance of this offer, or if you would like more details, please present yourself to 444 5th Avenue no later than 7 p.m. We look forward to welcoming you aboard.

Sincerely,

Basil Hickinbottom

Management

Getting job offers wasn't unusual. I was a Merlin and had been for the last ten years. The Merlin Group stood for Magical Enforcement Response League Intelligence Network. We were the magical police, if you will, like the FBI.

I'd always told Martin that I worked the night shift at McGillis Pub, the local pub in Greenwich

Village. He'd never suspected anything untoward. Of course, that was because he couldn't have cared less.

I'd heard of the Twilight Hotel. Hell, every paranormal—witch, werewolf, shifter, or fae—knew of that hotel. But getting a job offer from them was unusual. I'd never worked for them. Ever. And I didn't know anyone who had either. From what I knew, they were secretive and didn't like to hire out, which explained the mountain of curiosity I felt at getting this job offer.

I checked my phone: 6:15 p.m. "Still got time."

I stuffed the letter back in my pocket, hauled my bag up on my shoulder, and continued.

My blood pressure rose with excitement. Martin's broken-penis episode was forgotten as I only had room for one thought in my brain. Every hired witch knew the Twilight Hotel paid well. Maybe I could finally afford a car. Wouldn't that be something?

Maybe things were finally looking up for me—

My face smacked right into a wall.

A wall that smelled of musk and spices. It was a pleasant smell. I stepped back and blinked into the face of a handsome man with a square jaw and straight nose, the owner of the man chest I'd just assaulted with my face. Dark wavy hair brushed his broad shoulders, graying at the temples, which only made him more attractive. He was tall, the kind of tall that you had to let your head fall back to get a view. And it was quite the view.

He was hot. And he looked like he needed that glass of wine more than I did.

His eyes were dark and burned with a kind of intensity that had my insides churning. I kinda liked it too.

He wasn't human either. That part was clear from the rolling paranormal energy emitting from him. Big and strong like he was, no doubt this hot man-beast was a were. My money was on a werewolf.

"Watch where you're going," he growled, practically screamed, glaring at me like I was the most hated person in all of New York City.

Not so hot anymore.

I narrowed my eyes. "I would if you didn't take up so much space, *Wall*." He might have been built like a truck, which was how it had felt walking face-first into his chest, and maybe twenty years ago, I would have ducked my head and walked away. But I didn't. Life had made me hard.

And I'd broken a penis today. Go me!

The stranger glared at me, clearly not used to being challenged. Built the way he was, I was certain no one ever talked back. More than likely they cowered away. "The streets don't belong to you," he snarled.

"Don't belong to you either." If he was expecting an apology, he was going to wait a while. I was done apologizing in my life.

The hot man-beast watched me for a beat longer. "*You* crashed into *me*. You weren't paying attention to where you were going."

"Then you should have moved out of the way." I could do this all night. Well, not really. I had to go if I wanted that job. "And why didn't you? If you saw me coming, the gallant thing to do would be to step aside."

His nostrils flared with anger. "Why should I move for you?" He said it like the mere fact that he was standing there meant something to me, like he was someone I should know, someone of great importance.

As far as I knew, he was a rude, sexy man-beast. That was all.

"Clearly, you left your manners at home this morning," I told him. I refused to stare at his full, sensuous lips. Too late. I was staring. Damn. Those were some hot lips to go with the rest of his hot bod.

"You always walk around with your head in the clouds? That's how you get killed. That's how you get hit by a car."

I cocked a brow. "Problem solved. Right?" So why was he still here? Why wasn't he moving away from me?

The stranger watched me, his gaze intense. "You shouldn't be walking around here if you don't know where you're going."

I snorted. "Yeah. I don't need your permission, buddy. I'm late for an interview. Out of my way, *Wall*."

Confusion flashed in those damn fine eyes. He blinked and then walked away. My eyes, moving of their own volition, followed his fine behind until he disappeared through a multitude of humans meandering along the streets of Manhattan. Not one had any idea a werewolf walked among them—a hot, grumpy one. Yet I noticed how the humans moved away from him. They had no clue what he was, but even they could feel the ferocious, wild, and commanding energy emitting from him. He had an alpha vibe too. And I hoped never to see him again. Next time, I might not be so polite.

I let out a long sigh and started moving again, irritation fluttering through me. My body was burning up, like I'd had a sudden hot flash. Not exactly the composed, professional manner I wanted to present for the interview. I was probably red-faced. I'd look like I was nervous, which I was, but I didn't want management to know.

Damn the hot werewolf and his hot ass.

Just as I crossed East Thirty-Ninth Street, I took a few more steps and came face-to-face with 444 Fifth Avenue.

The large limestone façade had sandstone trim, and the design included deep roofs with dormers, terracotta spandrels, niches, balconies, and railings. It had a Gothic vibe, like something Dracula would have lived in, and I loved it. Above double glass doors were large, glowing white letters that read, THE TWILIGHT HOTEL. The main entrance had a double-height archway on Fifth Avenue. It was a glorious beast—all thirteen floors of it.

A soft shimmer fell over the building in a glittering spectrum of color. I recognized the glamour meant to keep any wandering humans from thinking they could get a room. To them, the building likely appeared as just a run-down, abandoned building or a building under construction—anything to make them move along and forget quickly.

My heart pounded against my chest, like a kid entering high school for the first time. I wiped my sweaty palms on my jeans before reaching for the handle.

It occurred to me then that I had no place to stay tonight or the nights after this one. Basically, I was homeless. All I had was the bag on my shoulder. I'd figure something out. I always did. Besides, things weren't so bad.

"Broke a penis today," I muttered, proud of myself. "Nothing can beat that."

Or so I thought.

With bated breath, I pulled the door open and walked in.

CHAPTER 2

The doors opened into a foyer and a spacious lobby, with high ceilings, lots of glass, gray paint, and rich red accents. A shimmer of sheer material slid over me, and I felt the familiar pulsing magic of a protection ward. Creating wards took some serious magic. Not all witches or wizards could create them, let alone such complex ones with so much power they protected an entire building.

The area was illuminated with soft light and had all the usual scents of a human hotel: air freshener and too many perfumes and colognes mixed together. Modern gray couches and chairs were placed throughout the space in designated seating areas. The only difference was the cold sharpness of paranormal energy.

The hair on the back of my neck prickled as I felt eyes on me. I looked over to find groups of people, paranormals, all watching me from their seats with curious expressions.

Adrenaline immediately spiked through my body.

A black-haired male witch was showing off his magic as his phone hovered and spun above the table while a redheaded female clapped enthusiastically. A band of older witches sat in the far corner with white and gray hair spilling out of their dark cowls, their knobby fingers wrapped around their drinks. Dark witches? Probably.

As I walked, a tall, blonde female in a leather jacket flared her nostrils as she sniffed me. Werewolf, if the scent of wet dog was any indication.

I passed a group of trolls gulping down pints. A cluster of male and female paranormals sat around a table topped with glasses filled with dark maroon liquid, which I seriously doubted was wine. Their unnatural good looks stood out among the other paranormals. Vampires. Everything was a blur of black eyes, pointed teeth, and fine clothing. Their faces were lovely yet feral. They whispered among themselves, and I didn't like how they were pointing and staring at me like they were wondering how my blood tasted.

I felt a spike in my blood pressure as I forced myself to keep my pace even, which was more of an I'll-whip-your-ass-if-you-get-too-close kind of saunter. No way in hell would I show these vampires the effect they had on me. Besides, I didn't want to cause a scene or call unwanted attention to myself in this hotel.

The Twilight Hotel catered to *all* paranormals. No

matter whether a Dark witch, vampire, troll, or some renegade werewolf, the hotel would grant refuge or lodgings, whichever was essential at the moment.

Part of me felt like an imposter, like I didn't belong here, and this was a huge mistake. Maybe the hotel had gotten me confused with someone else? With my luck, anything was possible.

A pale man with black hair stood behind a counter at the end of the lobby, typing on a tablet. My gut fluttered with nerves, and I strained myself to walk with confidence as I made my way toward the gleaming granite check-in counter. I didn't know why I was so nervous. This wasn't my first gig.

I took out my letter, smoothed it on the gleaming marble counter, and then dropped my hands behind it to hide my trembling fingers. "Hi. I'm here to see Basil." I'd already forgotten his last name. I glimpsed at the letter. "Basil Hickinbottom."

The man wore a fitted, expensive, dark gray, three-piece suit. The word CONCIERGE was pinned on the front of his jacket. Up close, his pale skin was practically translucent, and I could make out blue veins on his thin hands as he typed. He was slim and about a head shorter than me, and I could sense the paranormal energies coming off him. He looked around my age, but it was hard to tell when it came to paranormals. He could be in his forties just as easily as he could be in his seventies.

The concierge kept typing on his tablet and never looked up. "You must check in all weapons and all magical objects relating to weapons," he said in a drone-like voice. The slight flick of a gray tongue told me he was a shifter, possibly a lizard.

"Sure. I'm not carrying any weapons."

The concierge gave an exasperated sigh. His light eyes finally rolled over me and landed on my bag. "Did you not hear me? Do you not speak English? Shall I spell it for you? *No* weapons are allowed. Hotel rules." He then pointed to an A-frame floor sign next to the counter that read, NO WEAPONS ALLOWED—MAGICAL OR NONMAGICAL.

I narrowed my eyes. He was an annoying little bastard, but I wouldn't let him rattle me. I wasn't about to screw this up. "I told you. I'm not carrying any weapons—magical or otherwise. You can frisk me if you like," I added with a smile and raised my arms.

The concierge wore a frown on his face, the kind that seemed permanently etched into the folds of his skin like he'd used it so often that it was his only expression. "So what's in the bag?"

"My clothes."

"Why? Are you going on a vacation?"

I wasn't about to blab my personal life to a rude stranger. "I'm here about a job. I was asked to come here by management. To see Basil. I have a letter." I smoothed out my letter again.

In a blur, the concierge snatched my letter from me faster than I thought possible. "Hmmm." His eyes moved over my letter. "So, what kind of witch are you? Are you a White or Dark witch?"

Here it comes. "Neither."

The concierge gave me a pointed look and dropped my letter. "You can't be a witch without being a White or Dark witch."

I sighed. "I can."

The concierge snorted. "Maybe you're not a witch. Maybe you're just a loser fae who'll do anything to get inside the Twilight Hotel. That's it. Isn't it? Well, I've got news for you. We don't let the trash in. Get out, or I'll have you thrown out."

And here I thought my day was looking up. "I'm not going anywhere, and I don't have to explain myself to you." I snatched my letter back.

The concierge raised his brow. "And I don't have time to listen to stupid people."

"Really?" My anger flared.

"Really," challenged the concierge.

"What's going on here?" came a voice behind me.

I spun my back against the counter to see a tiny man with a tuft of white hair and a matching white beard. Round glasses sat on his nose, magnifying his eyes abnormally to make him look like an owl. His black suit was a stark contrast to his white skin, and he looked like a miniature version of Santa Claus in a suit, with the no-nonsense stare of a man who could see through any bullshit. The tag on his jacket read MANAGEMENT.

"Basil?" I guessed. A familiar wave of energy hit me, sending a swirl of prickles along my skin. The scent of pine needles, wet earth, and leaves mixed with a wildflower meadow rose to meet me—the scent of White witches.

When he gave a slight nod, I added, "I'm Leana Fairchild. I'm here about a job." My stomach twisted again, and I struggled to keep my face from showing how nervous I was.

The hotel manager seemed to relax a little at the mention of my name. "You're the witch. The Merlin?"

"I am." I looked over my shoulder and smiled at the positively furious concierge. Then, I turned back to the manager and pulled my bag around to my front. "I have identification if you want to see."

Basil, the manager, clasped both hands in front of him. "That won't be necessary," he said. "You're hired."

My eyebrows rose. "Uh… okay, great. Thank you. Can you tell me a bit about the gig?" I'd never been hired this quickly before. It had to be a record.

Basil's eyes rounded as he looked over his shoulder, and then he leaned forward and said in a low voice, "We've had two murders at the hotel. You're here to investigate. To find those responsible."

"Okay."

"It's very bad for business, very bad. We don't want to alarm the guests." Basil looked around again, his shoulders tensing like he feared he was about to get jumped.

"Can you tell me about the murders?" When Basil's eyes bugged out more at the loudness of my voice, I lowered it and proceeded, "Who were the victims?"

"Both guests and no connection as far as we

know," answered Basil. He looked up and smiled at a passing couple whose exquisite looks labeled them as vampires. "But that's what you're here for." I saw the concierge lean in to listen. "We discovered the first body three weeks ago and the second last week. Second and fourth floors. Rooms two oh two and four oh four. The bodies have been removed, but we otherwise left the rooms untouched."

"How were they killed?"

Basil turned to the concierge. "Errol. Give her the file, please."

Errol gave the witch an annoyed stare. "I'm not a servant."

"The file, now," growled Basil. "Don't push me, Errol. Not today."

At first, I wasn't sure Errol would get the requested file, but he bent behind the counter, pulled out a folder, and threw it to me.

I caught the file. "Thanks, Errol." I smiled at him as he grimaced. "I have a feeling we're going to be *great* friends."

"I'd rather slit my wrists," snapped Errol.

I laughed as I opened the file. Inside, I found copies of invoices and the victims' personal information. My fingers stopped at the two photocopied pictures—one male, one female. Both were covered in blood with severe lashes all over their bodies. A large, gruesome gap lay just below the male's ribs.

"Looks like he's missing some organs."

The female was in her twenties and in great condition. Well, before she was killed. It was hard to tell what killed them by just looking at the pictures.

Basil leaned closer. "I must insist on your full discretion," he said and then gave a tight smile at an elderly man who walked past the counter, looking as though he was trying to eavesdrop. "This whole… situation is bad for business. We can't risk the guests finding out. We might face closing the hotel if they don't feel safe here."

"Seriously?"

"No one will want to stay at the hotel if they believe they'll be murdered in their sleep."

"Good point. What about the pay?" I'd learned from experience never to agree or start a job without proof of finance or a signed agreement.

Basil pulled out an envelope from inside his jacket. "Here. This is one week's pay. After that, you'll get the same amount each week until the case is solved."

I opened the envelope and counted one thousand in cash. "Okay. If I accept the job, is there a way I can get a room?" I realized I was at a disadvantage after breaking Martin's penis. I had nowhere to live. "It might come in handy to be so close." Partly true, but I really needed a place to stay for a while.

Basil nodded. "I have a vacant apartment on our residents' floor. You can stay there for the duration of the job."

Okay. One problem solved.

I watched as Basil walked behind the counter and grabbed something from a lower shelf. Then he walked back around and handed me a key with a green tag. "You're on the thirteenth floor. Apartment thirteen twelve."

"Thanks." I pocketed my new key.

"So? Are you going to take the job?" asked Basil. I heard Errol muttering something, though I couldn't catch what he said.

I folded the file and stuffed it under my arm. "Sure. Yes. Yes, I'll take it."

"Good. That's good." Basil let out a sigh and said, "Because we just found another body."

CHAPTER 3

I stared at the body of a male lying on the floor next to the shattered pieces of a wooden coffee table. He lay in a puddle of his own blood, guts, and bits of clothing. The gray that peppered his chestnut hair at the temples told me he was in his late forties. His shirt was a little too tight around the middle, and his pants a little too short. His body was in a fetal position, and from the grimace still visible on his face, I'd say he died in excruciating pain.

I let out a breath. "Who did this to you?"

I knelt next to him. Splatters of blood stained the light gray carpet, and more blood soaked into the carpet beneath his chest. The ceiling light reflected on his rib cage, and I could see teeth marks. Sharp enough to eat through bone... someone would have to have strong jaws to snap through bones like that. They'd have to be paranormal.

Gauging by the slashing and many other deep lacerations on the body, it looked like he died in the same manner as the other victims in the hotel. Without weapons allowed in the hotel, I could only conclude that the killer used something innate to them, like their claws or their teeth. It could also be a curse. I'd heard of some pretty dark curses that could mimic a traditional knife-type weapon that could rip your body to shreds.

And I needed to be sure if I wanted to solve the case or get ahead. To do that, I'd have to pull on my own magic.

It wasn't that my magic had to be kept secret. I just didn't have the patience anymore to explain how my magic was different. My mother and grand-mother warned me at a very young age to try and keep it private—not secret—to avoid the stares and the trouble that seemed to follow me because I was different. Even in the paranormal world, folks feared things they didn't understand or were foreign to them.

I looked over at the window, to the darkening deep-blue sky. I still had about two hours before sundown, so I couldn't tap into my entire well of magic, yet, only part of it.

But it might be enough for this.

I took a breath, tapped into my will, and chan-neled the emanations, the forces beyond the sky.

Immediately, I was hit by a cold, throbbing energy from the body, followed by a faint scent of sulfur and something else much darker and more sinister.

"You're a Dark witch or possibly a White witch," I muttered. He'd practiced magic here before he died.

That was clear. But I wasn't getting any clear signs of what kind of paranormal did this. Could be a crazed werewolf or a werebear. Whichever, it was extraordinarily strong to be able do that to a body and had also bypassed the Merlins' magic. What could do that?

I spotted blisters on his side through a hole in his shirt and more on his arm. He'd put up a fight. The room was trashed and looked like a bomb had hit it. Chairs and tables were overturned, while broken glasses and ceramic plates with food still in them lay scattered on the floor. Cool air seeped through a broken window over black scorch marks marring the light gray walls, and the pile of feathers, foam, and fabric that dotted the floor had been a couch at some point.

"I'm sorry you died like this." I was sad at the death of a witch in his prime. It only fueled my desire further to solve this case.

I checked his pockets but found nothing, not even his identification. Weird. Maybe Basil took it. I'd check with him later. I needed this dead witch's name to further my investigation. Did he know the other two victims? He died on the sixth floor, where the others were killed on the second and fourth floors. What was the connection? Why was he killed? Who was he?

It was clear whoever did this had knowledge of powerful magic.

I stood and yanked out my phone to start taking pictures.

"You the new Merlin?"

The voice snapped my head around, and I found a tall, handsome male leaning against the doorframe of room 601, which I distinctly remembered closing.

A snug black T-shirt revealed tight muscles and a fit body. He wasn't as thick and muscular as the rude man-beast I'd bumped into earlier, but he had more of an athletic build, like a swimmer. His light brown hair was cut short on the sides and longer on top, fashioned in a modern style. His handsome face was wearing a smug smile, the kind that knew he was easy on the eyes and was used to the admiration of warm-blooded females. And I swore I could see a twinkle in his eye.

"I am," I answered, wondering who the hell he was. I wasn't getting "killer" vibes from him, though. More like he was out on the prowl for some casual sex, but that didn't explain why he was here.

At my answer, the handsome male strolled into the room and came right up to me, way too close, in my personal space.

I frowned. "And you are?" I'd have to knee him in the junk if he got any closer.

I was assaulted by his nearness, the smell of his aftershave, and a hint of pine needles and earth. The guy was a White witch.

Hot-guy flashed me a smile that would have had a group of single ladies throwing their underwear at him. "Nice," he said, rolling his eyes over me. "Never thought Merlins could be so pretty."

Heat rushed from my neck to my scalp. I wasn't

immune to handsome faces. I just knew they were trouble that I should steer clear of. Besides, I had a job to do, and this guy was in my way.

I cleared my throat. "What are you doing here?" I didn't like that he wasn't bothered by the dead witch at our feet. Who the hell was this guy?

"You married?" he pressed. "No? Got a boyfriend? Girlfriend?"

"Leave her alone, Julian," said a second voice from the doorway.

I pulled my eyes away from the witch called Julian and spotted an older female strutting into the room. Again, uninvited. Again, not looking a bit traumatized by the dead guy at our feet.

She had a mess of red curly hair that brushed against her shoulders. Her tan, weathered face said she liked to spend time outdoors. Her blue eyes were lined with crow's-feet, and her thin lips were pressed into a tight line. She looked to be in her mid-sixties and wore a long denim skirt and garden clogs, with a long necklace and pendant over a green blouse that she'd folded back at the elbows.

She walked right up to us, stepping *on* and then over the dead witch. She blinked up at me and smiled. "I'm Elsa." She shoved Julian back forcefully away from me. I liked her immediately. "Don't mind him. He's just horny. Controlled by that thing between his legs. He's annoying but harmless." She pressed her hands on her hips as she studied me. Her cheeks lit up in a rosy hue as she flashed an infectious smile that was welcoming and felt almost like family.

Julian snorted. "Depends on what you define as harmless."

"Told you, annoying," repeated Elsa, her smile stretching.

"And she's the annoying widow who likes to keep her dead husband real close." Julian tapped his chest, eyeing the locket attached to the necklace around Elsa's neck.

On closer inspection, it wasn't a pendant but a vintage brass locket, a form of Victorian mourning jewelry. Yikes. Was that a piece of her dead husband? I knew some witches kept a lock of hair from their deceased partners. I'd just never met one in person.

Elsa rolled her eyes like this was nothing new or worthy of mention. "So, you're the new Merlin, eh?"

The same wave of energy I got from Julian hit me. She was a White witch too.

I felt myself relax a little. Clearly, these two were not here to slice my throat but more to be nosy. "Yes. I'm Leana." My gaze went from a smiling Elsa to a grinning Julian. "Why are you guys in here exactly? Did Basil send you?" Irritation flickered in my gut. Maybe the manager thought I'd need some help in the witching department.

"Basil? Goddess no," laughed Elsa. "We came to see if you needed our help."

"Right." I eyed them again. Elsa was toying with that locket around her fingers, and Julian was going through the dead witch's drawers, picking up his clothes, smelling them, and putting them back.

Part of me wanted to tell them to leave. But they were the prying types, and those types knew things. Right now, I was in the market for information.

"So?" Elsa rubbed her hands together. "What can we do to help?"

My eyes went to the dead witch. "From what I gather, Basil wants to keep this under wraps. So my question to you is, how did you know there was a dead body here?"

"Lisa told me," said Julian, walking back to join us.

At my questioning brow, Elsa added, "She's one of many hotel maids our boy here is sleeping with. Come to think of it. I think he's been with all of them."

I looked at Julian, and he flashed me a dazzling smile. "What? It's all consented."

Oh boy. But I couldn't help the smile that tugged at my lips.

"She found him this morning," continued Elsa. "Died in a puddle of his own blood."

Something occurred to me. "You call me the *new* Merlin. Was there a Merlin for hire before me?" I thought it strange that Basil would hire a stranger when the hotel had Merlins working for them. If he wanted to keep the deaths discreet, why hire an outsider?

"Yes," said the older witch. She grabbed her locket with her hand, her face wrinkled in thought.

"Eddie, something? Or was it Franky? I can't remember."

"Where is he, and why isn't he here?" I didn't like that Basil decided to keep that information from me. Maybe this other Merlin was on vacation. Either way, he should have told me.

Elsa gave a nod in the direction of the dead witch. "You're looking at him."

My mouth fell open. "You mean…"

"He's the dead guy," said Julian. "Poor bastard. I was going to help him hook up with Danielle. She's a guest on the second floor. Nice, shapely werefox."

I frowned as I looked at Eddie, Franky, whatever his name was. This explained why Basil was in a hurry to hire me. I was going to have words with that tiny witch later.

The Merlin working the case was dead. This was not good. It meant that whoever killed him was more powerful, or he'd been taken by surprise.

Damnit. I should have asked for more money.

"Looks like Eddie got too close, and he got killed for it," said Elsa, rolling her fingers over her locket.

"I think his name was Franky," echoed Julian. "Yeah. Definitely Franky."

I nodded. "That's what I think." It made sense. The witch had definitely discovered something. But what?

Julian leaned on the opposite wall and crossed his arms. "You from New York?"

I shook my head. "From a small town in New Hampshire. Moved here about fifteen years ago with my husband, which I'm hoping to be my *ex*-husband shortly."

Elsa's eyes rounded. "Sounds like a good story right there. I'm feeling some anger from your tone. Did he do something to you? What was it?"

"He cheated," I answered, finding it strange that I was so open with them about my relationship. I'd keep the gory details for later. "I just want to get a divorce and get on with my life. He's human. I don't know how long that'll take."

Elsa's face brightened. "I can help you with that. I have friends in the human legal system. If you can get me all his information, I can have your divorce final within two weeks because he cheated, and we paranormals pull strings for things like that."

I felt a pang of tension release from me. "Really? That would be great." Great? That was phenomenal.

"So, where do you live?" asked Julian, his eyes on the carry-on bag I'd placed on the floor next to the entrance. "You homeless?"

I sighed. "Here for now. The thirteenth floor until I find something, I guess."

Elsa clapped her hands enthusiastically. "We live on the thirteenth floor too. All the residents do. We're your neighbors. Isn't that wonderful? I can't wait to introduce you to the others. Jade is going to love you!"

Julian gave a one-shoulder shrug. "The hotel doesn't want us mingling with the guests. We're told not to, but we never listen to them." He flashed me a million-dollar smile. "It's how I get all my dates."

The idea of being alone with a bottle of merlot and my thoughts wasn't sounding so great at the moment.

The scuff of shoes on carpet pulled my attention to the door. A group of three men and one woman dressed in black suits, sunglasses, and equipped with medical briefcases walked into the room.

"Well, well, well. The cleanup crew is here," said Julian, eyeing the female.

Basil had mentioned that a group would come by to take the body away discreetly. Not sure how they were going to do that. First, because how do you remove a body discreetly, and second, they looked like they belonged in a remake of the *Men in Black* movies. Nothing was discreet about these people.

With my arms crossed over my chest, I watched the cleanup crew take a few pictures and categorize the crime scene before one of the males pulled out a glass vial and dumped the contents over the body. A sudden prickling of energy rippled over my skin. And then Eddie Franky lifted from the ground in his fetal position, hovering in the air.

Magic. These guys were witches. Or at least, that one was.

Next, the female sprinkled some white powder over the dead witch, mumbling words I couldn't quite catch. Energy hissed and oozed through the air as if sheer power and magic had been extracted into an invisible haze. The white powder grew and spread over the body until it disappeared. Ha. She'd cast some invisibility spell.

Damn. I wish I could do that.

"Show offs," muttered Elsa, her face wrinkled in a scowl.

But I was seriously impressed. I was more impressed as I watched the three cleanup crew members walk out of the room, a thin, white translucent tendril tethered to the female witch's hand as I imagined her pulling the floating body behind her.

The body might be gone, but my work was just beginning.

"Who's this?" A woman stood in the doorway where the cleanup crew had just disappeared a moment ago. Her blonde hair was crimped, big, and stiff like she'd used a whole can of hair spray. Her eyes were lined with blue eyeshadow, and shiny pink lipstick coated her lips. She gave off a Cindy Lauper vibe with black fishnet tights, a white ruffled skirt, and a short denim jacket. Her arms were looped with white and black plastic bracelets. I couldn't guess her age. She appeared older than me but younger than Elsa. Clearly, she was stuck in the eighties and loved eighties' music and fashion.

"That's Leana, the new Merlin," answered Julian, giving me a proud grin.

The woman's eyes rounded. "No way."

I turned to Elsa. "And who's that?"

Elsa blinked at me. "That's Jade. The one I told you about. She's one of us."

"Us?"

"Part of the gang. The thirteenth-floor gang," answered Elsa, like it would explain everything.

"Right." I looked back at Jade, who was openly grinning and staring at me like she was fanning over one of her favorite singers from one of her eighties' rock bands.

Someone grabbed me, and I cringed as Elsa hooked her arm around mine. "Come on. Let's finish this with some food in us. And a soft spot to rest my behind while we chat. I, for one, think we need to talk."

I raised a brow. "We do?"

"Yes," said Elsa. "There's a lot you don't know about the hotel. Rumors. You're new, so it's not your fault, but you need us."

"She's right. You need us," agreed Jade from the doorway.

"*I* need *you*? How's that?"

Elsa tapped my arm. "You need what we know. Trust me. You want to know what we know."

I knew she was right. "Sure."

"Good. Let's eat." Elsa dragged me with her. "And we'll tell you everything."

I grabbed my bag and let her pull me out the door with Julian and Jade following behind us.

In the space of a few hours, I'd broken a penis, gotten hired for a new job, and found myself with a newly dead body on my hands.

It was turning into one hell of a day.

CHAPTER 4

We didn't go far. In fact, they took me to the restaurant next door to the hotel, a storefront under a gray awning. The sign right below said AFTER DARK.

The restaurant door banged behind us as we sauntered into the lobby. It housed a modern interior of dark gray seats and tables in an open-concept room with twelve-foot ceilings and exposed beams and pipes. The tall windows at the front let in the last of the evening light.

Two paranormal males and a female, dressed in suits, were standing in the lobby, their voices hushed. They glanced up as we passed them and then returned to whatever discussion they were having.

"Table for four?" said the cheerful young brunette in a white shirt and short black skirt, who greeted us at the entrance.

"Unless you want to join us?" purred Julian, and part of me wanted to slap that grin off his face.

"Yes. Four, please," I said, taking the lead.

The hostess smiled at me. She blinked, and for a split second, the pupils of her hazel eyes elongated to slits, like the eyes of a cat. She blinked again, and her human eyes were back.

"You're going to love it here," said a smiling Jade. "The food's amazing."

I glanced around, recognizing the familiar energies from all walks of paranormal life. It seemed the restaurant catered to us paranormals like the Twilight Hotel, but I hadn't gotten a glamour vibe when we'd stepped through.

We followed the pretty hostess as Julian moseyed a little too close next to her, to a table in the middle of the restaurant.

A male waiter came rushing our way, winding expertly through a sea of tables and chairs with a tray under his arm.

He rushed at Jade, expecting her to move. When she didn't, he gave her an annoyed look and growled, "Move, freak."

Jade flinched like she'd been slapped. Her face paled, her smile fading.

Anger fired up in my belly. I don't know why, but I felt a sudden overprotectiveness toward her. I wanted to grab his tray and smash it over his head. Twice. No, make that five times.

The waiter released a frustrated sigh and moved around a stunned and embarrassed Jade.

"Ignore him," I said. "People like him are not worth the time."

Jade gave me a tight smile as she dragged over a chair and sat. Pink spots colored her cheeks, and she'd lost that spark about her. I glanced at Julian and Elsa, whose faces mirrored my anger.

I pulled out my chair and let myself fall into it, realizing how exhausted I was—not physically but mentally. And sometimes that was worse.

"I need a glass of wine," I said.

"I'll have the waiter bring you a bottle of our house wine," said the hostess. "Red or white?"

"Red," interjected Elsa. She looked at me and said, "I know you prefer red."

I did. But how did she know that?

"Not that waiter," I instructed the hostess as I pointed to the asshat across the restaurant. "Someone else."

"Of course," she answered and then walked away.

I watched as Julian angled his head to get a better view of the pretty hostess walking away.

He caught me looking at him. "I'm going home with her at the end of this meal. It's a guarantee."

I tried not to smile, but my traitorous lips quirked upward. He was growing on me. "So," I said, leaning forward and glancing around at my new friends. Were they my new friends? Guess I would know soon enough. "What do I need to know about the hotel?"

Elsa interlaced her fingers on the table. "Well, for one, it's haunted."

Jade snorted but didn't say anything.

"Okay. What else?" A haunted paranormal hotel wasn't new to me. Ghosts and spirits were attracted to all things supernatural. The energies we gave off were more than the average human times a hundred. It only made sense they'd frequent these types of hotels.

Julian leaned back in his chair. "She means she thinks a ghost is doing the killing."

"A ghost?" I stared at the witch. "From what I can tell, the last victim was killed by brute force. Something powerful. Ghosts lack the physical strength. They don't have bodies. You need to have a physical body to kill someone like that." Or so I thought. But I could be wrong.

"Not necessarily," continued the older witch. "Some ghosts or poltergeists have the ability to manipulate physical objects. They can kill if they want to."

I watched the witch for a moment. "You think a ghost killed those guests and the Merlin?"

Elsa widened her eyes. "I do. I know it."

"Says the witch who still speaks to her husband like he's alive," said Julian as he crossed his arms over his chest.

Red blotches appeared on Elsa's face. "You'll never understand true love. All you do is screw and leave before your victim wakes up," she shot back.

Jade pointed her finger at Julian, and her plastic bracelets clacked around her wrist. "She's got you there, lover boy." She caught me looking at her, and she smiled. I was glad to see her smiling again.

Julian shook his head. "Love is messy. Besides, I'm not selfish. I like to share—share my body with the ladies. Why shouldn't they experience *The Julian*?"

I rolled my eyes and then looked at Elsa across from me. "Okay, let's say a ghost is killing these people. Do you have an explanation as to why?"

Elsa grabbed her cotton napkin and started folding it. "Not yet. But it explains why no one saw the killer coming or leaving the room. You can ask Basil to show you the feed from the cameras. You only see the guests coming and going into their rooms. No one else. It's a working theory."

"It's a stupid theory," Julian shot back.

Elsa clenched her jaw. "You got a better theory? Spill it."

Julian shrugged. "I think it's something to do with sex. A husband or wife caught cheating. Then they got whacked. Happens all the time."

Like breaking penises. "It does. But it doesn't explain why they killed the Merlin. And why two deaths so close together? What's the connection? What did Eddie or Franky discover? Was that the reason he was killed?"

"He found the ghost responsible," said Elsa. "And it killed him."

"What ghost?" came a deep, manly voice.

I looked up to an expression of intrigue on a handsome face that belonged to a muscled man, tall and virile, with tattoos peeking out from his sleeve down one arm. His dark eyes made me wonder what kind of lover he was in bed.

My heart slammed against my rib cage like a car hitting a cement wall.

Shit. It was the man-beast I'd crashed into earlier. He locked eyes with me, not bothering to hide the annoyance in his expression.

My eyes moved to his large hands. He held four glasses in one hand and a bottle of red wine in the other.

"You work here?" I asked.

"Sometimes," he growled. That same frown returned as he carefully placed our wineglasses, cut the foil below the lip of the bottle, and began to rotate the corkscrew. "What are you doing here?" He said it like I wasn't allowed to be here, like I should have asked his permission.

Anger rolled through me. "It's not illegal to have a meal in this city. My friends and I want to sit down and have a nice meal. You got a problem with that? Or am I not allowed to walk the streets *or* sit and eat?"

The man-beast leveled the cork out of the bottle and poured a little wine into my glass. "Taste it."

I frowned. "Giving me orders too? Wow. Full of yourself and rude. How wonderful."

Jade sucked in the breath through her teeth, and I could see Julian shifting in his seat while Elsa fondled her locket.

"You need to taste the wine," said the man-beast,

his voice low and dangerous. "If you don't like it, I can get another bottle."

Heat rolled off my scalp. I knew my face was probably red. What was it about this guy that made my blood boil? "Fine." I took the glass and sipped, not bothering to swirl it around a few times or give it a sniff, like I should have. But to my surprise, the wine was delicious. A perfect balance of alcohol and sweet fruit.

"It's good." I swallowed and put my glass back down, watching as he filled it and then proceeded to fill the others' glasses.

He set the bottle on our table. "I'll have another waiter come and take your orders in a few minutes."

"Good. You do that." The last thing I wanted was my meal to be ruined by this grumpy werewolf. I'd had enough of men and their drama for one night. I wanted some time to de-stress with some wine while not having to deal with this guy.

The muscles around the man-beast's shoulders popped and jerked. It was a nice display, but I was anxious for him to leave. He watched me a second longer, too long for it to be considered polite, and then walked away.

I laughed softly and reached for my glass of wine. "Still got it. What?" I said, staring at my new friends, who were looking at me like I'd just stripped out of my clothes and decided to walk around the restaurant.

"You've got some serious lady balls," said Julian, shaking his head at me. "Either that or you're crazy."

"I've been told both," I said, still smiling. "What? Why are you all staring at me like I've lost my mind?"

"That was the owner." Jade leaned over the table, her voice low. The quirks at the edges of her lips suggested she was holding in a nervous laugh. "Valen."

My insides churned. Great. Now I'd just made an enemy at a possible regular hangout. "Is he always this pleasant?"

"Worse." Julian watched me with a curious expression. "Do you know him? I kinda got a vibe that you did."

I shook my head. "No." Not unless you counted me crashing into him earlier.

"Damn." Julian ran his fingers through his hair. "I got all kinds of sexual tension from you two."

I choked on my wine. "Stop." I swallowed. "Trust me. There's nothing there." Who was I kidding? He turned me on in a way I hadn't felt in a very long time. Hell, more like never. But I squashed those feelings. I didn't need this right now. I had a job to focus on. Not sexy man-beasts.

"It did feel like there was history between you," said Elsa, an inquiring frown on her brows.

"It did," agreed Jade, that hint of a smile still lingering over her lips.

"None whatsoever." I took another sip of wine, maybe a mouthful. "I'd remember someone like him."

"He can be a bit grumpy," said Elsa as she took a sip of her wine.

"Asshole is more the correct term," said Julian. "Just don't let him hear you say it. He's got a temper to match his large size."

I wasn't sure what to make of that. "What's his problem? Why does he have to be this way?" I'd had enough assholes in my life. I didn't have the patience to deal with one more.

Julian swirled his glass of wine. "That's just the way he is. I wouldn't get on his bad side. Those who do... seem to disappear."

I laughed. "Is he like a mob boss or something?"

He nodded. "Or something."

Awesome. Now I'd really done it. Not only did I have to figure out who was killing the guests in the hotel, but I'd have to watch my back for the man-beast.

"So, the werewolf restaurant owner hates me. Maybe we should find another place to eat next time." I took another sip of my wine and then let out an inappropriate moan.

Elsa looked over her shoulder before answering. "Not a werewolf. A vampire," she said, her eyes wide.

I swallowed hard. "Really? He doesn't look like a vampire. I thought for sure he was a shifter. Were-wolf or a wereape." He definitely didn't have the unnatural good looks most vampires possessed. He had a more rugged edge. He was handsome. Just not over the top like most vampires. But if he was only *part* vampire, that might explain the harshness of his looks.

"He's not a vampire," said Jade, rolling her eyes. "Everyone knows he's a werecat. A tiger, I heard."

Julian gave a snort. "You ladies have it all wrong."

"Oh yeah?" Elsa crossed her arms over her chest. "What is he, then? If you're so smart."

"Easy." Julian popped a piece of fresh bread into his mouth. "He's a werebear. Just look at him. His size? Can't you tell?"

Elsa and Jade frowned at him, and I tried hard not to laugh.

"Whatever he is… what's his story?" I couldn't help myself. The sexy man-beast intrigued me.

"No one knows," said Elsa. "He just showed up about five years ago and bought the place. Keeps to himself. Not very talkative."

Julian tipped his head and finished his wine. "The guy's a jerk. He needs to get laid more often."

"Why do you come here if you don't like him?"

Jade shrugged and said, "The food's amazing."

And they were right.

I ordered roast duck with figs and moaned every time I brought the fork to my mouth. Elsa had a vegetable dish I couldn't remember the name of for the life of me, which looked like a big salad with nuts spread on top. Jade had fettuccini alfredo that smelled divine, and Julian had a giant steak with sweet-potato fries. When we were done, our plates gleamed like they'd just been washed.

After two bottles of wine and eating so much my belly looked like I was a few months pregnant, we paid our bills and made our way toward the main exit.

I was trying to act cool and walk a straight line while the restaurant's floor seemed to be moving. I spotted Julian speaking to that pretty brunette hostess. She grabbed his phone and typed something before handing it back, sex written all over her face. It was obvious they were going to hook up later.

I laughed as I shuffled toward the front door where Elsa and Jade were waiting for me. They could hold their wine better than me. Not fair. Maybe that came with more years of experience. I looked forward to that.

I felt better. Wine could do that to a person. After the day I'd had, I needed it. Turned out Elsa, Jade, and Julian were wonderful company—funny and kind, the way real friends should be. And informative. I hadn't felt this good in a long time. I hadn't realized how much I missed the company of others. I'd been so immersed in my work and too busy pretending my marriage was okay.

The skin on my back prickled like I'd been touched with electricity. The hairs on the back of my neck rose as I felt a pressure there, the same kind I got when someone was staring at me.

I turned around. Valen stood in the lobby staring at me, but he didn't look angry this time. His face was carefully neutral, but those dark eyes were as intense as before, perhaps more. Maybe that was the wine talking.

Too bad he was such a dick. He was nice to look at, so I kept staring, not wanting to turn away first. He was a fool if he thought he could intimidate me by staring—a handsome one but still a fool. I, too, could play the staring game. I was exceptionally good at it.

"Come on, Leana," called Elsa from the doorway. "You need to meet the others."

Valen, the man-beast, was still staring at me. Why? Who knew. Maybe he was contemplating ways to kill me.

The wine in my veins was still pumping and making me bold and foolish.

So, I gave him a smile and a finger wave before walking out of his restaurant.

CHAPTER 5

I'd never been on the thirteenth floor of any hotel or building. That was because most building designers were superstitious and avoided numbering a level as thirteen, like the plague. But this was a supernatural hotel where all things paranormal were embraced.

Still, I wasn't expecting this.

I stepped out of the elevator, stumbled, and righted myself with my carry-on bag around my shoulder, feeling much heavier than before as I gawked at my new residence.

The thirteenth floor had twelve doors, all open at the moment.

Music, TVs, and the sounds of people mingling reached me as I followed Julian and the ladies down the hallway. It opened up to us with an array of lights, music, food, and the paranormal, like stepping into a fairyland or something similar.

A few passing paranormals waved at us as they came and went from each other's apartments like it was the normal thing to do. I peeked into the first apartment to find an ample space occupied by an elderly gentleman sitting in an armchair, with a TV tray in front of him as he watched an episode of *Jeopardy*.

Across from his apartment, another room was filled with teenagers all bouncing and head bobbing to some music they were all listening to at the same time, though I couldn't hear a thing from the small white headphones pressed into their ears.

Next, was a female in her forties with too much makeup, leaning on the doorframe of her apartment while smoking a cigarette as she eyed Julian, like she wanted to strap him down to her bed and lick him all over.

"Julian, darling," she purred, her voice husky like someone who started smoking at the age of six. She took a deep drag of her cigarette. "You coming over tonight? I've got a bottle of whiskey we can share." Plumes of smoke rolled out of her mouth and nose as she traced a finger down her cleavage.

Julian rubbed the back of his neck, the top of his ears turning red. "Ha ha, Olga," he laughed awkwardly. "Maybe some other time. I'm showing the new girl around."

Interesting. It looked like Julian drew the line at smoking, crusty-looking ladies.

At that, Olga scowled at me like I'd just stolen her husband. "Who's she?"

I opened my mouth to answer, but Elsa beat me to it. "Leana. The new Merlin."

"The new Merlin?" Olga was still giving me the stink eye, but then she smiled. "You won't be here long."

"Was that a threat?" I laughed, tracing my finger down my much smaller cleavage. I couldn't help it. Damn wine. "By the way, you're smoking. You're the one who won't be here long."

Olga pinched her barely there lips together and spun around, slamming her door.

"Was it something I said?" I snorted. Crap. I had to remember to stop at two glasses of wine. Four. Well, four was going to get me into trouble.

Yet Julian had a tiny smile on his face when he looked at me. Guess we were friends now.

"Move!"

I flattened myself against the wall as twin ten-year-old girls in identical pink, sparkling princess dresses came skipping past us, the scent of animal and grass following them as energy bit my skin. They were shifters—werehorses or weredeer—and really cute.

I flinched as a dozen house cats came barreling down the hallway and vanished into an apartment on the right.

"Luke's cats," said Jade, watching me. "He picks up a stray whenever he goes out. He's got them trained to use his toilet. And he has some spell that brushes them daily, so you won't find any hair in his place."

I smiled. "Love cats." The truth was, I'd always wanted a cat or a dog. But I was never home. These furry babies needed love and attention. One day I would have a cat, catspiration. That was me.

"Elsa. I'm out of milk," commanded a tall, thin woman in her seventies wearing a long nightgown, her long, white hair flowing behind her like a cape.

"In the fridge, Barb." Elsa pointed to an apartment down the hall that could have been any door.

The tall woman walked past us and disappeared three doors down to what I could only assume was Elsa's place.

It was like the entire floor was one big family residence. It was weird—a good weird. And I loved it.

"Move!" chorused the twins as they skipped past us again. It seemed they had acquired a third wheel as I spotted a boy running clumsily after them.

"See?" Julian pointed to the boy. "That's how I started. Attaboy, Terry!" he encouraged. "Don't let them run away."

"You're the last apartment on the left," directed Jade as she strolled before us. She stood at the doorframe of what I guessed was my new home and posed with a hand gesture that would make Vanna White proud.

The number 1312 was stenciled in black just above the open door.

"After you," said Julian, bending from the waist.

I laughed and stepped into the apartment. I was half expecting it to be occupied by a horde of teenagers, but it was empty.

I walked down a small hallway into a decent-size living room and connecting dining room. The salmon-and-white wallpaper was peeling in long strips. The carpet was a dark green and felt more like sandpaper than actual carpet.

Moving on, just off the kitchen were three doors. Two were bedrooms, and one was the bathroom with light green tiles around the bath and shower combo.

It was furnished with lots of white and green-colored lamps and décor that looked like they belonged in the nineties. Not my style, but it was clean. I wouldn't have to buy anything, seeing as it was furnished. Being the last apartment meant that I didn't have neighbors on one side. And instead, I had extra windows, which meant more light.

I put my bag on the bed in the largest of the bedrooms and let out a sigh, my mind on the day I'd had, specifically on the two encounters with Valen, aka man-beast. I didn't know what it was about him, but my thoughts kept finding their way back to that burly man and that intense way he'd glared at me, like I'd stolen his spot at the gym.

I shook my head and left the room to join Elsa, Jade, and Julian in the living room.

"Laundry's in the basement," said Elsa. "The hotel only does the laundry for the guests. Not us rebels." She winked.

I came to sit next to her on the dingy yet comfort-able beige couch. "Easy enough. Didn't bring much with me anyway."

"Hello! Hello!" A generous-sized woman carrying

a plate of food came waltzing in. "Is this the new girl? Oh, she's pretty. Bet you can't wait to get in her pants, huh, Julian?"

Heat rushed to my face. I hated the attention and leaned back into the couch, trying to disappear.

"Her husband just cheated on her, Louise," said Julian, like that was supposed to explain it all.

The woman's eyes widened. "Well, well, well. I bet that's a fascinating story. I bet you have tons of interesting stories to tell. Goddess knows we need some good stories up here." Her green eyes sparkled. "I hope you gave him something in return."

I grinned. "I did. I took care of his package."

"Good." Louise chuckled. "Here. I brought some of my famous tuna tartare and my cheddar dip." She settled her platter of diced tuna served on a bed of sliced avocado and mounds of tortilla chips on the glass coffee table.

"I've got wine!" I raised my head and saw a woman about my age with short black hair and dark skin walking in with a bottle of wine hung from each hand.

She was followed by a man with gray hair and a short beard. He held up a six-pack of beer. "I've got the beer," he said joyously.

More and more people followed, carrying some kind of beverage or food. I blinked, my head spinning as I realized most of the tenants from the thirteenth floor were in my new apartment. Even the twins made an appearance, skipping around the room.

The rest of the night went like that: chattering, making new friends, drinking more wine, and eating until my stomach felt like a brick wall.

Around one in the morning, Elsa shooed everyone out and said her goodbyes. I wasn't twenty anymore and didn't bounce back as quickly after a night of drinking. I needed sleep, especially after the day I'd had, if I wanted to make good on the new job.

I stumbled into bed with a stupid tipsy grin on my face, finding it exceptionally comfortable.

I went to bed and dreamed of broken penises chasing me.

And a pair of dark, smoldering eyes.

CHAPTER 6

I didn't know how long I lay in bed, refusing to open my eyes. I knew once I did, it would mean I was awake. My head throbbed like I had miniature jackhammers smashing against my skull.

I felt a sudden pressure on my chest. *Martin.*

Martin was trying to choke me again. It wasn't the first time I'd woken to him with his hands wrapped around my neck, his idea of fun sex. He'd nearly killed me the last time, and I'd had a ring of nasty bruises around my neck to prove it. Enough was enough.

"Martin, stop!" My eyes flashed open in a jerk of adrenaline, and my breath came fast.

A wooden dog's face was staring at me. And when I say staring, I mean its eyes blinked.

"Ah!" I screamed, scrambled back, slipped, and fell hard on the carpet. When my head hit the side table, all fragments of sleep fell away. My husband—soon-to-be ex-husband—wasn't here. The room was different. The smells. And then it hit me. I wasn't in my old apartment. I was in the Twilight Hotel.

The toy dog rolled to the side of the bed. Its eyes blinked again as it stared down at me. "That's going to leave a nasty bump."

Holy shit. The toy could speak!

"Definitely had way too much to drink last night," I grumbled, blinking the sleep fuzz from my eyes.

"I'll say," said the toy dog, its voice strangely human and male. Its painted eyebrows twisted in a bemused expression. "You snore like a trucker in your sleep."

Okay. Now I was freaking out.

I sat up in a flash, my heart thumping in my throat and trying to squeeze through my teeth. The toy looked like a beige beagle with dark spots covering its back. Instead of legs, it had four red wheels, a metal spring tail, droopy wooden ears, a head that rotated on a metal joint, and a moveable jaw, like a ventriloquist puppet, which I suspected enabled it to speak. To speak!

This was definitely not a dream. The toy dog was real. It was male. And it was in my room.

"Who are you, and what the hell are you doing in my room?" I clasped my arms around myself, content I had a T-shirt on and wasn't naked. That would have been much worse. Still pretty creepy to wake up to a magical toy staring me in the face.

The toy dog wagged its tail. "The name's Jimmy."

I frowned at the toy. My pounding headache

etched around the backs of my eyes and made its way to my eyebrows. "What the hell do you want?"

The wooden dog blinked. "I came to see you, of course. The hotel's buzzing with news of the new Merlin. I needed to see you with my own eyes."

I didn't sense any dark, magical energies coming off the toy, but that didn't mean it wasn't sent by the ghost or whoever had murdered those people. "Do you belong to one of the kids?"

The dog's ears swung back. "I don't belong to anyone. I'm not a toy."

"You sure look like one."

Toy dog Jimmy's eyes narrowed. "I wasn't always like this. I was once a man, you know."

"That's even creepier."

Jimmy watched me a moment, and then he sprang off my bed and rolled out of my bedroom. "Get dressed. We've got work to do," he called back.

"Excuse you?" Part of me wished I was still sleeping, but I found myself getting up and locking myself in the bathroom. I didn't trust the damn toy.

After a shower, I pulled on a pair of dark jeans and a T-shirt before grabbing the bottle of Tylenol from my bag and walking into the living room. The air smelled of fresh coffee, and I found Jimmy on the counter next to the coffee maker.

"You don't have legs," I told him, wondering how the hell he got up there and then made coffee.

"How observant of you," snapped the toy dog. "Did anyone ever tell you how grumpy you are in the morning?"

"Yeah. My husband." I moved to the coffee maker and poured myself a cup. "How did you get on the counter?" And my bed, for that matter. Even more disturbing was that he'd made coffee without hands.

Jimmy swung his ears forward. "Magic."

"Funny." I downed two Tylenols with a sip of coffee. "You said you used to be a man. What's your story? Cursed?" I'd heard of people being trapped in animals before, but a toy dog was a first.

Jimmy's tail lowered. "I was thirty-seven, in my prime, when the sorceress cursed me. She loved me, see, but I didn't love her back. So, she decided if she couldn't have me..."

"No one else would." Damn. Poor bastard. "How long ago was this?"

"Nineteen fifty-four."

I choked on my coffee. "Damn. That would mean you've been inside that toy for..."

Jimmy sighed. "A very long time."

Okay. That did change things a bit. I couldn't imagine being stuck inside a toy for that many years. Here I thought I was in hell, stuck with my husband for the last few years of our marriage. This was a lot worse.

"Has no one ever tried to break the curse?"

"Many have tried, and they've all failed. It's fine. I've accepted my fate. This is who I was supposed to be."

"A toy?"

The dog frowned with his painted eyebrows,

which was really trippy. "A helper. A guide. I help people."

"Hmmm." I took another gulp of coffee and finished my cup.

"Elsa asked me to help you with your investigation," said the toy dog. "She's at her sister's place in Brooklyn, weeding her garden. Her sister has a bad case of arthritis."

"I usually work alone," I told him, though a guide or guide dog sounded pretty helpful since I still was new to the hotel and didn't know where everything was. Maybe this wasn't such a bad idea.

"Not anymore. Well, at least not while you're staying at the hotel. Your business is everyone's business."

"I noticed." Last night was an awakening. I set my empty cup on the counter next to Jimmy. "Did you help the last Merlin?"

"Eddie?" said the toy dog, his metal spring tail wagging. "I did. Good lad. Decent witch."

That was good news. "Do you know what he discovered? He found something out, and it got him killed. I'm sure of it." That was the only logical explanation.

"Well," said the dog as he rolled back in what I imagined was his attempt to sit. "I remember him saying that there was no connection between the two victims, excluding him, of course. And that the killer, or killers, killed only at night and somehow were able to move through walls."

"Move through walls?"

"Like ghosts."

I raised a brow. "You've been talking to Elsa."

The dog dipped his head. "It's the only thing that makes sense. We can see the victims entering their rooms. Only them. And then the maids finding them in the morning."

It was Elsa's theory. But I didn't buy it. "I'd like to see that footage. I'll ask Basil to show me."

"Eddie has copies on his laptop," said the toy dog. "He showed me."

"You know where the laptop is now?" I didn't remember seeing a laptop in the room. If I had, I would have grabbed it.

The toy dog nodded. "Yes. I'm betting it's still there. The maids haven't touched the room yet. They're afraid the ghost will kill them if they come inside the room."

"So much for keeping this discreet." If one of the maids had found the body of poor Eddie, I was sure the entire hotel staff knew by now. It wouldn't be long before the guests knew as well. But a laptop with notes from the previous Merlin was golden. It meant I would know what Eddie knew before he was killed.

It also meant I would be a target. It wouldn't be the first time.

"You're a Dark witch. Aren't you?" asked the toy dog after a moment. "You channel your magic through demons? Not that there's anything wrong with that. But are you?"

I looked away from the toy dog. It was too early

in the morning for that conversation, and the Tylenol hadn't kicked in yet. "I'm a witch. Let's just keep it at that."

The toy dog's ears swiveled forward. "Fine. Keep your secrets. It'll come out eventually."

He was right. It always did.

"So, is Martin your husband?" asked Jimmy.

"You're a nosy little creature. Aren't you?"

"That's how I know so much," answered Jimmy. "I make it my business to know what happens in this hotel."

I let out a sigh. My body tensed at the memory of Martin squeezing my throat last year, and the excitement in his eyes when I woke up to find him on top of me, me not able to breathe, which somehow turned him on. My blood pressure rose at the recollection. I felt sick, partly that I'd ever loved a monster like that. But mostly I was angry with myself that I didn't have the courage to leave all those years ago.

"He's my soon-to-be ex-husband," I found myself answering after a moment.

Jimmy rolled forward. "Ah. So, that's why Elsa asked me to drop off those files on the table for ya."

"What files?" I moved to the dining table and saw a manila envelope. A single Post-it note read *Fill out the forms and give them back to Jimmy.*

If Elsa was right, I'd be free of him in just two weeks. It seemed too good to be true. Hell, I needed a little bit of happiness in my life.

My heart leaped with the news. "Let's go, Snoopy."

"It's *Jimmy*," said the dog, though I could see the smile on his wooden face. He leaped off the counter and rolled to the front door, which—surprise, surprise—was wide open. "You coming?"

I smiled and grabbed my shoulder bag from the wall hook rack in the hallway. "Right behind you, Snoopy."

CHAPTER 7

It turned out Jimmy was right. The Merlin's room had remained intact. It wasn't even locked, to my surprise, as I pushed us through. I caught a glimpse of a maid, judging by the white-and-gray, short-sleeved uniform dress, looking over her shoulder at us. Her eyes widened in terror, and then she jerked her head back around before hauling her cleaning cart with a speed that suggested she was late for an appointment.

The guest rooms were smaller than the resident apartments. The main difference was they didn't have separate rooms, just one big space that included a bed, a small desk set before a window, a modest bathroom, and a kitchenette that hosted a small fridge and coffee maker.

The sound of wheels grinding caught my attention, and I saw Jimmy roll to a stop on the carpet next to me.

"So, where is it?"

"He hid it in the bathroom," said the toy dog as he rolled away.

"He hid it?" That wasn't good. It meant he knew someone or something was onto him.

"Yeah," called Jimmy. "In here. I can't reach it. You'll have to get it for me."

For him? I shook my head but followed him to the bathroom.

His ears swiveled forward. "Up there in the vent."

I stepped around Jimmy and then pushed up on my toes. Slipping my fingers under the metal casing, I pulled, and the frame came free. Setting it on the bathroom vanity, I stuck my hand through the vent cavity, and my fingers touched cold, hard metal. I yanked out the laptop and grinned at the toy dog.

"Not bad, Snoopy."

"You're welcome, Merlie."

I laughed. "Come on. Let's see what Eddie discovered and why he felt the need to hide his laptop."

I sat on the edge of the bed and flipped the laptop open. Jimmy leaped on the bed and rolled next to me. The computer turned on moments later.

"Shit. It's password protected." Of course, it would be.

Jimmy leaned forward and said, "*Trustnoone*. The one is the number one, and trustno is all lower case." At my questioning brow, he added, "What? I saw him type it more than once."

Seriously. This toy dog was proving to be an

excellent assistant or guide. And I was glad he was here. Without Jimmy, I'd never have found the laptop. And if, by a miracle, I had, it would have taken days to find someone to crack the password. I was happy Jimmy was here.

"Looks like Eddie was an *X-Files* fan," I said, remembering the countless times I'd rewatched the entire eleven seasons. "He had good taste."

I typed in *trustno1* and pressed enter. "We're in." The desktop had about fifty folders, some labeled with dates, some just letters that didn't mean anything. "He's not that organized. Wait—here." I clicked on the folder called MERLIN. "This is only a spreadsheet of the hours he worked," I said, feeling some of my excitement fade.

Jimmy cycled forward until his front wheels bumped my thigh. "Try that one. The one that says TH. Twilight Hotel."

I scanned the screen for the folder and then clicked on it. "Here we go."

The folder opened to a list of multiple files, documents, images, and more folders. I clicked on the pictures first. The first image was of a woman lying on the floor above a green carpet. It was hard to see her face from this angle, but I could just make out the frown and the squinting of her eyes, recognizing the pain she must have felt before she died.

"That's Patricia," said Jimmy. "The first victim."

I nodded. "I recognize her from the photo Basil gave me. Looks like she died in the same way as

Eddie." I flipped through the pictures until I landed on the second victim. A male.

"That's Jordan," informed the dog.

I studied the image. "The only thing that connects them all is how they were killed. Whoever did this killed them all the same way." It didn't say much, but it told me the killer was consistent.

After that, I clicked through more files and documents. "Where is it, Eddie?" I said to the screen. "What were you afraid of?" I wanted to know why Eddie felt the need to hide his computer. So far, I couldn't see anything that would give him a reason.

"Click the video file," suggested Jimmy. "It's where he downloaded the camera feed from outside the rooms."

Following the toy dog's instructions, I clicked on the folder that said VIDEO. Only two videos were inside. My pulse quickened as I clicked the first one.

The clip opened to reveal footage from a hallway of the hotel. The dim lighting and orange glow from the wall sconces were enough to make out the numbers on the doors. They all started with the number two, so I knew I was looking at the second floor. I sat there in silence with Jimmy and watched for a few seconds until, finally, a figure stepped out of the elevator. A woman dressed in dark clothing crossed the hallway and, with her key card, opened the door to room 202.

"That's Patricia," said Jimmy.

I watched as the door to her room closed and then nothing. I scrolled through the video, seeing people come and go, and finally, a brighter video as the morning sun shone through the windows.

"Here comes the maid," announced Jimmy.

Sure enough, I saw a maid push her cleaning cart to room 202, knock twice, wait, and then use her key card, unlock the door, and push in.

"Wait for it," said the toy dog.

"For what?" I asked, glancing at Jimmy.

"Look."

I stared at the screen just as the maid came crashing out of the room and ran off camera.

"See?" Jimmy shifted on the bed. "No one was in that room except for the victim and the maid. How do you explain that? Ghosts? Elsa seems to think so."

I shook my head. "I don't know. I don't think so. A vengeful ghost? Could be. But something doesn't make sense. She was killed sometime during the night. Same as Eddie and the other guy. All were killed at night and then discovered by the maids the next morning. Hmmm."

"What does *hmmm* mean?"

"It means if it was a ghost or ghosts, why doesn't Eddie mention that in any of these files? I mean, I haven't gone through all of them, but if he thought ghosts were responsible, shouldn't we have seen some evidence of that? There's nothing on ghosts in his notes."

"It doesn't mean it *wasn't* a ghost."

I shook my head. "No. But if it was a ghost, why here and why now? Why these people?"

"Good question." Jimmy rolled back. "What are

you thinking? If not a ghost or some kind of evil spirit haunting, then what? Who did this? The last I knew, living paranormals can't walk through walls."

"You're right. We don't."

"Like Dark witches?" pressed Jimmy. "You're a Dark witch. Right?"

Ignoring him, I leaned forward and clicked the play button on the other video. And just like Patricia, no one entered the room after Jordan did. Just the maid who came running out the following morning.

I didn't believe a ghost did this. I didn't think Eddie thought that either. I thought something in his computer got him killed—something we hadn't seen yet.

I scrolled through the video again, all the way until Jordan walked inside his room, shut the door, and then let it play. Scrolled a bit. Let it play. And then—

"Wait a second." My heart sped up as I moved through the video frame by frame.

"What? Did you see something?" Jimmy leaped up onto my lap. "What?"

I looked down at the toy dog, thought of smacking him off my lap, but then thought better of it. "Here." I moved back, pressing a few frames with the left arrow key on the keyboard. "Here. Look." I moved from one image frame to the next. "See how the light from the moon reflects on the wall here?"

Jimmy rolled forward until the tip of his wooden nose hit the screen. "Yeah."

"Watch." I pressed on the next frame. "See. It doesn't match."

Jimmy whistled and rolled back. "Holy smokes. Someone tampered with the video feed."

"Exactly." I beamed. "This is no ghost. I'm sure of it. This is someone very much alive. I'm willing to bet Eddie figured this out too. It's what got him killed."

Jimmy stared at the screen. "Look. The time frame didn't change."

I stared at the video. The bottom of the screen read 11:31 p.m. "I know," I said, moving through the video again to where I'd spotted the glitch. The clock never lost time. "That would have been a dead give-away. They made sure the clock stayed correct throughout the video. It was probably missing a few minutes near the end, but no one noticed."

"You're like a modern Sherlock Holmes. Does that make me Dr. Watson?"

"If this helps solve our case, you can be anyone you want, Snoopy."

Jimmy laughed, which sounded so human that it was almost like he was right here next to me in his human form.

I stared at the toy dog. "Who has access to the cameras?" I had a feeling I was onto something.

"As far as I know, Basil and the security chief," answered the toy dog.

I smiled. "That is excellent news, my friend. It narrows down our list of suspects."

"We have a list?"

"Now we do." I scratched under his chin, only

realizing then that I didn't know if Jimmy felt anything. He was a wooden toy dog, not a real puppy.

Jimmy closed his eyes in delight. "Julian owes me twenty bucks. He bet that you wouldn't find anything. And you found something big."

I wasn't sure if I was more offended that they had put bets on me or that Julian didn't think I was up to the task.

I looked at my new partner, wondering where he slept, if he even slept. Did he have a room or an apartment, or did he just wander through the hotel all day and night. I wanted to ask him, but that could wait for another time.

"Let's go." I jumped up. Jimmy leaped off my lap easily onto the floor, and I grabbed the laptop, securing it under my arm. I wasn't letting go of this baby. Besides, I left my own computer back at my old place, and I wasn't going back.

This find was excellent news. I didn't take Basil as the murdering type, but if he had access to the camera feed, he was now on my list of suspects, along with whoever this security chief was.

I grabbed the door handle, yanked it open, and smacked into the chest of none other than my favorite man-beast.

CHAPTER 8

I stepped back, my face flaming from irritation and embarrassment because I'd just smeared it against some of his chest skin. "What are *you* doing here?" I really had to stop meeting this guy this way. I really had to stop thinking about him too. And dreaming about him. And why the hell did he have to smell so nice?

The man-beast wore a shirt that did nothing to constrain the muscles that pulled against it, like they were begging him to tear it off. It was buttoned low, which explained why part of my face had splattered against his man-beast chest skin. My eyes flicked at the tattoos peeking from the collar of his low V-neck shirt. He wore a pair of dark jeans that fit his slim waist and were snug against thick thighs. He looked predatory, ready to fight and kill something. Like I said, man-beast.

I quickly tore my gaze away from his distracting, extremely virile chest.

Valen, the said man-beast, looked mildly surprised at my tone. "I was asked to come here and take a look."

"By who?" I looked past him and saw two pretty women huddled together, both dressed in identical white-and-gray maid uniforms, both twenty years my junior. Now I understood. I was pretty sure he had lots of women drooling in his wake. He had that alpha thing down to a T. It was hot. Not hot enough to tempt me, though. Okay, maybe a little. Yeah, I was a total liar.

Jimmy rolled ahead and stopped at my feet. "Hey, Valen. What's up?"

"Jimmy," said Valen in the way of greeting my new friend. So, they knew each other. Interesting. I had a feeling Jimmy knew a lot more than he let on. He was proving to be a valuable ally.

"Everything smooth over at After Dark?" asked Jimmy.

The large man nodded. "It is."

"I heard there was a fight between two shifters last Friday," continued Jimmy. "I heard it got bloody. Heard one guy busted a few ribs and the other lost some teeth."

A muscle feathered along Valen's jaw as he kept his eyes on me. "I took care of it."

"Of course you did," answered the dog, rolling around Valen's ankles and stopping next to his left foot. "Your restaurant. Your fists."

Valen's dark eyes shot to the laptop tucked under my arm. He looked at me. His unwavering stare beat into me like the pounding of a drum. Tingles washed over my scalp and spread over my skin.

This man was dangerous. Not because of his size and bulging muscles. It was more in his presence, the energy he gave off. Something deadly and brutal glinted in his gaze, concealed under his rugged and handsome exterior. He was like a lion. Unpredictable and lethal, which set me on edge.

He said nothing as he brushed past me and entered the room. That damn fine cologne touched my senses, and I had no choice but to inhale some. I expected the two maids to follow, but they stayed outside in the hallway, their faces tight with fear.

I followed him. "What are you doing?"

Valen strolled into Eddie's room and went straight to the bed. He lifted the mattress with one hand, like it weighed nothing more than a bedsheet, and looked under it. Thick muscles flared along his back in quite the show. I wondered why the women weren't in here enjoying the view.

"There's nothing there, apart from bedbugs," I said, though I hadn't thought of looking under the mattress. Not very thorough in my investigation.

Valen let the mattress fall and then went through the drawers of the two night tables, clearly looking for something. "You're Leana, the new Merlin."

"That's right." I wasn't thrilled that he'd been asking about me. "And you're the grumpy, rude restaurant owner, Valen." There. I knew his name too.

Jimmy made a weird sound in his throat. "You two know each other?"

"No," Valen and I chorused with the same amount of ire. Okay, that was weird.

Those dark eyes rested on me again. His face was carefully blank of any expression. "The last Merlin died in this room."

I narrowed my eyes. "Who told you that?" My gaze went to the two maids clustered together in the hallway, both avoiding my eyes. Clearly, the two maids had blabbed. If he knew about the deaths, it wouldn't be long before the guests in the hotel knew. No way could Basil keep this quiet much longer.

Valen crossed the room and opened the cabinet of the kitchenette, the coffee maker and cups rattling above it. I was next to him in a heartbeat.

"You shouldn't be here. This is my case."

Valen shut the cabinet door and turned to me. "Your case."

"That's right," I said, my heart thrumming in my chest. Jimmy rolled past me and joined the two maids in the hallway as I turned my attention back to the large man. "I've been hired by the hotel to look into the Merlin's death." I didn't want to say too much. I didn't trust this guy. He was giving off all kinds of different vibes, and none of them were trustworthy. For one, I didn't like that he was snooping around Eddie's room like he was looking for something.

"Have you discovered anything?" asked the man-beast.

"Right. Like I'm going to tell you." The nerve of this guy.

"So you haven't discovered anything."

"I've discovered that you're very rude to strangers," I shot back, my free hand on my hip.

"I could say the same about you," said Valen, his eyes narrowing slightly.

My temper rose, and I reined it in. I did not want to start a fight, especially while on the job and with a very dangerous-looking man. "You should leave," I told him. "You're messing up my crime scene." I wasn't sure how much authority I had with the hotel. Basil and I never really discussed it. I was hoping I had carte blanche, as I usually did whenever working on a case.

His intense gaze was making me uncomfortable. I leaned my hip against the cabinet. And when I went to steady myself with my right hand, it hit one of the coffee cups.

I blinked as the cup slid off the counter.

Valen's left hand shot out so fast, I only saw a blur, and then he placed the cup back on the countertop.

I jerked, squeezing the laptop against my armpit. Okay, so this guy was fast. Vampire fast. My skin prickled and danced with fear and a little excitement. Something was seriously wrong with me. I blamed it on my soon-to-be ex-husband's years of neglect in the bedroom.

"How long have you been a Merlin?" asked Valen suddenly in the silence, leaning back and studying me. He crossed his arms, the muscles on his chest bulging, clearly wanting out of that shirt.

I didn't want to answer, but I did anyway. "Ten years. I know what I'm doing. This isn't my first murder case."

"So you've worked on a case like this before?" asked the man-beast, his voice carefully neutral.

I frowned. "I've worked on many cases. Never one like this, but every case is unique. I have to treat them as such." I wasn't liking where this conversation was going. He shouldn't be grilling me. *I* should be peppering *him* with questions.

Valen stood there, watching me. "You're different from the other Merlins."

My battle to stop flushing wasn't going well. "Really?" I snorted. "In what way? That I'm not afraid of you? All those muscles don't scare me."

I thought I saw a tiny smile form on those thick lips, but in a flash, it was gone, replaced by a tight mask of indifference. "I seriously doubt you know many Merlins." Just like there weren't many powerful witches, even fewer of them became Merlins. We were a select few.

Valen's gaze went sharp, and for the briefest of moments, a look of pure, primal hunger flashed over his face.

I stiffened, and then my traitorous body fluttered in response to whatever that was. And it wasn't fear.

"You're married to a human," stated Valen, like this was old news. His face again, carefully blank. "Interesting choice."

My lips parted in surprise. "Soon to be unmarried," I shot back, pricks of unease working through my body. I didn't particularly appreciate how he'd said "interesting choice," like I'd lowered myself by marrying Martin. Maybe I had. But I didn't like having it thrown in my face. "You've been checking up on me?" I wasn't thrilled that this stranger knew personal things about me when I knew pretty much nothing about him, apart from the fact that he was usually a prick and owned a restaurant that served fantastic food.

"It's my business to know about strangers in my city," said Valen. "We don't like strangers."

"*Your* city?" I gave him a hard stare. "Are you saying you own New York City?" Wow, this guy was infuriating. He was pushing all my buttons.

Valen flicked his gaze across the room, not really settling on anything. "No. I don't own the city. But the Twilight Hotel is in my territory. I'm responsible for the paranormals in this sector. What goes on in here is my business."

This conversation was all kinds of weird. I knew there were paranormal bosses, alphas, and heads of clans and packs in certain large city districts like Manhattan, but I'd rarely had to deal with any of them. I also knew that paranormals tended to disappear if you pissed them off. "Listen. I don't know who you are or if any of that is true, but I know I have a job to do. You're messing with it right now. You're making it impossible for me to work." I made a mental note to investigate this man-beast, along with my case. He'd checked up on me. It was only fair that I returned the favor.

A female voice rose in pitch from the hallway. I couldn't make out what she was saying, but I was pretty sure Jimmy would give me a rundown later.

Valen's intelligent gaze regarded me for a beat. "Did you like the duck?"

My eyebrows shot up, completely taken off guard by that question. "Huh?"

"The roast duck with figs... was it to your liking?" Valen's deep voice rumbled, and I found myself entranced by it.

I blinked. "Yes. It was good. Very good." Why the hell were we talking about food?

The man-beast watched me again, almost like he was wondering if he should put a hit on me. That, or rip off my clothes. I thought he was going to say something, but he moved past me and headed right for the bathroom.

Only when I stood in the bathroom's doorway did I realize that I'd forgotten to put the metal vent back. Whoops.

Valen's eyes went to the duct cavity in the wall and then back to me, resting on the laptop again.

"Stealing hotel property?" Valen's gaze bore into mine. "That's a crime. Even here."

At that, my face was scorched like I'd doused it in molten lava. "I didn't *steal* anything. This is my laptop." I was a terrible liar. It didn't help that I stuttered and avoided his eyes. *Nice one, Leana.*

But it didn't explain why he suspected it wasn't

mine. If I didn't know any better, I'd say he knew Eddie had hidden his laptop somewhere in this room. He'd come for the computer.

I thought he was about to rip into me about the computer, but he said nothing. Without another word or glance in my direction, Valen walked out of the bathroom and into the hallway as I made my way to the door. I stood there, Jimmy at my feet, watching the man-beast and the two maids step into the elevator at the end of the hallway.

Valen looked my way. Our eyes met and held for a beat as the elevator doors slid shut.

"What can you tell me about that guy?" I asked Jimmy as I pulled the door to the room shut.

"A lot," answered the toy dog.

"Good."

We'd made good progress by finding the laptop and seeing that the video was tampered with. But I couldn't suppress the feeling that Valen somehow knew something about the murders. What was his connection?

I only knew for sure that he'd come for Eddie's laptop. I was certain of it. Did he know about the videos? Was he here to destroy the evidence?

I was going to find out.

CHAPTER 9

"Have you seen Basil?" I leaned on the front desk, careful not to hit the laptop still tucked under my arm.

"Why are you looking for him?" Errol was picking his nails with a letter opener, a bored expression on his face.

"Because I need to speak to him. Where is he?"

"Why?"

I gritted my teeth. "Hotel business."

Errol let out a dramatic sigh. "*I'm* the hotel business."

"Not this one."

"Tell me why you want to see him, and maybe I'll tell you."

Part of me wanted to jump over the desk and strangle him. "You're particularly shitty this morning."

The concierge made a face like I'd just spat on his expensive suit. "I don't like you."

"Come on, Errol, this is important," shot Jimmy from the floor. "Just tell us where he is."

"I don't respond to wooden toys. Go find a child or something. Or better yet. Go jump in a fire."

I laughed. "How the hell did you get a job in hospitality?"

Errol's pale face reddened. "Because I'm *excellent* at my job."

I pushed back from the counter. "Looks to me more like whoever hired you is a moron."

"That would make *me* the moron," said a voice.

Crap.

I turned slowly. An average-looking man with a forgettable face stood behind me. Most of his scalp showed through his thinning hair, and he'd attempted, very poorly, to comb over the strings of hair he had left. Dark circles marred his eyes, like someone who hadn't slept in years. It was hard to guess his age due to his sickly looking face. Maybe fifty? Sixty? His skin was oily, and his dark suit looked like he'd picked it from a thrift shop. In his hands hung a stained cloth and a bottle of disinfectant.

"I'm Raymond. The assistant manager of the hotel. How can I help?"

I felt a little relief wash through me. "Hi. I'm Leana."

Raymond was nodding. "Yes. I know who you are."

"Good. We're looking for Basil. Have you seen him?"

Raymond moved over to me, nudged me off the counter with a shove of the cloth in his hand, sprayed where I'd touched it, and began to scrub the surface.

I wasn't sure if I should be insulted. He was paranormal, no doubt, but all I was getting from him with the scent of vinegar and bleach. The dude was a germophobe.

"He left for some personal matter," said Raymond as he buffed the same spot continuously. "He'll be back later in the afternoon." He eyed the spot one final time and then looked at me, blinking pale eyes. "There. Must keep the hotel looking its best at all times."

Jimmy snorted, winning a glare from Raymond.

"Sure." He was a strange creature.

Raymond raised his bottle and aimed it at me like he was about to spray. "Shall I take a message? Or maybe I can help you."

"It's fine. I'll wait for him to get back." The fewer people who knew about the footage, the better.

"As you wish." Raymond cast his gaze over the lobby, his eyes settling on something, and he took off. He crossed the lobby to a group of guests lounging on the couches and sprayed his disinfectant on a coffee table to the many outbursts of annoyance from the guests.

"Come on. Let's check with security," called Jimmy from the floor.

I followed behind the toy dog as he rolled ahead. He stopped at a black metal door just off the lobby. The sign on the door said HOTEL SECURITY.

I knocked once and pushed in.

The first thing that hit me was the strong cigarette smell. The second was how tight the space was, like the size of the bathroom in my new apartment. The back wall was covered in floor-to-ceiling screens. A desk sat before the screens, topped with four laptops. The largest man I'd ever seen was squeezed into the only swivel chair. Dark hair covered most of his face, and light eyes peered from under thick brows.

"Yes?" said the man in a thick voice that matched his frame. "What do you want?"

I took a step back. My heart pounded at the threat in his voice and the way he was looking at me. He could easily snap off my head. The scent of wild animals hit me. Yup. This guy was a shifter. Werebear, judging by his size.

"Oh, hi, Jimmy," said the large man, his demeanor switching in a second to something soft and even possibly brotherly. "I didn't see you there. You here for another game of chess?"

"Hey, Bob. Not today." Jimmy rolled inside the room. "Bob's a werebear," informed the toy dog. "But don't let his size scare you. He's a big teddy bear."

"Mmm," I said, still a little taken aback by his enormous size.

"We want to ask you about the security cameras," the toy dog went on.

"Ah. You want to know about the murders?" His eyes looked me over. "You the new Merlin?"

"I am." *Please don't eat me.* "Can you show me the feed from those nights? Start with room four oh four." The clip was still fresh in my memory. I didn't take Bob for the murdering type, maybe just the killing type. But unless I could clear him, he was one of the only people I knew who had access to the cameras. And by looking at his setup, he could easily have altered the video. I wanted to see his reaction with my own eyes.

Bob moved a beefy finger over the keypad of one of the laptops. He clicked on something, and then one of the larger screens on the wall flashed. Suddenly I was staring at the same footage I saw on Eddie's laptop.

"Can you fast-forward to around 11:31 p.m.?" I instructed.

Bob did as I asked without a second thought, and then we were looking at the same spot where it jumped frames.

"Did you see that?" I squeezed around the desk and pointed to the frame. "Stop and go back a few frames."

Bob did as I asked. "What am I looking at?"

"The lighting." I pointed at the screen. "Look. It changes. Someone erased a part of your footage. The time frame was also manipulated. There's no difference in time. Just the video."

Unless Bob was an Oscar-quality actor, he was genuinely surprised and shocked at what he saw on the screen. Then… then he got mad, and that was truly scary.

He jumped up, the floor and walls shaking with his brute force. The top of his head hit the ceiling, though he barely took notice. "Who would do that?"

"That's the million-dollar question," said Jimmy. "Or is it billion-dollar question these days?"

"Bob?" I squeezed back around the desk. "If I were to take a chunk out of the video recording, how would I do that? How would I manipulate the feed?"

"Yeah," agreed Jimmy. "How would someone do that?'

Bob looked from me to the laptop. "You'd have to change the original. Go into the editing program and manually change it."

I tapped my chin with a finger. "So you'd have to be *inside* this room to do it."

The big man frowned. "Yes."

"Unless they did it remotely. Could they?" I asked. With so many hackers these days, anybody could be a potential hacker.

Bob shook his head. "Our network system is not like the human networks. You can't log in remotely, and you can't hack it from outside either. It's protected. Magically protected. Wards and such. There's only one way someone did this—inside this room."

"You've got cameras in here?" I looked around, hopeful.

"No. Sorry."

"Apart from you and Basil, does anyone else have access to this room?" I asked, following his logic. So whoever changed the feed had to get into this room and get past Bob, which was no easy feat.

Bob looked troubled as he squeezed his large behind into that chair. It was a mystery that it fit and didn't crush the chair under his weight. "Just me and Basil."

"Who works this office when you're on break or when you go home?" Jimmy asked, pulling the question right out of my mouth.

Through his thick beard, Bob's lips pursed. "No one. It's just me."

"So there's a time when no one is in here," I said out loud. Someone could have easily waited for Bob to finish his shift and made their way in to sabotage the footage. Which meant we weren't any closer to finding who that person was.

"Thanks for your time, Bob," I told the giant werebear. We weren't going to get much else.

Someone had screwed with the footage. I just didn't know who. I doubted it was Basil. He didn't look like the type who would know how to navigate and edit digital footage and then make it nearly impossible to catch, but I was still going to talk to him.

Teeth flashed, and I jerked back, only noticing that big Bob had just smiled at me. To anyone else, it could have looked like he wanted to chomp down on my head.

"Anytime," said Bob.

I started out the door. Jimmy rolled along next to me but then halted and spun around. "Did anyone else ask about the cameras?"

Bob blinked as he thought about it. "The other

Merlin before you and Basil."

"Thanks."

I closed the door behind me. "Looks like Eddie knew something was up."

"Looks that way," answered the toy dog.

I looked around the lobby. It was around ten in the morning, and the hotel was buzzing with guests. One glimpse in Errol's direction, at the frown on his face while listening to a couple speaking to him at the front desk, made me smile.

We walked through the lobby. Well, I was walking, and Jimmy was rolling next to me. Not a single person looked our way. No one seemed bothered by the fact that I was waltzing around with a wooden toy dog at my feet in a fancy hotel, but this wasn't the average human hotel. This was a paranormal one.

"Do you want to put the computer in one of the hotel's safes?" inquired Jimmy as he rolled to a stop.

I stared down at my wooden friend. "The hotel has safes?"

"Yup. It's where the guests put their valuables, precious stones, jewelry, magic wands, orbs, weapons that were confiscated—that kind of thing. I'm sure it'll be safe."

I thought about it. "I think I'll keep it with me for now. I still have to go through it. There's still a lot I don't know about Eddie." I tapped the computer under my arm. "I think I'll take him to bed with me."

Jimmy laughed. "Where do you want to look next?"

"I have some errands to run. I need to stock my

fridge. And I need clothes. I kinda left in a hurry from my old place. You wanna come with me? I can stuff you in my bag. No one will notice."

The dog's tail bent down almost between his back wheels. "Can't. I can't leave the hotel."

"Ever?"

"Ever."

"Have you tried?" Of course, he had, but I wanted to know.

"Many times, and it's always the same."

"What?"

"Excruciating pain," said the toy dog. "And if I stay outside longer than a few seconds, I will die."

I narrowed my eyes suddenly, a bitter taste in my mouth as anger flowed through me. The fact that the sorceress had done this to this poor man bothered me. "What was her name? The sorceress."

"Doesn't matter anymore." Jimmy rolled away. "See you later, Leana." I watched as he rolled down the lobby, no one bothering to look at him.

"Wait!" I called. "How do I get ahold of you? Do you have a room or something?"

Jimmy halted and spun around. The wooden toy dog looked sad for a moment, if that were even possible. "Just holler, and I'll find you."

I watched with a heavy heart as my new friend rolled away. Not only was he a prisoner in a toy dog's body, but he was also a prisoner in this hotel.

I felt a rush of hate for this sorceress. She might still be alive. And if she was, I would find her and have words with this bitch.

CHAPTER 10

My first stop was Macy's on West Thirty-Fourth Street. With my cash advance, I was able to buy a crapload of new underwear, bras, T-shirts, jeans, socks, bath towels, and some cotton sheets for the bed. I even bought a new leather shoulder bag for the laptop, so I could carry it properly without any nosy man-beasts asking too many questions.

Speaking of said nosy man-beast, I needed to know more about this Valen character and why he wanted the laptop in question. Was he working for someone, or was he trying to get his hands on the evidence himself?

It didn't help that I found him ridiculously attractive, with all those manly muscles and big, rough hands that I was sure would feel amazing on my skin. Yeah. I was losing it. Just a few days ago I had walked in on my husband banging some woman and had walked away, and now this handsome, dangerous dude was haunting my thoughts.

I blamed it on my hormones. Premenopause, or whatever it was, made your woman hormones go out of whack in your forties.

The truth was I didn't need a man to feel complete or comfortable in my own skin. I just needed me. I was my own hero. But that didn't mean I didn't think they were pretty to look at. I didn't trust them, especially after being with Martin, but I wasn't so naïve to think all men were bastards. I knew some were good guys, but most of the time, the good ones were already taken and settled with families.

I was lonely and had been for years. And with my luck, I would stay that way for another while. Good thing I had this new job to keep me busy.

On my way, I stopped at the small bodega on the corner of Park Avenue and East Thirty-Seventh Street and got some groceries to last me a few days until I had to go out for more. Of course, I popped into the nearest wine shop and grabbed two bottles of whatever they had on sale.

A glass of wine would be welcomed with all the research I had to do tonight, mainly with Eddie's computer. I wanted to know what he knew before he died. Maybe I'd find more than just the video feeds. Perhaps he'd discovered something else, and I needed to know.

By the time I made my way back to 444 Fifth

Avenue, the clock on my phone said 6:53 p.m. No wonder I was so hungry. I didn't have breakfast, and I'd forgotten to have lunch.

I swept my gaze around the street. The hotel was nowhere in sight. Damn. I'd been so immersed in my thoughts that I'd walked right past it and didn't even notice.

"Definitely need to eat," I muttered to myself.

I turned on the spot and walked back a few steps, only to realize I *was* at the correct location. My eyes flicked to the green street sign with the words stenciled in white that read Fifth Avenue. Then my eyes settled on the restaurant After Dark. I was standing *right* in front of the restaurant. The Twilight Hotel should be there, right there, but I was staring at a dark alley. No hotel. Nothing.

"Oh shit."

Panic licked up my spine. Was this how the humans saw it? What was going on? I knew the hotel was there, but for some reason, I couldn't *see* it anymore.

My heart rate shot through the roof. I couldn't panic right now. Humans were all around me, and the last thing I wanted was to draw unwelcome attention to myself.

I took a deep breath, gripped my shopping bags, hauled my new leather bag on my shoulder, and walked forward. I might not see it, but I'd feel it.

I walked straight with my right hand in the air. I got a few looks from some humans walking past me.

They probably thought I was some crazy lady or I'd lost my sight.

But when I'd reached halfway down the alleyway, seeing the sign West Fortieth Street at the other end of the block, I started to panic. I'd crossed the entire block without feeling so much as a solid wall.

"This is bad." What the hell was happening?

With my bags gripped tightly in my hands, I turned around and doubled back, going right back the way I'd come, all the way back to the wide sidewalk on Fifth Avenue... but nothing. It was as though the hotel had never existed.

Fear pounded through me, making me irrational. Had I imagined the whole thing? Was I so messed up with my marriage that I had created this part to help me cope? Of course I had a wild imagination, but I was pretty sure I'd lived this experience. Hell, I'd slept in the damn hotel.

No, something was definitely wrong. Somehow the hotel wouldn't reveal itself to me anymore.

"Maybe I need a password. A magic word." Yeah, I wouldn't be surprised if Basil had forgotten to tell me that I needed a special password to get back into the hotel after spending more than a few hours out. It made sense.

I dropped my bags on the ground and rubbed my hands. "Open sesame," I muttered and got a few laughs from a passing group of teenagers.

"Abracadabra," I tried again, waving my fingers for good measure, but still nothing. I didn't even feel the magical pulsing of the glamour that hid the hotel from human eyes anymore.

"The Twilight Hotel. Reveal yourself!" I said and waited. Soon my fear was replaced by irritation and a bit of my sanity. I stomped my foot on the ground. Yup, very mature. "Open up, you damn hotel, or I'm going to clog all the toilets!"

Nope. Still just an alley.

I let out a breath and rubbed my eyes with my fingers. "I can't freaking believe this."

"You lost?"

I flinched but kept my hands covering my eyes. I didn't need to see the person to know it was the man-beast from the restaurant next door.

"Go away," I said, still hiding my eyes. When I heard his chuckle, I dropped my hands, spun, and glowered at him. "What's so funny?"

Valen, being himself, stood with his arms crossed over his broad chest, amusement flashing in his dark eyes. "You can't find the hotel. Can you?"

Shit. If he knew, that meant I was right. I needed a password or something. Heat rushed to my face, a mixture of embarrassment and the fact that he was so damn fine and right next to me.

A black leather jacket hung over his broad shoulders, drawing my eyes down to his narrow waist. His dark jeans fit his long thighs perfectly, and the T-shirt did nothing to hide his muscled chest.

I puffed out some air. "Of course I can see it." I totally couldn't.

His dark eyes fastened on me. "Really? Then why aren't you going inside?"

"I thought I'd get some fresh air first."

Valen raised a brow. "You mean some exhaust fumes?"

I flashed him a smile. "Nothing like the toxic air to unclog my pores."

Valen laughed again, the sound a deep rumble that sent delicious tingles over my skin. I found myself liking how it sounded. Crap. I had to stop this. He was bad. Hot bad, but still bad. And he knew about Eddie's laptop, which put him on the list of "possible suspects."

When I realized he must have seen me lose my cool and walk up and down the alley like someone who'd lost her mind, more heat rushed up from my neck and settled around my face. And now I was sweating. Excellent.

I glanced at him again, realizing he'd been staring at me. His eyes were intense as they beheld me. I felt mesmerized by them. I couldn't help it. I felt a pull toward him, even if he was lethal.

"If you *can* see it," challenged Valen, "then go on ahead. Go in."

"Why? So you can stare at my ass? I don't think so."

Valen smiled. It transformed his face from ruggedly handsome to a whole new level of sexy.

He stared at the ground, laughing silently. "You're a witch. Right?"

"Yes. We've already been through this. I'm a Merlin. Remember?"

The corners of his eyes crinkled with laughter. "And you don't know when someone puts a spell on you?"

Oh shit. I swallowed hard. *There goes my reputation.* "You think? No. Are you serious?" What he said made much more sense now that I thought about it. Why hadn't I thought about it?

Valen nodded as he glanced in the direction of where the hotel was, though I still couldn't see it. "Someone spelled you so you can't see the hotel."

Now that I knew what had been done to me, I recognized the faint magic as it swept around me, crawling over my skin like hundreds of ants until it faded all together. I wasn't much for glamours, but I knew of them. I knew whoever had put this spell on me was an experienced magical practitioner with a high level of magic. Especially to put a spell on me without my knowledge.

I stared at him. "How would you know this?"

The big man shrugged. "The Twilight Hotel will forever ensure that all of us paranormals can find it. It's always visible to us unless a spell keeps it hidden. Like you right now. You looked like a human looking for her lost cat."

Damn. So he had been watching me.

I clenched my jaw and looked in the direction he was staring. Someone inside there had spelled me. Motherfrackers.

"So, there wasn't a password to get back in?" I felt

like a fool. A big ol' fool. Maybe that person had been watching me make a fool out of myself the whole time too.

"No password," said the man-beast with laughter in his voice. "Just a spell. Or whatever magic you witches use."

"This isn't funny," I snapped.

"Yes. It's very funny."

I sighed. "And here I thought I was having a good day." I glanced at him. "Was it you?" What? I had to know.

At that, Valen chuckled, his wide chest jumping up and down. "I don't do magic. Not my thing."

I raised a brow. "All paranormals have some magic flowing in them. Whether it's the wild magic of shifters or the cold magic of demons."

Valen's face went still. "It wasn't me. If it was, why would I be here now?"

Good point. "So, what's *your* thing, then? You know about me. It's only fair I know about you."

Valen just kept staring at me with those damn dark eyes. I could still see a spark of laughter in them. The guy was having a blast at my expense. Great.

"Who would do this?" I asked after a moment, but I knew the answer as soon as the words left my mouth.

The one who'd committed the murders, that's who. They didn't want me back inside the hotel because I was onto something. I knew about the cameras. And this spell led me to believe I was about to discover more.

The fact that they did this to me only made me want to solve the case even more.

I was going to find these bastards.

We stood in an awkward silence for a while, my heart making music in my ears in the swirl of conflicting feelings while my entire body thrummed with heat that had nothing to do with my warm jacket.

Valen bent down and grabbed my bags. "Come on. I'll take you inside," he said finally, his tone caring and soft, which threw me off a little.

I didn't say anything as I followed closely behind him, not wanting to miss anything. If he should disappear, I'd find myself alone again and unable to find the hotel entrance.

I felt a little more relaxed that he didn't look or sound angry. I took that as a good sign.

I'd barely noticed the change in air pressure as the world around me changed. Suddenly I was staring at the inside of the hotel and not eyeing an alleyway.

"Is the spell gone?" asked Valen, and I turned to meet his eyes.

"Yes. You were right. Thank you," I added a little awkwardly.

He opened his mouth to say something but then stopped. Steadying himself, he tried again. "Here." He gave me my bags.

I took the bags from him, and before I could thank

him again, he'd turned his back on me and made his way out the front doors.

I watched him go, more confused than ever about this guy. Why did he help me get back inside the hotel if he was truly bad? It could be to throw me off, to make me *think* he was one of the good guys when in reality, he wasn't.

I watched him through the front lobby windows until he turned left and disappeared.

CHAPTER 11

The smell of cooking had my mouth watering as I entered my apartment. The door was already open wide, which was why I'd smelled the cooking before I saw it.

The sound of voices wafted over to me, both male and female. I reached the end of the hallway and walked into the kitchen.

Elsa stood at the stove, the sleeves of her orange blouse folded at the elbow as she mixed a tall stainless-steel pot on the burner.

Julian lounged on the couch. He had one arm around a young woman with long, blonde hair, who I didn't recognize, and a beer in the other.

Jade was busy setting the table with wineglasses. She wore a black, vintage Def Leppard T-shirt with baggy jeans and had her hair in a punk-esque updo with a black bow. She saw me and raised a glass in salute. "Hey, Leana. Hope you're hungry. Elsa's making her famous chili con carne."

"Oh, hi, Leana," said Elsa as she smiled at me over the steam of her chili. "Hope you like spices. Oh. You eat meat. Right?"

I laughed. "I do." I was trying to cut back, but I didn't want to take away her thunder.

"Leana, this is Carmen," said Julian, raising his beer. I gave the pretty blonde a smile, but she seemed to be only interested in Julian.

I looked around. "You guys bought food? And wine?" I couldn't believe these witches' generosity, and I barely knew them.

"Of course we did," said Jade, flashing her big smile at me. "You're family now."

A surge of warmth wrapped around my heart and tightened my throat. My eyes burned, and I quickly looked away.

The sound of wheels whirring on the carpeted floor brought my attention behind me as Jimmy rolled into the apartment.

"How did the shopping go?" asked the toy dog, his spring metal tail wagging behind him. He might not be a real dog, but he was cute as hell.

I raised my bags. "Good. Let me drop this off." After putting the bags containing my new clothes, sheets, and towels in my bedroom, I returned to the kitchen and set the bags with the food and wine on the counter.

Elsa looked at me. Splatters of chili spotted her face and her blouse. "Dinner will be ready in about fifteen minutes. Need to let the chili cool for a bit. If it's served too hot, it'll just spoil the flavor."

I smiled at the older witch. "Thank you for doing this. You guys are amazing."

"Have some wine," said Jade as she handed me a glass of red.

"Thanks. I really needed that." I took a sip of the wine, moaned a little at the fruity taste, and started to stack my fridge with the fruits and vegetables I'd bought earlier.

Jade came to stand next to Elsa, hands on her hips. She leaned over and said, "You're putting in too much cayenne pepper."

"Don't be ridiculous. I've made my chili thousands of times. I know what I'm doing."

I joined the witches at the stove. "Can I help?" It was a strange feeling having people cooking dinner for me, let alone having my apartment filled with people.

The last time I had people over at my place, it was with my husband. He'd invited his parents for dinner about five years ago. Let's just say the evening didn't go so well. I ended up excusing myself, lying that I had to work, just to escape their condescending stares and hateful remarks that I hadn't given them any grandchildren yet.

Not for the lack of trying. But after countless tests, I was told I was barren. The initial shock of being told that I couldn't do the one thing I was supposed to be able to do as a woman sent me into a deep depression. It didn't help the marriage, either, and Martin pulled away after that. I was damaged goods to his eyes.

Needless to say, that was why I'd immersed myself with work. Those wounds healed as I accepted the cards I'd been dealt. It took years, but I was finally happy again.

Elsa pointed a finger at me. "You just relax. We'll take care of everything."

"Go sit," said Jade, pushing me out of the kitchen. "We've got this."

"Okay, okay," I laughed. They didn't have to tell me twice.

My eyes found my divorce papers tucked neatly on the counter next to the fridge, and I made a face. I did not want to ruin the night by filling those out. I'd handle them tomorrow.

I grabbed my wineglass and moved to the living room. Julian was whispering something in Carmen's ear, making her giggle. Giving Julian and his lady friend some privacy, I slumped into the chair next to the window. The sounds of the busy street slipped in from the open window, carrying a bit of cool air.

"So, how are you finding the hotel so far?" Jimmy rolled to a stop at my feet.

I set the wineglass on my lap and looked down. "I like it. It's not what I imagined. It's better. Well, apart from the three deaths."

The toy dog swiveled his ears forward. "Glad to hear it. It does grow on you after a while." His eyes flicked around the room.

I wanted to ask him how long he'd been at the hotel, but then I remembered that he'd been cursed all those years ago. I didn't want to make him any sadder than he was.

I leaned back in my chair. "What can you tell me about Valen?" I figured this line of conversation was better. Better for me, of course.

The dog's jaw flapped down. "Lots. What do you want to know?"

"Everything," I told him. "Start with his history. Who is he? Where did he come from?"

"Well, I'll tell you what I know," began the toy dog. "I know he moved here from Chicago after his wife died from ovarian cancer."

"Oh no." My heart tugged at his words, and I found myself nodding and speaking around a rather tight throat. I knew all too well what losing a loved one to that horrible disease was like. Even paranormals weren't immune to some of the human diseases, cancer being the major one.

"Bought the restaurant next door," continued Jimmy. "Fixed it up and made it more modern, or so my spies tell me."

I gave a little laugh. "You've got spies?"

"Everywhere," said the little toy dog. "I have eyes and ears outside this hotel." After a moment, he added, "I think he needed a change. A new place that didn't remind him of the past."

"Must have been horrible for him." I was sure it also contributed to his short temper and irritability. Losing a loved one changed a person.

"I'm sure. He dates, nothing long-term, and I don't remember ever seeing him with the same woman more than once. He told me he'd had enough of high-maintenance women and all the drama. Wants no commitments."

I laughed. "You asked him?"

"Yeah. I mean, we already have a man-whore in the hotel. We don't need two."

"Heard that," called Julian from the couch, though when he caught me looking at him, he winked, seemingly delighted at the nickname.

I turned my attention back to Jimmy. "What can you tell me about his business? Not the restaurant, the other part. He told me that he's responsible for the paranormals in this district. What is that about?"

"Well," said the toy dog, his left ear swiveled back. "I'm not really sure. The guy is very secretive. But I think he meant it more like as a paranormal. It's his duty. He feels a responsibility to keep others like him safe."

"Doesn't explain why he showed up at Eddie's old room," I said. "And how he knew there was a hidden laptop."

Jimmy rolled back. "That I don't know."

"Does he have people working for him? Like the maids?" I asked, remembering the two pretty maids from this morning.

"Possibly," answered Jimmy. "Or the maids might just be some of his lady friends."

"Right." Damn. Just how many women did this guy sleep with? "So, he's like an alpha?"

"Yeah, I guess," said the dog.

I leaned forward. "What kind of shifter is he? No

one seems to be able to give me a straight answer." I had thought werebear at first, but now after meeting Bob, I wasn't so sure. He didn't give off the same kind of energy that Bob did. Whatever Valen was, he was different.

"Beats me," answered the dog. "I went through all the list of shifters and weres with him once, but he never told me. Believe me, I kept asking him that the whole first year he'd moved here. Never let it slip once."

I pursed my lips in thought. "Sounds like he doesn't want anyone to know." And in my experience, if you hid something, it was because it was bad, and you didn't want others to know about it. So, the question was, what was Valen hiding? Because he certainly felt the need to hide his animal self from us.

The dog cocked his head to the side. "You're a witch. Don't you have a spell that could reveal that?"

I shook my head. "Not that kind of witch."

Jimmy's jaw fell open to ask the obvious question, but Elsa interrupted him.

"Dinner is served!" she called and clapped her hands. "Let's eat before it gets cold."

I leaped to my feet, wine in hand, and looked down at Jimmy. "You don't eat, right?"

"No," said the toy dog, not sounding a bit saddened by the fact. "But I do like to watch."

I frowned. That sounded kinda dirty.

I moved to the dining table, Jimmy in tow, and sat next to Julian and his lady friend.

The table setting wasn't fancy. If fact, there wasn't

one, not really. The centerpiece was a giant pot of chili surrounded by six bottles of wine. A collection of different place mats was set in the designated spots. It was a mismatch of tall and short glasses, some plastic with faded patterns. The utensils were dull and old. The plates, well, they looked like they were from the 1970s. Not a single plate matched another. The only thing they had in common were the scratches.

And I loved it.

It was like us, a mismatch of witches, none of us the same, but we fit remarkably well together.

"Oh. We're missing a chair?" said Jade, scratching her head. "I'll go get one from my place." She disappeared while Elsa filled each bowl with a generous scoop of chili and reappeared moments later with a chair she squeezed next to Elsa's at the end.

I helped myself to some salad, a mix of yellow and red tomatoes, cucumber, and diced feta cheese, dripping with olive oil and balsamic vinaigrette.

Next, I tore into the chili. It took every bit of effort not to moan as my taste buds exploded with all the wonderful flavors. Elsa could cook up a mean chili con carne.

"Mmmm," I said to Elsa around chews. "Excellent chili. What's in the sauce?"

Elsa's smile widened to her ears as she poured herself a substantial amount of wine. "Ah. It's my secret." I couldn't help but notice that she'd wrapped her hand around her locket as she'd said it.

Jade stood up suddenly and raised her glass of red wine. "I'd like to make a toast."

Following her example, we all took our glasses and raised them.

Jade's eyes fell on me. "To Leana. Welcome to the family."

"To Leana!" chorused the voices around the table.

"To me," I said, the tips of my ears burning as I finished the toast with a large gulp of my wine through a colossal smile.

For the first time in a long while, I felt welcomed and a part of something, like a real family. I could get used to that nice, comfortable, familiar feeling.

"Help!"

And then maybe not.

I spun around in my seat to the sound of a terrified voice and recognized the elderly, tall, thin woman wearing a long nightgown.

"Barb?" Elsa shot to her feet, and so did I. So did everyone. "What's the matter?"

Barb's eyes widened in terror as she clutched the front of her nightgown. "Demon!" said the older woman. "There's a demon in the hotel!"

Guess my wine was going to have to wait.

CHAPTER 12

Everyone in the room looked at me with expectant expressions mirrored on their faces.

Right. I was the Merlin.

I stepped around my chair and came to face the older woman. "Are you sure it's a demon?" The odds that a demon was in the hotel were slim to none. I'd felt the wards the first time I'd stepped through into the lobby. They seemed carefully crafted by probably some of the most powerful witches or wizards to keep malevolent demons from entering. The hotel was a sanctuary, a safe haven where paranormals went if they had a demon on their tail.

The Veil also protected our world, like an invisible supernatural layer. But sometimes the Veil had cracks called Rifts, where demons got through.

Unless someone had *let* them in.

Barb's fear turned into anger, her wrinkled face making her look harsh. "I know a demon when I see one. I've been a witch longer than you've been alive, girlie girl."

I stared at the older witch, seeing her eyes clear, and she seemed alert. "Okay. How many demons?" I was still not 100 percent sure she'd seen a real demon, but it was clear she *believed* she had.

Barb let out a sigh. "One. Just one, I think."

I was nodding as I started for the door. "Where's the demon?"

"The ninth floor," said the older witch as I rushed out of my apartment.

I stopped at the elevator, changed my mind, instead, pushed the emergency exit doors, and hit the staircase. By the time the elevator reached the top floor, I'd already be on the ninth.

I took the stairs two at a time. The adrenaline coursing through my body helped my thighs push me forward. I wasn't twenty anymore, I wasn't as fast as I used to be. I had to rely on my profound hatred for demons to fuel my legs. I was fit, but I wasn't an athlete.

My breath came fast as I pulled open the door to the ninth floor and stepped into the hallway. I stopped to listen as I blinked into the darkness, looking for signs of the ceiling lights but saw none. The faint whisper of water running through pipes answered back. Then nothing. The dim scent of sulfur lay in the air followed by the pulsing of something cold and vile and not of this world. A demon. The old witch had been right.

I looked to the window at the end of the hallway.

It was small, and I could just make out the dark, clouded sky through two tall buildings.

With my heart pounding in my ears, I stepped forward. The sound of glass crunching under my boots stopped me dead in my tracks

"Okay. Who turned off the lights?" I muttered into the darkness. I yanked out my cell phone and switched on the flashlight.

I looked to the side wall, and as my eyes adjusted to the darkness, I could make out the two adjacent light fixtures, their glass bulbs shattered.

Not knowing which hotel door the demon had slipped through, I walked to the first door on the floor and checked the knob. Locked.

The sounds of feet running and the click of a metal door opening and closing spun me around with my heart in my throat.

The emergency exit door slammed shut as Jade, Elsa, and Julian clambered into the hallway behind me.

"What are you guys doing here?" I hissed. Not that I didn't appreciate the help, but I was the Merlin here, and I didn't want my new friends to get hurt.

Elsa slipped forward. "You're going to need our help," she said, tapping her locket as though it might contain some great power.

"We might not be Merlins like you," said Jade, "but we can help."

"We can," Julian reiterated. When my flashlight rolled over him, he was wearing a long leather duster that I'd never seen on him before.

I opened my mouth to tell them to go, but looking at their defiant faces, I doubted it would make a difference.

"Just don't get killed," I said as I turned back, staring at the dark hallway. The cold pulsing in the air intensified, matching the throbbing of my heart in my chest.

"Where is it?" asked Julian. "Where's the demon?"

Screams erupted from down the hallway. "Follow the screaming," I whispered and started running.

I rounded the end of the hallway and took a right. Soft-yellow light shone from the only door that stood ajar, the faded sticker indicating 906. I rushed to the door and pushed it farther open as quietly as I could to step inside. The air was filled with the stench of blood—not exactly the best sign. The room was lit with nothing more than a table lamp that wasn't knocked down.

A body lay on the ground not ten feet from me.

Damn. I rushed to the bundle. She was lying on her side. Female—from her sheer size and the width of her shoulders under the thin, black jacket she was wearing—at least what was left of her.

My lips parted as I ran my eyes over the body. Because, yes, it was a body. No one could be alive and look like that.

The skin over her face, hands, and neck was torn, like something with long claws had attacked her, and she lay in a puddle of her blood. A large gash was torn through her abdomen. A hole meant something inside her had been taken out. Yeah. Pretty gross.

"Oh my," said Elsa, terror flashing across her face.

Jade knelt next to the body, careful not to get any blood on her. "What could do such a thing?"

"Demon," said Julian, taking the word out of my mouth.

"He's right," I said, pulling my eyes away from the dead woman and looking around the room. "So, who let it in? Did someone summon it? And where is it now?" No way could a demon slip through the wards of the hotel. No, I was willing to bet someone had let this sucker in, and I had to find it before it killed anyone else.

As if on cue, another scream erupted from somewhere on the ninth floor, raising my neck hair.

I jumped to my feet, not waiting for anyone as I hurled out of the room and dashed toward the still-screaming male voice.

A door to my left stood open, and I rushed in.

The first thing I saw was a man pressed against the wall, a hand clutched to his bleeding chest. The second was a creature that looked like an overgrown lizard.

The monstrous, mismatched nightmare of scales, fur, claws, and fangs had a collection of black eyes in the front of its flat skull. Its tail ended in a thick talon that whipped menacingly from side to side.

"That's a gutuk demon," said Elsa, joining me at the entrance. "Nasty bastards. Killing machines."

I raised my brow, impressed at her insight. "You know your demons."

"Among other things," said the witch.

The demon wailed and drove itself into the air with its powerful lizard legs, hurtling toward us with frightening speed.

I drew up my will, channeling the emanations and harnessing that celestial energy beyond the clouds. I felt a tingling as it answered.

A spool of blinding-white light curled up in my palms and wove through my fingers in a slow crawl.

And then I let it rip.

Blazing white light soared forth from my outstretched fingers, and I directed it at the demon. It hit the beast in the face, covering the gutuk's body in a sheet of white light.

A shriek of pain came from the gutuk, and then it fell to the ground in a heap of charcoaled, blackened flesh and ash.

"Holy shit," breathed Julian, his eyes wide as he stared at me. "What the hell was that?"

I looked over at Jade and Elsa, who were both staring at me with equal amounts of fascination. Well, I'd done my magic in front of them, so no point in avoiding this anymore.

I opened my mouth to answer. "My magic is different."

"No shit," said Julian.

I took a breath and said, "It's—"

A scream split the air.

Crap. "There's more than one," I said. My eyes

found the still-bleeding man. "Can someone stay with him?"

"I'll look after him," said Elsa, waving us away. "You go. Hurry."

I doubled back and was out the door in a flash. Well, not really. More like half a stumble and a decent jog.

The odds of another demon inside the hotel proved my theory that someone had let them in. No way did two demons slip inside a highly warded establishment.

I made it back into the hallway.

Make that three demons.

Two vile creatures turned at the sound of my approach, just as I caught a glimpse of a mess of black hair as a door slammed shut at the end of the hall.

I could see them, even in the dim light, and I wished I couldn't. These were different than the demon I'd just evaporated. They were naked and horribly misshapen humanoid monsters—hideous, foul, and heavily muscled.

Damn. I wasn't paid enough for this shit. I should have asked Basil for double what he gave me.

"What are they?" asked Jade.

I shrugged. "Ugly bastards." I had no idea. "Naked, ugly bastards," I corrected.

"How many more of these things are there?" Julian was next to me, his hands inside his coat pockets.

"Two," said Jade. "Can't you count?"

I shook my head at these two witches. This wasn't the time to start bickering.

One of the demons, the closest one, charged.

I rolled my shoulders, getting ready, and stepped forward to meet it.

It leaped, swinging one of its long, misshapen arms, ending in talons, at me. I tapped into my will and channeled the celestial energy. I felt a slight tug, and then with a throb, my cosmic power went out.

Uh-oh.

Instinctively, I ducked and rolled as I felt talons pull the top of my hair. I slammed into the wall, my breath escaping me.

"What the hell, Leana?" cried Julian, moving forward and catching the demon's attention.

I pulled myself up. "It happens sometimes. It's not a clear sky tonight."

"What?" yelled Julian, his focus still on the advancing demons.

The same demon that came at me rushed toward Julian. It leaped at him in a blur of grotesque limbs, bringing forth a stink of feces.

Julian pulled his hands from inside his coat, and two twin glass vials shot from his outstretched palms. The demon took them in the chest.

After a clap like thunder, an explosion threw the demon back and up into the air. It was held there for a moment, wreathed in a ring of blue energy. It thrashed and howled, its misshapen limbs flailing and kicking.

And then the demon exploded in a mess of black blood and guts.

Dripping bits of demon rained down around us, landing with little, wet plopping sounds on the carpet, walls, and doors.

Julian caught me looking and grinned. "I'm a potion master. Poisons are my specialty."

Huh. I'd never have guessed. More like love potions were his thing.

A door to my right cracked open to reveal a startled-looking face belonging to a middle-aged man.

"Close your door and lock it," I warned him as I pushed to my feet.

The door slammed in my face as another opened down the hall from us.

"I'll go," said Jade as she ran to the young woman who was staring at the mess in the hallway, with a confused expression.

A scream sounded near us. The voice was young, possibly a teenager. The cry turned high-pitched and then became a strangled sound.

I made a wild dash toward the scream, rounded the end of the hallway, and halted.

The body of a young witch, maybe twenty, lay on the floor in the hallway, her feet hidden inside what I believed was her room. She'd tried and failed to escape.

She rested in a large puddle of her blood, forming a sticky pool around her. Her face was covered in a mask of blood and ribbons of torn flesh. Bile rose in the back of my throat.

Another gutuk hovered over her, eating strings of what looked like her intestines. It had ripped open her throat, too, and gotten her jugular. Her beautiful light eyes stared upward at nothing, glazed and dead.

My vision turned red.

The gutuk turned and looked up at me, strips of the young woman's flesh still hanging from its mouth.

Fury bloomed in my chest. Emotions were always the key to reaching more power. I drew on the celestial magic again, focused all of my will on it, and homed in on one single goal—obliterating the demon.

Putting all my rage into it, I let it go.

Two balls of pure white light hit the demon.

The blow knocked it off the woman to collide with the floor, rolling like a flaming sausage from hell. The white light filled the hallway, illuminating it like sunlight. Heat from the white energy rose, and I took a step back, watching as the demon's body snapped in half and then disintegrated into a pile of ash.

Breathing hard, I sagged with a bit of tiredness. Channeling so much power was like running a marathon, and a sudden weakness in my limbs made me sway.

The ding from the elevator sounded down the hall followed by the aggressive thumps of feet.

Errol came round the corner, his face a mask of

horror and disapproval as his eyes met mine. "Who's going to pay for all of that?"

"Bill me," I said.

Julian walked forward. His eyes were on my hands, which had blazed with white light only moments ago.

"What the hell was that?" asked Julian. "What kind of witch are you?"

"That was starlight," said Elsa, coming around to join us with Jade. "Leana is a Starlight witch."

CHAPTER 13

"What the hell is a Starlight witch?" asked Julian for the third time, sitting on the couch facing me. When we'd returned to the apartment, his date was nowhere to be found, but he seemed more interested in my magic than missing out on sex.

Only Jimmy remained, wagging his tail like a real dog, thrilled to see us back. I wanted to squeeze him. He was so cute. But then I'd remembered that inside that wooden puppy was a grown man, which might have made things a bit awkward.

We'd waited for the cleanup crew to come and take the two bodies away, which was about five minutes after Errol had arrived at the scene, complaining about the mess. Guests were spying on the whole thing from the safety of their rooms. It'd be impossible to keep this attack quiet. Now Basil would have a full-on panic on his hands.

"I'm going to get sacked," Basil had said,

appearing on the scene moments after Errol, his hands on his head and looking as though he was about to keel over.

"You're not going to get sacked." I patted him on the shoulder as I watched the same female witch from the cleanup crew, I'd seen yesterday, sprinkle the same white powder over the dead witch. The body had shimmered before vanishing. Not that it mattered. Nearly the entire floor was out watching these developments. "This is not your fault."

"Of course it's my fault," said the tiny witch, his voice rising in hysterics. "I'm the manager. I'm supposed to make sure guests are safe. *This* is *not* safe! This is death. Demons loose in the hotel? It's never happened in over a hundred years since the hotel's been open for business. This is a catastrophe."

I felt for the small witch. Clearly his job was essential to him, just as mine was to me. "I'm going to find who's responsible. It's why I'm here." Two people had died on my watch, and I wouldn't let it happen again.

Basil turned his face and looked up at me. His expression twisted in what looked like a mix between nausea and fear. "You'd better hurry. If you don't stop these killings soon, we'll have to send everyone away and close the hotel."

Okay. No pressure. "Everyone? Even those of us in the apartments?"

Basil nodded. "Everyone. The hotel cannot afford to lose any more people."

His statement only cemented the urge to find out

where the demons were crossing over as well as those who'd either summoned them or let them in.

Now back in my apartment, with the air still smelling of chili, I'd taken a quick shower to wash away some of the demon bits that were still stuck to me and then joined my friends in the living room.

I pulled my focus away from Julian and stared at my glass of wine, the one I hadn't finished. "Well, it's—"

"Isn't it obvious?" stated Jade, sitting crossed-legged on the floor right in the middle of the living room. Her crimped hair stood on odd ends like she'd stuck her finger in an electrical socket. "Her magic lies in the stars."

Julian whistled. "That's impressive. How come I've never heard of a Starlight witch before?"

"Because they're very rare," said Jade. She leaned forward, excitement rippling through her. "We know living beings generate magical energy; life force itself is a form of magical energy along with the human heart and emotions," continued Jade. Jimmy sat next to her on the floor. She reached out and petted his head.

"Her inner nerd witch is coming out," said Elsa with a smile. "Brace yourselves."

"Souls are also a source of magical energy," Jade continued. "There's the power of the elements. Elemental magic, like what we use, and ley line magic. Then you have magic with the help of demons by borrowing their magic."

"And magic in potions, like Julian here," said

Elsa, tipping her glass of wine at him as he sat next to her on the couch.

Jade rocked forward. "There's power in words, magic words, just like there's power in sigils and seals—if you're a strong enough witch, that is. All witches are born with some level of magical powers inside them, some innate energy given to us by our demon ancestors. Still, not all witches are created equally in strength and magical abilities. Some are born with almost zero powers and are practically human." Jade wiggled her bent legs. "But starlight magic, well, it's power from the stars and constellations, *celestial* power," she added, her eyes wide.

I shrugged it off, feeling a little self-conscious that I had everyone's attention. "You make it sound wonderful. Too bad it's not a reliable source of magic like elemental magic or potions."

"What do you mean?" asked Julian. "I saw you blast that demon. We all did."

"And you also saw me not being able to do squat." I leaned back in my chair and crossed my legs at my ankles. "My magic is limited to a specific group of stars, the ones closest to us, a triple-star system called Alpha Centauri. And it's limited during the day. See, even if the sun is technically a star, it's a bully star. It blocks me from drawing my power from the other stars during the day."

"The sun cockblocks you," said Julian, his lips pursed in a smile.

"Exactly. Which is why starlight magic is best drawn at night," I continued. "Especially when the sky is clear. If it's cloudy like tonight, it's harder to draw and not very reliable."

"So what you're saying is," said Julian, leaning forward. He tipped a short glass with a clear liquid that was either vodka or rum to his mouth and took a sip. "If it's a clear night sky, you're basically unstoppable."

I laughed. "It's when my magic is strongest. Yeah. But like I said, sometimes it can be unreliable."

The sound of metal thumped on the ground as Jimmy wagged his tail. "Wow. I feel like I'm meeting a celebrity."

I burst out laughing. "Good one. Most celebrities aren't broke and homeless." Not that I was at the moment, but I had been.

The toy dog cocked his head. "You'd be surprised."

"Are you the only Starlight witch you know? What about your family?" asked Jade.

"I don't have any family," I told them, my chest squeezing. I was never comfortable with this conversation. "My mother passed away a long time ago, and I never met my father. My mother never talked about him, and she died before I had a chance to ask her. She was a White witch, like you. No siblings. No aunts and uncles. So to answer your question, I've never met another Starlight witch. I just know there are some. We're just rare, I guess."

After that, the silence was so heavy around the apartment that I could almost feel it against my skin like a mist as all of us became lost in our thoughts.

My conversation with Basil came back to me. "Does the hotel have any enemies? Like competing hotels?"

Elsa shrugged. "Not that we know of. The only other paranormal hotel near here is in Boston. The other is in Chicago. Why? What are you thinking?"

I shook my head. "Just something Basil was saying. Sabotage from other hotels, maybe? He told me that if I don't stop these killings, he will have to close the hotel and send everyone away."

"What!" Wine flew from Jade's mouth. "But... where are we supposed to go? This is our home. I've lived here for twenty-three years."

"There goes my casual sex with the ladies on the lower levels," muttered Julian.

Jimmy's head swiveled my way. "What exactly did Basil say?" I noticed the tinge of fear in his voice. If we all had to be forced out, what would happen to Jimmy?

I shifted my weight, unease gnawing in my belly. "Exactly that. He was going to lose his job and that if I don't stop these killings soon, he'd have to send everyone away and close the hotel."

"But what about Jimmy?" asked Jade, echoing my thoughts. "He can't leave."

The toy dog pivoted his ears back. "I'll be fine. I'll have the entire hotel to myself." However, his voice said the opposite.

This wasn't very good.

"Some of the tenants have never lived anywhere else," said Elsa, red spots coloring her cheeks, and I envisioned her blood pressure rising. "Closing the hotel would put us on the street. Families here have children and the elderly. We're like a big family. I've had the same neighbors for as long as I can remember, and now we'd have to be separated."

Jade was running her hands over her thighs, a pained expression on her face. She looked scared. She was more terrified at the prospect of losing her home than facing a demon.

Though Julian was trying to play it cool, his eyes were fixed on his glass. He looked tense and paler than usual.

They were terrified of losing their home, friends, and family. And I'd be damned if I was going to let that happen. I happened to like it here too. I wasn't ready to give it up.

I set my wineglass on the side table. "The hotel won't close. I won't let that happen. Look, there's still time to stop what's happening here."

"Do you have an idea of who's behind this?" asked Jade, her voice hopeful as I felt all their eyes zero in on me.

I sighed through my nose. "Not yet. But someone is letting in demons. You saw it yourself tonight. Only a very powerful magical practitioner could do it. Someone with the knowledge of how to bypass the wards in the hotel. Someone with enough skill to bend the Veil enough to let the demons slip in. Or they could be summoning them from inside the hotel."

Elsa shivered and rubbed her hands over her

arms as though she was cold. "You think a witch inside the hotel is summoning demons?"

"I do," I said. "I think the one responsible is here, inside the hotel. You can't summon a demon from the outside and hope it'll get through. It wouldn't. Just like the demons that actually do escape the Veil can't get in with the wards in place. They're too powerful." I leaned forward. "The only way in is from the inside. And somewhere inside this hotel is a gateway for the demons to cross over—a hole, a crack, whatever you want to call it. A doorway somewhere lets them through."

"Okay," said Julian. "Say that's true. Then it means we have some crazy-ass witch or wizard letting in demons while we sleep. Nice."

"Is there a connection between the previous deaths and tonight?" asked Elsa.

I shrugged. "I'm still working on that. So far, it looks as though the killings were random, no real logic behind them," I said. "Except for Eddie. He was a target because he knew too much. He found out that someone had sabotaged the security cameras." Once the words came out, I sort of let it all out. I knew I could trust Jimmy, and my gut told me I could trust everyone in this room. "Which tells me that whoever's behind this is doing it on purpose. There's a reason they've opened the gates from hell and let the devils in."

"But why?" asked Elsa. "Why would they do this to us?"

"To close the hotel," answered Julian before I had the chance. "To get rid of us."

"But why do they want that?" asked Jade, her back stiff with tension and fear. "We haven't done anything. We just live here. We don't hurt humans or other paranormals. Our lives are very boring."

"Speak for yourself," said Julian. "I happen to lead a full and very vibrant lifestyle."

Jade made a good point. And it was the only real lead so far. Now I had to find out who would profit from the shutting down of the Twilight Hotel. But first, I had other more urgent matters to attend to.

Because the real culprit was still out there, and none of us were safe until I stopped them.

I cleared my throat and stood. "I need to go."

"What? Now?" asked Elsa. "It's nearing midnight."

"Yes. I do my best work at night. It'll be easier for me to draw on my magic. And I'll need all of it if I need to look for possible cracks in the Veil. Or traces of a summons."

Julian stood. "I'll come with you."

"Me too," said Jimmy.

"No," I told them, smiling.

Elsa pressed her hands on her hips. "You can't inspect the entire hotel on your own. It's too damn big."

"With many secret doorways," interjected the toy dog.

I stared down at him. "Secret doorways?" I wasn't

sure if that was true or if Jimmy was just saying that so he could come along.

The toy dog's head bounced. "There's a lot you don't know about this place. I've been here a long time. You need me."

He made a good point. So far, he'd proven to be a perfect partner.

"Okay. Jimmy's with me," I said, and the toy dog started to spin around my ankles. "But I need the rest of you to stay here and keep an eye out. Protect the tenants on this floor should anything happen."

"You think more demons are in the hotel?" Jade's eyes were round.

"It's a possibility," I told her. "Tonight might be just the beginning. There could be more. We just don't know." I pulled out my phone and checked its battery life. I still had about forty-eight percent left. "Call me if you see anything."

"We will," answered Elsa. "Be careful."

"I will," I said, dropping my phone back into my pocket. "Same goes for all of you. No one is safe until I stop whoever's behind this."

"Let's go, Leana." Jimmy zoomed out of the living room and was already at the door by the time I stepped around the coffee table.

I walked down the hallway toward the elevator. I knew two things for sure tonight. First, I knew that more people would die if I didn't find those responsible. And the second, I was on their target list now that I had proof someone had sabotaged the cameras.

I smiled. *Come and get me.*

CHAPTER 14

"Why the basement first?" Jimmy rolled next to me, his wheels crushing the small dirt and pebbles on the cold cement floor.

"I like to work from the ground up," I told him.

The basement was huge and ran the length of the building, with many hallways and doors leading to many rooms. The ceiling was low, and the cement floor smelled of urine and cigarette ashes. I smelled the musty, moldy scent of old things long abandoned as well as a few traces of cigarette smoke and perspiration. Halogen lights hummed and buzzed overhead.

We checked the first room. Shelves and filing cabinets lined the walls. A couch and some chairs sat in a corner next to a coffee table littered with magazines and boxes. More books and boxes cramped the shelves. A room without windows was depressing. I could never work here. It was cold, and I didn't want to stay here any longer than necessary.

Jimmy rolled to a stop and looked up at me. "How do you plan on checking the entire hotel? How are we going to find this crack in the Veil?"

"I'll send out my senses," I told the toy dog.

"Like what? Witchy instincts?"

I gave a short laugh. "There's that. But I'm talking more about my magic. Here. Let me show you."

I stepped out of the room and waited for Jimmy. Then, I closed my eyes and tapped into that well of magic, to the core of power from the stars and the constellations high above me.

The air buzzed with raw energy. My hair and clothes lifted as I felt the humming of power from the stars, waiting to be unleashed.

With a burst of strength, I pulled on the stars' magical elements and combined them with my own. Energy crackled against my skin, tingling like cold pricks.

My back arched as a giant slip of that power ripped through me. I was careful not to take too much. Too much would kill me.

I opened my eyes and stared at the ball of brilliant white light that hovered over my hand.

And then I blew on my palm.

The globe rose in the air, hovering just above the ceiling, and then with a pop, it burst into thousands of tiny stars of light. Then, with a final push, the miniature stars shot forward, leaving a trail of bright light in their wake like pixie dust.

"What *is* that?" asked Jimmy, the wonder in his voice nearly a palpable thing.

"My starlights. My starlight magic," I told him. "I can manipulate the starlight into smaller versions. They're like sensors. I feel what they feel."

The toy dog blinked. "You'll be able to sense if they find any more demons."

"And if there're any cold energies here in the basement. If there's a crack in the Veil, I'll sense it. And if someone's stupid enough to make a summoning circle here, I'll sense that too."

"And if we find them? Then what?" inquired Jimmy.

"Then," I exhaled, my body shaking as I kept my focus on my starlights. "I'll kick their ass and bring them in. Let the Gray Council deal with them. My part will be done by catching them. What they do to them after that isn't my problem."

The Gray Council was the governing body created after centuries of conflict between the paranormals. It consisted of one member from each paranormal race, whose mandate was to keep the peace between the races. They were also the owners of the Twilight Hotel and similar establishments.

"I can't wait to see that," said Jimmy. "Anything?"

I sent out my senses to my starlights. "Not yet. Come on. We've got a lot of ground to cover."

"I've got all the time in the world," said the toy dog, riding ahead. "So, are you more powerful with a full moon?"

I chuckled. "Yup." A full moon wasn't only when all the crazies came out but when rituals were most potent, when magic was its most vital, and when the Veil that kept the demons from entering our world was the weakest.

But it was also when my starlight was strongest. On a full moon, well, you better watch out.

I smiled and followed behind him. I was still getting used to working with someone. Having worked alone for more than ten years without a partner, I was set in my ways. But having Jimmy with me proved to be worth it. He was like a scout, a spymaster. The toy dog knew all the "secret" doorways and rooms in this hotel that might host some vile persons wanting to harm the hotel and its tenants. Plus, he was good company, and he laughed at my jokes. What was better than that?

We walked along, every now and then, I'd pull on my starlight, see if anything vile and demon-esque came back at me, but nothing so far in the basement.

"There at that spot right there," commented the toy dog. "Was where I first saw Evonne Dubois, the famous sorceress."

"Right." No idea who he was talking about.

"She was busy... you know... with one of the locals, a much younger werewolf," continued Jimmy. "In 1962, Harry Tarrio came to stay. You know. The vampire turned actor? And then in 1983, the Ogre twins came to stay at the hotel... unfortunately, they ate one of the maids. It's hard to control your inner ogre..."

As I listened to Jimmy commenting on various

other famous paranormal stars who visited the hotel through the years, I found myself thinking of a man-beast with dark, intense eyes and a smile that set my panties on fire.

Totally inappropriate at the moment, but my mind had other plans. He infuriated me, yet I felt an attraction to him. I was drawn to him, and the fact that no one seemed to know what kind of paranormal he was made him more appealing. Mysterious. Here I was on the job, hunting demons, only moments out of a bad and extremely long relationship, and my head was full of Valen. Valen. Valen. I even liked saying his name in my head.

Yup. I totally needed therapy.

After three hours of searching the hotel, even the ballroom—yes, an actual ballroom—the kitchen, and Jimmy's secret rooms, I'd discovered no traces of a crack in the Veil or a demon summoning. Whoever had done this had done an excellent job at getting rid of all the evidence. Immaculate, really. I was beginning to fear that we weren't going to find anything.

"Anything?" asked Jimmy as we walked out of the elevator and found ourselves back on the ninth floor.

Again, I sent out my starlight, and again they swooped around the hallways like hundreds of white pixies out of sight. Tiny ripples of cold energy prickled my skin as my starlight answered back. It wasn't much.

"Just the traces from the attacks. Nothing else." I

was tired, exhausted, sweaty, and shaking. I was beginning to feel the effects of hours of pulling on my abilities and, by doing so, draining my magic and energy. Channeling my starlight magic like this was taking its toll. Soon I'd have nothing left to pull on. I'd have to rest and let my magic rest as well.

The thought of my bed made me walk slower. I had to drag my legs forward, feeling like they were filled with lead.

"Don't forget the envelope," blurted the toy dog.

I wiped the sweat off my brow. "The what?"

"Your divorce papers. Don't forget to fill them out and give them back to me."

"Yes. I have that to look forward to. I'll do them in the morning." If Elsa could get me a divorce in two weeks, she would be a real miracle worker.

"I'll remind you again if you forget," said Jimmy.

I laughed as we rounded the corner. "Thanks. I'll probably n—"

I halted. "Wait." The cold hit as my skin erupted in goosebumps. I felt as though I'd just stepped into a man-sized refrigerator.

The toy dog rolled to a stop. "You got something?" he whispered.

I nodded. The thing with my starlights was I felt what they felt, and right now, they felt something bad. Very bad. The energy they were giving off was cold, dark, and evil.

I pressed myself against the wall and slowly peeked around the corner. My starlights were plastered against a door, making it seem like it was made of light. Something was inside that door.

I pulled on my starlights, and then I let them go. The light on the door faded, and I could see the black number stenciled on the top, 915.

"Something's in that room. Could be a demon. Could be where all this started." I hadn't felt it before. I'd been too busy fighting off the demons to take notice. But something was there.

"Well, let's go see," began Jimmy, and then he halted as I stiffened.

The door opened.

My heart leaped in my throat at who I saw stepping out.

Valen stepped out of room 915 and shut the door behind him just as the last of my starlights vanished.

If he'd seen them or felt them, he didn't show it.

My heart suddenly pounded a lot faster than before. My abdomen contracted like my intestines were playing jump rope in my gut as my eyes rolled over him slowly. He was wearing the same clothes I'd seen him in earlier. I saw the confidence, broad shoulders, muscular arms, and that hard chest I'd been lucky enough to feel with my face. I found myself incapable of looking away.

But then his head turned our way—

I pulled back my head and hid against the wall. "Quick. Stairs," I whispered, but Jimmy was already rolling ahead of me toward the emergency exit door.

I ran as quickly and quietly as I could, which, let's face it, was little more than a lousy waddle, and my steps were loud. I wasn't a small nor a light woman in any aspect. I grabbed the door and pushed it open. Once Jimmy was inside the stairwell, I pressed it closed as softly as possible.

I kept my hand on the door. "What is he doing in that room?" I stared down at Jimmy, who moved his head as though he had shoulders and had given me a shrug.

I pressed my ear to the door, listening for any indication that Valen was headed our way. I prayed to the stars he wasn't.

A heavy tread came near, and I held my breath. But then the tread stopped, and the vibration of metal wheels and cables grinding echoed as the elevator jerked to a stop. I heard the sound of the doors opening and closing and the same twisting of metal on metal as the elevator set in motion again.

I cracked the door open. The hallway was deserted. No sign of Valen.

"Come on." Holding the door for Jimmy again, the two of us rushed back along the hallway until we faced door number 915.

"I know Valen," Jimmy was saying. "He's a good guy. I know it. He wouldn't do this."

"But you don't," I told him, going for the handle. "You told me only a few things about him and his past. But the fact is, you don't even know what kind of paranormal he is." He could be a witch or a wizard. It wouldn't be that hard for someone of high caliber to disguise their magic. A good glamour would do it, which would explain why no one could figure out his paranormal race. He was hiding it.

And here I was fantasizing about his damn fine lips and his enormous hands when he could be the guy letting the demons out.

One way to find out.

"If there's nothing in here," I began, though I seriously doubted it, "you can go on thinking he's a good guy."

I turned the handle, found it unlocked, and pushed in.

The first thing that hit me was the cold like the temperature had dropped ten degrees from just outside the door. And then there was the smell, the putrid stench of rot, carrion, and death—the scent of demons. Next, the faint scent of candles found me, along with something else. Blood.

A large blood circle sat in the middle of the floor with the head of what looked like a goat lying in its center. Runes and sigils painted in blood marked some spots around the circle's exterior. Burning candles sat on the floor, each strategically placed around the circle.

Next to the circle on the wall was a large smear of black tar, tall as a man. I knew what that was. I'd seen it before.

"That's a Rift," I said. "What's left of it. A demon portal, a doorway into the Netherworld."

Jimmy froze, his ears halfway through a swivel.

"Don't worry." I walked and stood right in front of the Rift, dragging my finger in the tar-like substance. "It's closed. Nothing can come in or out." But I knew without a doubt this was the place where the demons had escaped from. And it looked like someone had opened the Rift with a ritual—the someone being Valen.

The toy dog seemed to relax a little. He rolled toward the blood circle and whistled. "Demon balls. Would you look at that?"

I turned and looked at the circle. "I hate to say it, but your friend Valen's not looking all that innocent right now." I didn't like admitting it to myself either.

The dog twisted his head up at me. "I'll admit it is strange to find him here. I just don't understand why he'd be involved in something like that."

I exhaled. "Well, for one thing, if he did do this, and it's looking a lot like he did, he's some kind of witch."

"You think so?"

"My guess would be a wizard. A Dark wizard."

"But it doesn't explain why he would do this," said the toy dog. "Why he would have these demons kill the guests? What reason would he have?"

I thought about it. "Maybe he wants the hotel for himself. He's an entrepreneur. Maybe he's got ideas for the hotel. What better way to get it at a cheap price than when it's plagued by demons."

It made sense, but it left a bitter taste in my mouth. I'd never take the guy as a psychotic killer. But I didn't know him at all.

"Jimmy." I knelt next to the toy dog. "I need you to keep this between us for now."

"You don't want me to blab about Valen?"

I shook my head. "No. Not until I get more proof. Something's still off here. Something's bothering me. And until I can put my finger on it, I'd rather not say anything. I don't want Valen to know that I'm onto him. He's got a lot of friends here. I'm sure he'll be the first to know if we tell anyone. So don't tell the others."

"I won't," answered Jimmy. "Even Basil?"

"Even Basil. I'll tell him when I have more proof."

The fact that Valen stepped out of the room wasn't solid proof that he opened a Rift, I didn't actually *see* him performing the ritual, but it proved he was involved. How else would he have known about the room?

I pulled out my phone and started taking pictures of the blood circle, the runes and sigils, and what was left of the Rift. When I was done, I swiped the screen on my phone and then tapped it.

"Who you calling?" asked the toy dog.

"Basil. He needs to know I found the source of our problem."

Jimmy was silent after that. I knew he was struggling with the idea that Valen was responsible. I felt sorry for him, but the evidence was undeniable. We'd both seen him leaving the room.

I'd discovered where the demons had come from. Seeing as the Rift was closed, no more would be showing their faces tonight. But I knew this wasn't over.

I didn't want to admit it. Hell, I really, really didn't, but the proof was staring me in the face.

Whether I liked it or not, Valen was involved. He was implicated in opening a gateway to the Netherworld and had let the demons out.

Oh dear.

CHAPTER 15

Three weeks had passed since the night Jimmy and I had gone inside room 915 and discovered the Rift, and so far, there had been no more demon attacks.

I'd patrolled the hotel every night, searching with my starlights for any signs of demon activity, and had discovered only a few teenagers bumping uglies in one of Jimmy's secret rooms, which apparently weren't that secret, and a group of old paranormal males gambling in a smoke-infested, body-odor-laden room in the basement level of the hotel.

Every night I'd worked until dawn, knowing demons couldn't be on this side of the Veil come morning unless they wanted to suffer their true deaths. Not that I minded either.

Yet my nights had been uneventful, to say the least. I'd even dined six times at After Dark, hoping to get some information out of Valen or maybe corner one of his waitresses, but he'd been conveniently absent, and everyone refused to speak to me about him. They all got kind of the same deer-in-the-headlights expression and walked away.

But he was still my number one suspect. Hell, at this point, he was my *only* suspect.

By the time I rolled out of bed—and I actually did roll—the clock on my phone said 1:34 p.m.

The aroma of coffee pulled my legs from the bedroom to the kitchen.

"Oh good, you're up." Elsa came at me with a fresh cup of delicious-smelling coffee and a manila envelope in the other. "Here," she said, handing me both. "I've got some good news for you."

"Excellent news," said Jade, coming around the kitchen table with an Iron Maiden black T-shirt and some pink highlights in her hair. "You'll see. Open it."

"Give the poor witch a break," called Julian from the living room. His long legs were stretched over the coffee table as he lounged and watched a soccer game. "She's been working all night like me."

Elsa scoffed. "No, you haven't."

Julian flashed a grin. "I've been working all night on Janet Vickers."

I took a gulp of coffee first, hoping the caffeine would unstick the crust from my eyes. Next, I set my mug on the counter and, using both hands, tore the top of the envelope. "You did it." I looked at a grinning Elsa. "This is my divorce decree. I can't believe it. I'm divorced. I'm really divorced." I did a little dance.

"Thank the heavens," said Jade, lifting her mug in a salute.

"Now you're free to screw any hot guy you want," said Julian. "Or lady."

I blinked and stared back at the paper, my hands trembling slightly. I was both happy and a little bit sad. Not because I was officially divorced, just that it took me so long to do it. I should have done it years ago when I'd first suspected Martin of cheating on me. But at the time, I'd been afraid of being alone.

Not anymore. I was a different woman now. And I wasn't afraid of being alone. I just needed me.

I stared at Elsa. "I can't thank you enough."

Elsa's cheeks turned a little pink. "Ah"—she dismissed me with a wave of her hand—"it's nothing. Besides, I didn't do the work, my friend. Nimir did. And it was her pleasure to help."

"Well, please thank her for me." I set the paper down, feeling a sense of lightness and freedom. It was an awesome feeling.

Jade leaned on the counter next to me. "Did you find anything last night? Any more demons or Rifts?"

Of course, I had told my friends about the blood circle and the Rifts I'd found in room 915. I just left out the part about Valen. For now.

"No." I took another sip of coffee. "Just old Craig and his buddies in the basement again. And, of course, one of them was naked."

"Nice," laughed Julian.

"I wasn't prepared to see the naked man parts of an eighty-five-year-old."

Jade widened her eyes, a twinkle of a smile happening around her mouth. "Oh dear."

Julian slapped his thigh and let out a laugh. "I'm playing tomorrow night. I'm going to break these old-timers."

My eyes found Elsa, who smiled as she rubbed the locket around her neck with both hands. My heart gave a tug. She missed her hubby dearly. Part of me wanted to know what had happened to him, but this wasn't the time to ask. If she wanted me to know, she'd tell me.

The sound of wheels turning pulled my attention to the doorway.

"So, who's ready for the ball tonight?" Jimmy came rolling my way, a grin on his face, the way only a stiff, wooden dog could.

I swallowed another mouthful of coffee. "I'm sorry. Did you say ball?" I laughed. "Good one."

Jade clapped her hands together. "The Midnight Ball! It's tradition. Every year on the last Friday in September, the Twilight Hotel throws a ball."

I blinked. "You're serious?"

Elsa moved next to me and picked up a black piece of paper from the counter I hadn't noticed. "Here. This was on your doorstep this morning. We all got one. Everyone in the hotel is invited."

I took the invitation. Gold letters were stenciled elegantly on the black paper:

Dear Leana Fairchild. You are cordially invited to the
MIDNIGHT BALL
An evening of cocktails, music, dinner, and dancing
Hosted by the Twilight Hotel
Friday, September 30th
From Midnight to 4 a.m.
Vampire Hall
The Twilight Hotel, Manhattan, New York

I'd heard of the Midnight Ball over the years. Every paranormal in the city had. The rumors had it as being a lavish, magical affair you'd never forget. But you needed an invitation. And now I had one. I just wasn't sure I wanted to go. I wasn't the ball-going type, if there was such a thing. Hell, I'd never been to a ball or anything similar. The only thing that came to mind was Martin's cousin's wedding I'd attended four years ago at some snobby country club in Upstate New York. I got so bored I made friends with the wine table and couldn't remember how I got home. Not my proudest moment.

"It's the most sought-out event of the year," said Elsa as I looked up from the invitation and met her eyes. "Anyone who's anyone in our paranormal community will be there. Leaders. Heads of councils. Everyone. It's a great way to make new connections. And for you, it could mean new clients."

"And single ladies," said Julian. "I always leave with at least a dozen new lady friends."

I snorted. "I bet you do."

"And… you need to celebrate your divorce,"

said Jade. "This is a big deal. What better way than to dance until the wee morning hours?" She wrapped her arms around an invisible dance partner, waltzed out of the kitchen, and spun around the living room.

I stared at the invitation again. "I don't think hosting a ball right now is a good idea," I began, wondering what the hell Basil was thinking. I could only wager he was thinking if he hosted the ball, the hotel wouldn't look like it was infested with demons and hopefully would stay open.

But this was dangerous. Foolish. My investigation was still ongoing. Nothing was over yet. My inquiry into Valen hadn't been conclusive, but it didn't mean he wasn't involved. I just needed more time.

Elsa pressed a hand on her hip. "Why not? I think it'll lift everyone's morale. We need this. *I* need this."

I sighed, not wanting to burst her bubble but feeling an obligation to do so. "Because demons might still be wandering the hotel. Unless you want them to come to the ball."

Elsa narrowed her eyes at me. "There haven't been any demon or monster sightings for the past three weeks. They're gone. You found the Rift. It was closed. Right?"

"Right."

"So that settles it," continued the witch. "The person responsible is gone. They were found out and left. They know you're here. I think whatever scheme they were planning didn't work, and they've gone for good."

"Me too," said Jade, still spinning around the room with her imaginary dance partner.

I shook my head. "They're not gone," I said, thinking of Valen as I met Jimmy's worried eyes. We still hadn't told them about seeing Valen, nor would we until I had more. "I might have temporarily stopped them, but they're not gone. This isn't finished. Maybe I can get Basil to cancel—"

"No!" Julian, Elsa, and Jade shouted at me.

I raised a hand in surrender, a smile on my face. "Okay. I won't. If it means that much to you."

Julian pressed a hand over his chest. "Sex with beautiful women always means that much to me."

"Good. It's settled." Elsa gave a nod. "You'll see. You'll come, and you'll have a wonderful time. You'll dance and drink. You'll meet new people and forget about all that demon business for one night. I think you need this distraction more than us."

She wasn't wrong about that. "I can't. I'm working."

Elsa pressed her hands to her hips. "Not tonight, you're not."

"You can skip one night. Can't you? Oh, please, Leana." Jade joined me next to the counter, staring at me like she'd just lost her beloved puppy, and I was the only person in the world who could find it.

I let out a puff of air. "You're torturing me here." Then something occurred to me. "Is it a masquerade ball?" For some strange reason, that idea made me nervous.

"No," answered Jimmy. "Though some do wear

the masks. Henry and Harriette Moonspirit always wear masks at the ball. It's up to you, but it's not an official masquerade ball."

"Well, okay. Not sure that makes me feel any better about it."

"You're just a bit uptight because you need to get laid properly," said Julian, standing up and coming around to join us in the kitchen. He flashed me a smile. "Don't worry, Leana. I'll hook you up."

I frowned, not sure if he meant with him or some other man-slut, but he wasn't off. I hadn't been with a man in a very long time. I probably had cobwebs down there.

Maybe he was right. Maybe I was just a little uptight and needed to unwind. Maybe a ball was exactly what I needed to relax. One night off the job wouldn't be disastrous, but I was still unconvinced.

Julian put a hand on my shoulder. "Trust me. I'll get you laid by the time the ball plays its last song."

Oh boy.

"Jimmy, help me here." I looked over to the toy dog, my partner for the last three weeks. Surely he could help me out. Surely he saw the danger in hosting a freaking ball right now.

Jimmy wagged his tail. "Sorry. But I'm going too. It's really a nice ball. You're going to love it. Promise."

Jade clapped her hands together. "So, you're coming?"

I opened my mouth to answer, but Elsa cut me off. "Of course she's coming."

I rubbed my eyes. "Look, even if I wanted to come, I can't. I have nothing to wear."

Elsa pursed her lips. "That's not a good enough excuse. We'll find you something."

"But it's *tonight*. I have nothing to wear to a ball. And I'm pretty sure I can't wear jeans."

"Of course not, silly," said Jade. "You need to wear a dress. It's a *ball*."

I raised both hands. "I don't have one. I don't have anything that's ball appropriate." The only dresses I had were back in my old apartment with my ex-husband, who'd probably burned them when he got the divorce papers. The thought of his angry face made me smile.

"Fine." Elsa grabbed my arms and dragged me to the bathroom. "Go take a shower, and then we're taking you shopping."

CHAPTER 16

Vampire Hall was a vast circular room festooned with draperies of the Gray, White, and Dark councils and shields with grotesque faces, figures, and armorial emblems.

Ornate vases hung on the wall, displaying huge arrangements of red and white flowers, and similar bouquets sat in bowls around the room. Windows stretched the walls, and pretty much anything that didn't move was draped in garlands. A few small tables had been set out and were covered with bright linens. Little bits of glittering confetti sparkled on the tabletops. Ornate bows adorned the backs of chairs.

Glass lanterns sat in the middle of long tables, stacked with food and drink, adding a soft radiance to the scene's effectiveness.

It felt like I had stepped into a world made of ancient fairy tales and dreams come to life. I'd checked the ballroom every night on my rounds, and it generally looked nothing like it did tonight. It truly had a fairy-tale vibe, and I loved it.

A string quartet was set up at the far wall up on a dais. The mood in the room was lively and joyful. Couples were dressed in lavish gowns or colorful suits and tuxedos, some in the modern style, while some had more of a medieval flare with layers of skirts and lace.

Just like Jimmy had said, I'd spotted a few people with masks on. Some were dancing. Some were standing in groups near the tables at the room's edges, conversing happily with others in similar masks.

"You look beautiful," came a voice down around my feet.

I looked at Jimmy and smiled. "Who put that bow tie on you?" I asked, staring at the silver bow tie wrapped around his neck. "You look nice. Perfectly handsome."

"Thank you," said the toy dog, his tail wagging enthusiastically. "Jade put it on for me. I always wear one to the Midnight Ball. Reminds me of when I used to wear a suit, back when I was... when I was younger."

My throat tightened at the pain in his voice. "Well, you look great."

Jimmy tilted his head back. "Your dress looks... it looks like starlight. Is that why you picked it?"

"Hmm?" I looked down at myself and brushed a hand over the silver gown with a tight V-neckline bodice held with spaghetti straps and embellished with crystals. A fitted skirt with streams of satin pooled around my feet. The gown was made of material so fine and so delicate that it shimmered like liquid stars. I couldn't stop staring. I could see a subtle but unmistakable pattern of stars etched into the silk. The gown, well, it *was* divine.

Jimmy was right. The way the light was hitting it made the dress sparkle. It did look like starlight. I didn't even realize it until this moment. "I guess it does. Doesn't it?"

It had not fit perfectly at first, and since there was no time for a seamstress to work miracles, Elsa had spelled it.

"Don't worry," she'd told me earlier in the dressing room. "I've got a dressmaker spell that will fix all the gaps and make it as snug as though the gown was made just for you."

So, once the dress was on, and Elsa had cast her spell, a few seconds later, it fit me like a glove. I'd left my hair down with some last-minute big curls, a bit of lip gloss, and mascara, which had made my dark eyes pop with a thin line of kohl over my top and bottom lashes.

"Ah, there's Matias," said the toy dog. "I've got a bone to pick with him."

I laughed at his pun. "You better save me a dance."

"I will. Later." And with that, Jimmy zoomed across the ballroom, avoiding dancers with skill, like he was a race-car driver swaying through obstacles.

I looked down at my dress again. I felt pretty and

feminine, something I hadn't felt in years—maybe a decade. In my line of work, dresses weren't the go-to attire for fighting and vanquishing things that went bump in the night.

A shape danced in my peripheral vision. A man stood just off the entrance, his back to the wall. A tuxedo that might have been in style in the early 1800s hung on his thin frame. Raymond, the assistant manager of the hotel. He looked as excited as me to be here, and I had a feeling he was forced to show up. Kind of like me as well.

I spotted Julian looking like a hot version of 007. A voluptuous brunette in a tight, black cocktail dress sat beside him in the seating area pushed against the far wall. She sat primly with her back straight and her breasts out. They looked like they might pop. Julian seemed oblivious to the gathering of people around him. Instead, he made a show of staring openly at her enormous cleavage.

I laughed as I walked to the table with rows of empty wineglasses. A waiter stood behind it at the ready.

"A glass of red wine, please," I told the young waiter, a vampire, if his incredible good looks were any indication. He looked like he should be on the cover of some fashion magazine and not serving wine.

He gave me a coy smile as he handed me my drink, openly staring at my breasts. They weren't much, but he could stare all he wanted.

I took a small sip of wine, not too much because,

technically, I was still on the job. I turned and observed all the strangers in the ballroom, looking for one in particular. I would be a liar if I said I wasn't wondering if Valen would show up, but he wasn't here. Maybe only hotel guests and tenants were allowed.

I caught a glimpse of Basil in a heated discussion with Raymond, his tiny arms raising and falling. *Oh dear. I wonder what that's about.*

I made to move just as Elsa stepped into my line of sight. She wore a navy-blue-velvet gown that moved like liquid night as she neared. Her hair was pulled back smartly into a low bun, her locket tucked neatly between the girls.

"There you are," she said as she joined me. "We were beginning to think you'd pulled a fast one on us."

"I wouldn't spend money on this dress if I wasn't going to show," I told her with a smile. "At least for a little while." That was the plan. I was going to stay about an hour, and then I was going to sneak out, change, and go about my job.

Elsa's eyes brightened. "So? What do you think? Isn't it marvelous?"

I matched her smile. "It's beautiful. Very enchanting. Far better than I had imagined."

Elsa exhaled. "I could have told you that."

"You guys!"

I looked over Elsa's shoulders to see Jade rolling our way. Yes, I said, *rolling*. She wore a pink taffeta dress with a full skirt at the knee, off the shoulder with a sweetheart neckline. Her hair was curly, like she'd given herself an instant perm. Sizeable white plastic earrings hung from her ears. She'd completed her outfit with—no, not pretty sparkling heels to match her dress—but with roller skates.

She was one odd lady, and I loved it.

Jade dragged her left foot behind as she pulled to a stop right before us. "You'll never guess who's here!" she said, slightly out of breath.

"Who?" Elsa and I asked at the same time.

"Samuel Constantine," said Jade. She made a dreamy face.

"You're kidding?" Elsa craned her neck and looked out into the dancing crowd.

"Who's Samuel Constantine?" I asked.

Jade beamed at me. With her roller skates on, she was taller than me. "Only the most famous paranormal bachelor in all of New York City. He's a werewolf, and he's rich. Look, there. He's the one in the black tux. Isn't he dreamy?"

I looked in the direction she was pointing and saw a tall, fit man in his sixties. He was handsome in a Sean Connery way. I could see why my friends thought him attractive. But apparently, so did the four other females surrounding him at the moment.

"You've got competition," I said.

Jade flashed me a smile. "Well, I so happen to be rolling over there next, and maybe I'll just lose control and plow right through them."

"Oh!" Elsa clapped her hands together. "What a

great idea. Make sure to strike them so they can't get back up."

I laughed. These two were seriously deranged.

"Hello, ladies," came a female voice, and I turned to see a tall woman with a pointed face in a black gown that looked as expensive as the diamonds she wore around her neck and in her ears. Her pale skin was pulled and stretched tightly over her features, making her appear older than she probably was. Maybe she was forty. Perhaps she was sixty. Her blonde hair was styled in glorious waves. As she approached, the scent of pine needles and wet earth emanated from her. She was a White witch and a powerful one.

"Adele," said Elsa in the way of greeting.

I noticed how fast Jade lost her smile and that spark she'd had in her eye. I'd never seen this witch before. I wasn't so sure I liked her if she could put my friends in such an uncomfortable state.

Adele looked over Elsa's dress and then Jade's, her face pinched tightly in disapproval. She held herself in the way the rich and noble do, as though the rest of us are peasants and servants at their beck and call. "You're both wearing the same dresses from last year's ball. Really? Couldn't you have worn something new? Are you struggling that much these days?" The smile in her voice made me want to grab one of Jade's roller skates to hit this woman in the head.

Elsa shut down and started to rub her locket between her fingers, her cheeks flushed. Jade was staring down at the floor, slowly swinging her body from left to right, like she wanted to bolt.

Adele flashed a fake-looking smile my way, the kind that showed too many bottom teeth and never reached her eyes. "And who might you be?" She was staring at me with open curiosity. "Are you a guest at the hotel?"

Irritation pounded through me. I didn't like this witch. In fact, I think I hated her on the spot. "Leana Fairchild," I told her, my voice strong and steady. "I'm the new Merlin the hotel hired."

"I see." Adele was still smiling, though I noticed the slight narrowing of her lips. "Your name does sound familiar. Where is your family from?"

I knew she was trying to decipher whether I was from a powerful witch family, wondering if it was a good idea for her to continue talking to me or if I was a good connection for her. I doubted it.

"Not from New York," I said, wanting her to leave so my friends could have a good time.

Adele stepped closer, right into my personal space, which I didn't appreciate. However, I stayed where I was. "You're a witch. But the energies you emit are... strange. Not White. Not Dark. What kind of magic do you practice?"

"Witch magic," I said, and Jade snorted.

"Hmmm." Adele was still watching me like I was a rare jewel. "I just might have to make some inquiries about you."

"Inquiries?" I looked at Elsa and Jade, who both seemed to pale. Why? Because she had money?

"Yes," said Adele. "I sit on the White witch council."

Ah-ha.

"I am curious to know about you, Leana Fairchild," she said, saying my name like she was committing it to memory.

I shrugged. "Inquire away." I had nothing to hide. Being a Starlight witch wasn't a crime in our world. And I didn't like this witch. I didn't care that she sat on the council and could easily take my Merlin license away. I wasn't giving her anything. I hated bullies.

"Leana," said a deep, masculine voice behind me.

I didn't have to turn around to know who that voice belonged to. My heart rate increased as I spun slowly toward it.

Hot damn.

Valen wore a black suit and tie that could scarcely hold all the muscles. The material had a shine to it and molded perfectly to his body. His dark hair was slicked back in a ponytail, accentuating his high cheekbones and smoldering dark eyes. I'd thought he was handsome in a rugged kind of way before, but seeing him dressed like this boosted his looks a hundredfold. It took me a few seconds to stop staring and to get my head back on straight.

"Valen?" A sputter of relief shot through me that my voice was steady and didn't betray my stupid hammering heart. I hadn't seen him since the night he stepped out of room 915.

The sexy man-beast held out his hand. "Would you care to dance?"

Oh shit. Oh shit. Oh shit.

I had not expected this. Hell, I didn't even expect him to be here. Why *was* he here? I'd been waiting for weeks to speak to him. He was here now.

Adele was staring at Valen like he was a man-lollipop she wanted to lick all over. But Elsa and Jade were beaming at me, clearly wanting me to dance with the mysterious restaurant owner.

What does a witch do in this situation?

She accepts, of course.

"With pleasure," I said and placed my hand in his.

CHAPTER 17

I let Valen guide me to the dance floor, his hand warm and rough, and I hated that it sent delicious little thrills through me.

When he found his spot, he turned, holding on to my hand, and put his other hand on my waist, nudging me closer. The heat from his touch soaked through my dress's fabric as I draped my left hand on his shoulder.

If you'd ask me, I couldn't have even told you what music was playing right now.

Valen led with confidence on the dance floor, and I found myself falling in rhythm with him. Obviously, this wasn't the first time he'd danced or even attended this type of ball.

Women stared shamelessly at him, and I even spotted a female licking her lips sensuously at him as we twirled past. Even some of the men stared, but Valen never took notice.

I had two left feet, but Valen didn't seem to notice

that either. In fact, all he did was stare at me. The heat of his gaze was intense.

My face flushed, and I ignored the silly butterflies assaulting my stomach.

"So, where have you been?" I thought having a conversation now was better than the uncomfortable silence between us. Might as well get it over with and pull the Band-Aid off.

A smile tugged on those damn pretty lips, and the hand at my waist curled around the small of my back. "You've been looking for me?" His warm breath caressed my face, smelling of mints and something spicy I couldn't place.

I swallowed. "Yes, as a matter of fact, I was. I am. I was looking for you." Damn, I sounded like a blathering idiot. "I wanted to ask you something."

Valen was still smiling at me. "What did you want to ask me?"

I couldn't outright tell him that he was my number one suspect. It was over if I told him I saw him leave room 915. I needed more proof—a real motive as to why he was doing this. Was he working for someone else? Was he doing this alone? I had my suspicions, but I needed to make sure.

"How's the restaurant business going?" I asked instead, aware that I wasn't getting any of the witch vibes from him being so close. I could sense prickles of energy rolling off him, like most paranormals, but the specific type impossible to pinpoint. He could pass for a werewolf or any kind of shifter. But I didn't know any shifters or weres who were capable of that level of magic. And he could be a powerful witch or wizard with a glamour.

"It's going," he answered, clearly not wanting to discuss it. "You look beautiful tonight."

Ah, hell, the way he said it had my traitorous heart flapping like it had sprouted wings.

"Uh... that suit suits you well," I said, totally missing the mark. My tongue seemed glued to the floor of my mouth. It sometimes happened when I got nervous.

Valen's luscious lips spread into a smile. "Thank you."

Stupid tingles erupted over my skin, and I cleared my throat. "So, are you planning on expanding?" I tried again.

His dark eyes seemed almost black as they skimmed over my face and landed on my lips before snapping back to my eyes again. "Is that why you were looking for me? Do you want to invest in my restaurant?"

"No. Even if I wanted to, I don't have the money for it." The only cash I had was what Basil had forwarded me. "I was just wondering if you were going to expand your business. Maybe you're looking for another building? Or maybe wanting to venture into something else?"

Valen's thumb rubbed my back, and I felt a pool of desire flutter through my core. "Why? Why so interested in my business affairs?" I heard no annoyance in his voice at my questions, just interest.

I shrugged, trying not to inhale that musky

cologne or aftershave he was wearing. "Just curious. You are a curious guy. Some might even say mysterious."

Valen gave a small laugh and looked away. "Not really. If you knew me, you wouldn't say that."

I took the opportunity to look at him while he wasn't staring at me. He had a tiny scar above his right eyebrow and another on his neck.

Our fronts were almost touching now. I hadn't even noticed that he'd pulled me tighter. My body was getting confused between the cold air-conditioning and the heat pumping off his spectacular body.

I realized I was enjoying the feel of him, his hands, and his closeness. I also realized he could be the psychotic killer who let in demons that killed people. I was losing my mind.

"I heard you got a divorce," said Valen after a moment.

I stiffened. "How did you know about that?" I didn't think Elsa or my friends would have told him. Maybe the hotel staff had overheard me talking about it.

"Word travels fast in the Twilight Hotel," said Valen, his lips twitching as he tried but failed to hold back a smile. "Nothing ever stays secret here."

But you're *keeping secrets.* "I did get a divorce. Some might say it was my fault for marrying a human over our people. But I can't change that now. It does nothing to dwell on the past. Gotta move forward."

"What happened between you?"

Wasn't he a curious man-beast? "Just a falling out. Drifted apart, you know, the usual. I'm just glad it's over." I did not want to talk about my ex, or his cheating ass, with Valen. I was here to talk about him, not me. Funny how he managed to turn this interrogation around.

We danced in silence for a while after that, both stealing looks at one another when we thought the other wasn't looking. The music stopped, but Valen never let go. And then another slow tune played, and we kept on dancing.

"I wanted to talk to you as well," said Valen after a moment, his jaw clenching as his hold on me tightened.

"Really? About what?" I felt a nervous tickle at the back of my neck. Had he seen Jimmy and me? Had he felt my magic?

The man-beast sighed, and I felt myself leaning forward. "I wanted to apologize."

"Apologize for what?" Jade rolled past us and gave me a thumbs-up with her free hand, a large glass of wine in the other.

He leaned forward, his gaze was penetrating as it beheld me. "The first time we met on the street…"

"When you were incredibly rude."

Valen flashed me his perfect teeth. "Yes. I was incredibly rude. You caught me on an off day. It was… I was…"

"An ogre?"

"Angry," he answered with a laugh, and I found

myself wanting to hear him laugh over and over again. "Maybe I was an ogre. I had gotten bad news. I was upset. I went out to walk it off. And then you were there, and you bumped into me."

"Which isn't a crime."

"No. It's not." Valen pulled me tighter, my heart thumping so hard I was sure he could feel it through the fabric of our clothes. He stared into my eyes. "I'm sorry I was rude to you. Can you forgive me?"

I thought about it. "No," I said playfully, catching myself as I realized I was flirting. This guy was messing with my head. I didn't know if it was my hormones or how my body reacted to him, but this was dangerous.

I had to move away. I had to go. I had to stop dancing…

But nope. I didn't.

I felt eyes on me and looked past Valen to see Adele watching us, or rather, watching me. A tall, bald man stood next to her. I didn't like the way he was staring at me like he was onto me or something.

I pulled my eyes away to find Valen still observing me. "What?"

"Who are you looking at with a frown?" he teased, that thumb rubbing of his returning on my lower back. Damn that magic thumb.

"A witch called Adele," I said, trying my best not to look over at her again. "Don't like her. Don't like the bald guy next to her either."

"Declan," answered Valen without even a glance in their direction. "They both sit on the White witch council. Both pricks. Powerful, though. I'd steer clear of them if you could."

Damn. Was I starting to like him? Why was he being nice all of a sudden?

"Too late for that." I exhaled. "I think I just made two new enemies by the way they're looking at me."

"Are you worried about your Merlin license?"

I looked at him. "You seem very aware in all things witch." *Because maybe you* are *a witch?*

"I like being informed." He watched me for a beat. "Did she threaten you?"

I shook my head. "Not in so many words. But she did say she would *inquire* about me, whatever that means. Who my family is and how high it stands on the paranormal hierarchy."

"And where does it stand?"

I pursed my lips. "At the bottom."

Valen laughed again, and I felt mesmerized by the sound. He was very different from the first day I'd crashed into him. He was kind, attentive, and incredibly sexy. No, he'd been sexy the first time I'd slammed my face into those rock-hard pecs. I stared at his chest, wondering what it would feel like to trace my hands over them.

Valen was full-on rubbing his hand on the small of my back, which was distracting. "What else did she want to know?"

"What my magic source is," I told him, flicking my eyes again and finding Adele and her pet bald guy still staring. "It must be love 'cause they can't stop staring."

Valen gave a small laugh. "Which is what? What's your magic?"

I flicked my eyes over his face. "I'll tell you all about my magic if you tell me what you are?"

At that, Valen visibly tensed and then shut down. His smile was gone, the intensity of his gaze nonexistent. He was all taut, like the man-beast on the street. When he moved back, I felt a physical loss of heat from him, and I found myself disappointed.

Okay, so I'd found a touchy subject. But his reaction was proof I was right. He was hiding his true identity. The question was, why? Why hide it if not because you were up to something untoward?

Like opening portals and letting demons into the hotel.

Valen's attention snapped to something behind me, and more tension rippled over his broad shoulders. He stopped moving, let me go, and moved away from me. Okay. Now I was curious.

I turned and followed his gaze. And then, as if on cue, a man came barreling into the ballroom, howling. Couples shouted and jumped back to give him space. I tried to hear what he was saying, but I couldn't make it out from the screaming in between words and the loud music still coming from the band.

Then the music stopped. And I caught one word.

"Demons!" shrieked the man, blood oozed from a scratch on his neck. "Demons in the hotel!"

Well, shit.

CHAPTER 18

The ballroom, which had been a glorious, enchanted event with happy chatter and food and drinks, was now a full-on panic show.

Everywhere I looked, paranormals were making a mad dash for the exit. I spotted a male with a large gut climbing his way over two smaller paranormals on their knees on the floor. If they were too slow to react, people got punched, slapped, and kicked by the rushing horde. Shouts and screams replaced the wonderful music that had been playing just a few moments ago.

It was a freak show.

"Leana!"

Jade rolled my way, Elsa running behind her with impressive skill in her high heels, her eyes round like twin moons.

"What's going on?" Jade tried to put the brakes on, miscalculated, and came flying into my chest.

Good thing I'd seen her coming and reached out to stop her.

"I don't know." I steadied her and then let go before turning to Valen. He was gone, though. I cast my gaze over the room, but it was impossible to spot him with all the paranormals scrambling to get out. He'd abandoned me. Figured.

"There goes my sex tonight," said a disappointed Julian as he joined us. "And it was hinting on a threesome too. Just my luck. That demon owes me big."

I rolled my eyes and rushed over to the bleeding man as fast as the dress would allow. He'd fallen to his knees. Some paranormals who'd stayed were watching him, but no one got close, as though his bleeding were contagious.

I knelt and heard a rip. Ooops. There went my expensive dress. "What happened?"

The man's face slid from human to something not quite human. I blinked, and it was back to his normal, petrified visage. Sweat covered his pale face, and if I didn't know any better, I would say he was about to be sick. The wound from his neck didn't look too bad. He'd need stitches, but he'd live.

"Demons," was all he said. Then his mouth continued to flap, but nothing else came out.

"Yes, you said that. But where? Is anyone else hurt?" I know he said "demons" plural and not demon singular. "How many were there?" I needed to be prepared.

The man began to shake. "I... I don't know. Three? No, six."

When it came to demons, three versus six was a colossal difference. "Three or six? Which is it?"

The man shook his head but didn't answer.

Basil bobbed into view, his face redder than I'd ever seen it. It took on a dangerous purple color at the sight of the injured man. "This is the end. I'll never recover from this," he said in a weak voice. "Everyone will remember this night as the night Basil let the demons into the Midnight Ball."

I stared at the tiny witch, seeing how much he liked to overdramatize the situation and how he made it about him.

Basil took out a handkerchief and patted his sweaty forehead. "I'll never work again," he said, his voice taking on a higher-pitched tone by several octaves. "I'll be shunned from all the important events and social parties. I'll be ridiculed."

I rose slowly and glowered at him. "Get ahold of yourself," I growled. "You're the manager here. You're making the guests freak out with your little meltdown. It's bad enough without your hysterics." So, maybe this wasn't the way to talk to your boss, but someone needed to. I'd slap him if I thought it'd help.

At first, I thought he would fire me right on the spot, but then his face brightened a bit. "Yes. Yes, you are right, Leana. I... I need to set an example. I must stay calm and collected. *I* represent the hotel."

"Is there a healer on staff here?" I asked. My eyes flicked to the nasty gash on the man's neck.

Basil nodded. "Yes. The cook. Polly. She's our healer. Best one on the East Coast."

"Good. Then you should go get her." I looked at a handful of guests loitering around the ballroom and the lobby. "You should take the guests back to their rooms."

Basil glanced around the ballroom. "Of course. I need to take care of the guests. I'm the manager, and that's my responsibility. Yes. That's what I am. The manager."

"The healer first, Basil." I watched the slight witch hurry out of the ballroom, unsure he heard me. Raymond greeted him, and the two of them ushered the last of the guests out and into the lobby.

"Here. For his neck." Elsa handed me a handkerchief she'd pulled out of her bag.

I took it and placed it on the man's bleeding wound. "Keep pressure on it," I told him and waited until he did as I instructed. His face was pale. "What floor did you see the demons on?"

The man blinked a few times. "Twelfth floor." His voice was just a whisper, and that worried me.

"What room?" I waited, but he didn't answer. Well, the twelfth floor would have to do. I stood and looked at my friends. "Can you stay with him until the healer comes?"

"We will," said Elsa, a frown on her face. "But you're not going after the demons alone. Leana?"

"Yeah, you need us," said Jade, rolling slightly to the left. Her face was flushed from all the wine she'd drunk and the excitement of what was happening. Her eyes were slightly unfocused. She was tipsy. A tipsy witch going after a demon would get herself killed.

"Thanks, guys, but you've all been drinking. You're in no shape to fight demons with me."

Jade frowned at me. "I've only had two glasses."

"Four," corrected Elsa.

A soft ticking sound spun me around. "Jimmy? What the hell happened?"

My toy dog friend shuffled his way forward on three wheels. One of his back wheels was missing.

"I was trampled on," answered Jimmy. "I'm missing a wheel. I can't find it."

"We'll look for it," said Julian, motioning Jade to follow him.

"I'll see you later," I told them, and then I was off, running as fast as I could out of the ballroom while cursing the stupid dress that wouldn't allow me to move as quickly as I would have liked.

I got to the elevator and stepped on the hem of my gown multiple times, my heart pulsating violently in my throat. "This is ridiculous."

I slammed my finger on the elevator button. I didn't have time to go to my room and change. There was just one thing to do.

Resolute, I reached down, grabbed a fistful of the skirt, found a seam right at the knee—and pulled.

The sound of fabric tearing was loud in my ears as I kept pulling until I'd freed a ring of fabric around myself. With a final tug, the material ripped off. A breeze tickled my upper thighs, and I realized I'd ripped off more fabric than I'd intended. If I were to bend down, everyone around me would see my tummy-control, grandma undies. Too late to do anything about that now. I stepped over the material and caught Errol from the front counter shaking his head in disapproval, his face pinched in disgust.

"Don't like what you see? Then don't look." The elevator was stuck on the seventh floor. "Damn it." I kicked off my heels and ran toward the stairwell door across from the elevator.

I hit the first set of stairs two at a time. Look at me go! Adrenaline fed me with superstrength and stamina. But as I got to the fifth floor, my thighs burned in protest, and I could only run up the stairs one at a time. I needed to work on my cardio.

When I reached the eleventh floor, my thighs feeling like jelly, I heard the screaming. It was coming from one floor above me.

With a cramp from hell in my side, I climbed the stairs as fast as I could. I halted at the door to the twelfth floor, my heart pounding in my ears. Would Valen be here? Is that why he left so abruptly? To erase the evidence? I hated to admit it wasn't looking good for the handsome shifter, witch, whatever he was.

I didn't want to fight him, but he wasn't giving me much choice.

I tapped into my will, reaching out to the stars and pulling on their energies, their galactical emanations. The tickling of starlight power buzzed in my core. It was ready. I was ready.

I pushed open the door and stepped into the hallway.

But Valen didn't meet me.

It was much worse.

CHAPTER 19

Bodies were strewn across the hallway like discarded old rags. The scent of blood and rot was nauseating. At first glance, I saw four bodies. No way of determining if they were alive or dead. They'd been screaming moments ago, and now they weren't. I hadn't gotten here fast enough.

A grunt pulled my attention up.

And there, standing at the end of the hallway, was a trull demon.

The trull demon was about six feet tall and nearly as wide. Its flesh was red and raw like it was turned inside out. Its features twisted grotesquely with a mouth that could fit a whole chicken. It was more apelike than humanoid, its talons skimming the floor where it stood, hunched back and waiting, next to the corpse it had been feeding on.

Trull demons weren't the sharpest tools in the Netherworld shed either. They were big and dumb. But where they lacked brains, they made up for it in strength. It only took one powerful strike to break your neck.

I wrinkled my nose at the stink of sulfur and carrion. I hated trulls. They were mean and just wanted to rip you apart for fun. But it was here now. And I knew I'd find a new Rift here somewhere that wasn't there last night. I had to close it before more of these bastards walked out.

"Eat. You," said the trull, around a mouthful of fishlike teeth, its voice croaky and wet.

"I don't think so," I told it, my eyes resting on the body it had been feasting on before I'd interrupted it.

"Witch. Eat. Good," said the trull, speaking in low, crude tones, and I brought my attention back to its putrid face. "Me. Like. Witch."

"How wonderful. You like the taste of witch." Bile rose in my throat at the idea of this thing gorging on my body.

The trull's yellow eyes rested on me. "Eat. Witch," it said again.

"I heard you the first time. But it's not going to happen. I won't let it. See, I'm going to kill you."

The trull demon stretched its face back to a vicious smile. "Hungry." The demon's throat vibrated in what I could only guess was delight. Its eyes shone with fury and a savage hunger.

Yikes. I flicked my gaze over him, but I couldn't see if there was another trull or any other kind of demon. The man had said "demons," so I was betting more were here.

"Did you bring any friends with you?"

The demon cocked its head, eyeing me like it was contemplating which part of me to feast on first.

My eyes watered at the stench of rot, like I'd rubbed them with a fresh slice of onion. "Man, you stink. Do you bathe with sewer water? Or do you use poop as your bodywash?"

The trull demon grinned at me, and then it lunged.

"Oh shit."

It pounced at me, slashing with talons and fangs so swift, it would have killed most humans. Good thing I was born a witch.

Dancing back on my toes, I pulled on my magic and flung out my hands.

Bright light emanated from my palms and fired at the trull, hitting it in the chest.

The creature wailed, thrashing as the white light grew until consuming it entirely. The light crackled, drawing a scream of rage from the trull. The next second, the trull fell to the floor in a heap of burning flesh until nothing was left of it but a pile of ash.

I exhaled a breath. "There. That wasn't so hard—"

Something hard struck me in the back just as I was assaulted by the sharp pain of teeth perforating my scalp.

Teeth perforating my scalp?

"Ah!" I let out a girly shriek as I grabbed something cold and slippery—while trying not to freak out more—on the back of my head. I ripped it off and tossed it.

Then I reached up and felt warm liquid where the thing had sunk its teeth into my head.

The thing I tossed... well, it was a thing, a demon thing. Small, the size of a house cat, but where a cat was cuddly and exotic, this creature was quite the opposite.

Its black eyes were unnaturally too large for its head, and it had a long neck and batlike ears. A short nose sat above a mouth filled with teeth. Its fur, well, it had tufts of black grime-infected hair over its dark green skin. Its feet ended in sharp yellow claws. And unlike a cat, it didn't have a tail.

A gremlin demon.

I'd never actually encountered one. I'd just seen a picture of it somewhere I couldn't remember.

My scalp throbbed where the gremlin had taken a chunk. "You bit me, you little shit."

The gremlin stood on all fours and hissed at me, not unlike a cat but deeper and creepier.

Keeping my focus on the little bastard, I called to my starlight again, aimed my hand and—

I stumbled forward as something hit me in the back again. Not something. *Some things*. And then the backs of my thighs. My waist. And, of course, my head again.

I looked down at the gremlin demons latched on to my legs, opening their mouths as they sank their teeth into my flesh.

Okay. I was going to have a girly freak now. The idea of tiny little teeth and claws all over me was horrible, I'd admit. There. I wasn't all strong all the time. Sometimes I needed a good ol' freak-out.

I screamed as I felt teeth sinking into the flesh all over my body. I blinked as a green shape threw itself at me from the ceiling and landed on my shoulder.

"Get off me!" I screamed again, grabbing the gremlin on my shoulder and throwing it as far as I could. But it didn't matter. I had another six latched on to me, their teeth and claws tearing at my skin.

Panicked, I grabbed and yanked the gremlins off me as fast as I could, not waiting for their claws to slash me or sink their teeth into my flesh. I slipped on something wet, possibly blood or something even grosser. A gremlin on the ground hissed at me, ready to leap, but I sidestepped and kicked it in the face.

The fact was, I was losing. What the hell was I supposed to do now?

Blood pounded in my ears as I spun around. Then I threw my back against the wall, hearing the crunching of bones and then feeling its teeth let go as its weight lifted from me.

I shivered. "So, so gross."

I cried out in pain at what felt like twenty needles which pierced my scalp again and sliced at my ears. My eyes watered, and I reached up and swiped with my free hand, hitting something solid—a gremlin— and some pain stopped. I rubbed the top of my head with my hand, and my fingers came back slick with blood.

"I'm not getting paid enough for this shit." I was

seriously going to have a talk with Basil about a raise.

A door to my left cracked open, and a male teenager with a face full of zits stared at me, open-mouthed and wide-eyed.

"Shut your door!" I howled at him and cringed as I felt more teeth sink into my thighs.

I gritted my teeth as tiny clawed hands worked their way over my face. How many were on me now? Ten? Twenty? I had no idea.

But I couldn't keep doing what I was doing. The more I yanked them off me, the more seemed to launch on me.

If I didn't do something quickly, these little bastards were going to chew me to death. Or, at the very least, blind me by poking my eyes out.

I only had one thing left to do. I'd only done it once before, but they'd left me no choice.

With my heart thrashing, I took a deep breath and called to the magical energy generated by the power of the stars. I felt a tug on my aura as it answered.

But this time, I didn't release it. I kept it with me. Inside me.

My breath came in a quick heave as a jolt of power spun, overflowing my core to my aura. Magic roared. A gasp slipped from my mouth, and energy from the stars flooded me. The rush was intoxicating, and then bright light exploded into existence.

The starlight magic raced all around and through me in an invisible kinetic force.

The bright light was all I could see as it consumed

me. I was a star—a brilliant star. And like a star, I burned with energy.

The gremlins weren't thrilled.

They screeched in pain as starlight power thrummed in me. I heard a sudden collective intake of tiny breaths, and then the gremlins fell, like wasps sprayed with insecticide, and landed on the floor in soft plops.

I released the starlight with a breath, blinking in the bright light until it subsided and I could see the hallway again.

I stared, breathing heavily for a moment and trying to see if any of the gremlins stirred. But I doubted it, given the crispy piles of charred meat that was left of their bodies. The starlight had taken care of that. The gremlins would never move again.

I looked down at a substantial burned mark on the carpet at my feet. Yup. I'd done that. It was one of the reasons I didn't use the starlight that way. It tended to burn whatever was near me.

"Leana? Where are your clothes?"

And my clothes were part of the said things—one of the major reasons I didn't use starlight on myself.

I glanced up to find Elsa, Julian, Jade, and Jimmy stepping off the elevator. Elsa had Jimmy in her arms and laughter in her eyes.

Fantastic. Here I was in my birthday suit for all to see.

Julian's smile made my face burn. "Nice." He stared at me in a way that people didn't do in polite company. And then he clapped. Actually clapped.

I was in hell.

Jade clamped her hands over her mouth, but it did nothing to hide the choking sounds that bubbled in laughter.

All I could think of was thank God I'd waxed my bikini area and hadn't decided to go native like I had for the last eight months. 'Cause, *that* would have been embarrassing.

I wrapped an arm over the girls and squeezed my legs together. "Can I get some clothes, please?"

CHAPTER 20

I woke a few hours later with a migraine from hell, which happened when I used the starlight on myself, and with scratches and bite marks to about 60 percent of my body. It was not a pretty sight. My face was swollen and red from the gremlins' venomous claws and teeth—little bastards.

"Stop fidgeting. Do you want me to help or not?"

I sat on a chair in the middle of the kitchen, wearing only a bra and underwear, and stared at the generous woman with red cheeks and bright green eyes, wearing a traditional white, stained chef jacket, a little too tight around the middle. She sported blonde pigtails under a toque blanche and an infectious smile, though at the moment, she was glaring at me.

"I'm trying," I snapped. "It burns." I motioned to the large jar of a pink substance that looked like Pepto-Bismol in her left hand. She was smearing the substance on me with a basting pastry brush.

Polly, the healer, pursed her lips. "It's a healing ointment. It doesn't hurt. Stop fussing. Or do you want to look like you've fallen face-first in a wasp's nest?"

Jade snorted. "You do look like that."

I exhaled. "Fine. Okay."

"I've gotta see this." Julian came around the living room with a chicken sandwich in his hand. It didn't bother me one bit that I was half-naked in front of him. He'd already seen me rare and bare.

Polly giggled as she carefully painted my face, ears, neck, and parts of my scalp with her pink healing ointment.

"Smells like poo," I told her.

"And it works like a charm," she snapped back.

She was right. It did burn for about half a second, and then I felt a nice cooling sensation afterward. But I wasn't about to tell her.

"Okay. Stand up and spread your legs," ordered Polly, swinging the basting brush in her hands.

"What?" I cried, mortified. What the hell was this?

"Just kidding," said the healer. Jade burst out laughing, and I gave her the stink eye. "But I do need you to stand. I can see many teeth marks on the backs of your thighs. You're lucky they didn't do more damage. It's a miracle you got out of that alive. Gremlin demons are like piranhas. You fall into a group of them, and you're left with only your skeleton."

After standing for another twenty minutes while

Polly finished brushing her ointment on me, she stood back and said proudly, "There. My best work yet."

"Okay." Not sure what to say. "Thanks."

Polly grinned, so genuine and glorious that I found I had to smile back. "Okay." She smacked her hands together, casting her gaze around my apartment. "Who's my next patient?"

"Me."

I turned slowly to see Jimmy jerk-rolling-limping, if that was even a thing, toward us. His tail was bent behind him, and his ears swiveled down. He looked miserable.

My heart fell to my feet at the sight of him. It was bad enough that he was stuck for all eternity in the body of a toy dog. But a broken toy dog? That stung.

"Here's the broken wheel." Elsa moved and placed a wooden wheel on the table. Then she bent down, picked Jimmy up, and set him on the table.

Polly jammed her hands in her chef's jacket and pulled out what looked like a glue gun. How it fit in her jacket was truly a mystery, and I had a feeling her coat was spelled with deep pockets or something.

"Don't worry, Jimmy," said Polly as she bumped her stomach against the table and leaned on her elbows. "I'll have you rolling again in no time."

Jimmy stayed silent, which only made me feel worse. Who knew what was going on in his head? I prayed to the goddess that Polly could fix him.

I watched as the healer squirted a rainbow-colored substance that glittered in the light, not unlike fairy dust, onto the broken wheel. Next, she carefully placed the wheel onto the axle and squeezed some more of the rainbow-colored goo while muttering a spell under her breath. After a flash of light and a soft boom, she placed Jimmy back on the floor.

"There," she said as she straightened. "Good as new."

Jimmy rolled a few feet forward, testing his new wheel—or rather, his old wheel, which was now fixed. "Thanks, Polly," he said, his voice grateful, but I could sense some sadness there too.

"My pleasure, sweetie," said Polly as she wiped her brow with her free hand.

My throat constricted as I watched Jimmy roll away and turn right out of my open apartment door to disappear down the hallway.

Polly saw something on my face. "He'll be all right."

"Will he?" That wasn't the feeling I got. "You seem very skilled with that thing. Is there anything you can do to un-curse him?" I studied Polly as she jammed her magical glue gun back into the large pockets of her chef coat. I wondered what else was in there.

Polly beamed. "Thank you. I take that as a compliment from a Starlight witch. Yes. I know all about you." She lost some of her smile with a sigh. "Unfortunately, the curse on Jimmy can't be undone. At least, not with any tools I possess. Don't think I haven't tried over the years. I have. I've contacted my healer friends and some of the most powerful witches on the East Coast. None of us were able to remove the curse."

"Who can?" I wasn't about to let it go. Something about cursing that man into a toy dog as someone's idea of a sick joke made my blood boil.

Polly blinked and said, "The one who cursed him is the sorceress Auria. And before you ask, no one has seen or heard of her in over sixty years. I believe she's dead."

I didn't believe that for a minute. And at that moment, I promised myself I would find this sorceress and make things right again for Jimmy.

"Well, if there's nothing else, I need to get back to the kitchen," said the witch-cook.

"Thanks, Polly." Elsa grabbed her into a hug.

"Yes, thank you," I told her as she waved goodbye and made her way out.

Curious, I walked into my room and went straight to the mirror that hung on the wall, expecting to see my face with streaks of thick pink cream, but there was nothing. My skin had consumed Polly's ointment, or it became invisible after a while. Still, the scratches and bite marks on my face were much less visible and were already healing. Some I noticed were completely gone, without even a trace of a scar. Wow. Basil wasn't kidding. Polly was an amazing healer.

I grabbed a clean pair of jeans, a T-shirt, and a jacket, and stuffed my feet into a pair of short, flat boots. Then I pulled my hair into a messy bun at the top of my head before walking out of my bedroom.

"Where are you going?" Elsa had her hands on her hips. "I don't think you should go anywhere right now. You need to rest. You don't want to overexert yourself after what happened last night. You *were* attacked by demons."

"I'm perfectly fine." I grabbed my shoulder bag from the wall hook rack in the hallway and looped it around my neck. "I need to speak with Basil. I want to know what he plans on doing with the hotel." Last night, after Jade and Elsa had found me some spare clothes, I'd searched the rest of the twelfth floor and discovered another Rift. The portal seemed to be closed, but that didn't mean there weren't more doorways all over the hotel.

The guests were in danger. With the body count that kept climbing, they couldn't be in the hotel while demons were roaming at large. Not until I caught the culprit. I didn't like it, but Valen was the only suspect at this point, and he needed to be stopped.

Jade stepped into the hallway, a grilled cheese sandwich in her hand. "Hey. Apparently, most of the guests fled the hotel last night. We're the only ones left—the tenants. I heard that Mr. and Mrs. Swoop from apartment thirteen oh three left as well. It'll be a Midnight Ball we won't soon forget."

The fact that most of the guests had left was good news. But to keep everyone safe, the hotel had to evacuate everyone. Even us, the tenants.

"I'll be back later."

I left my friends in my apartment and took the elevator down to the main floor. My thighs were sore from all the climbing last night, but other than that, I felt good. Polly was indeed a miracle worker.

"You're still here?" sneered Errol as I passed the front desk. "I thought they would have fired you by now. You can't even do your job. And now, more people died. We should ask for a refund."

My anger flared, but I kept my mouth shut and headed for Basil's office just off to the right of the front desk. I didn't have the time or the energy to deal with stupid people.

"Basil..." I knocked and pushed in at the same time. "I need to talk to you." I blinked and stared at the empty desk and chair. His landline phone was off the hook, the receiver dangling off the desk like someone had dropped it and forgotten to put it back. At first glance, I thought he wasn't here, but then the soft whimper pulled my attention around.

Basil sat on the floor, his back against the wall. And in his hand was a half-empty bottle of bourbon.

"I'm finished," said the small witch, his words slurred as his bloodshot eyes rolled over me, not settling on anything. His face was red and blotchy, and he looked like hell.

I moved closer. "Have you been drinking all night?"

"I'll never be a manager again," garbled the witch. "So many dead. Dead. Dead. Dead."

I exhaled, shaking my head. "Listen, you can blame yourself all you want, but you still need to pull your head out of your ass. There're still people in the hotel. And while people are here, their lives are in danger. Basil?" I wondered if the witch could comprehend what I was saying or if I was wasting my breath.

A tear slipped from his eye. "Gone. The guests are gone."

"Not all of them. And the tenants are still here. Well, most of them."

Basil gave a fake laugh and raised his bottle. "What would you have me do? They hate me. They all hate me. I'm the laughingstock of New York. The worst manager in history at the Twilight Hotel." His wandering eyes finally settled on me. "They're closing the hotel." He hiccupped and then said, "I got the call this morning. One week. The Twilight Hotel will be no more."

I rolled my eyes. "I'd love to join you in this pity party, but I've got a job to do. And that's to ensure that the remaining guests and tenants leave the hotel —alive. It's not safe for them anymore."

Basil pinched his face together like he was struggling to make a coherent thought in his inebriated mind. "What do you want?"

"You need to evacuate everyone in the hotel. The sooner the better."

The witch blinked a few times, and I waited a few seconds' delay for the information to sink into a drunk mind. "What? You want me to force everyone out?"

"I do. It's not safe. They can find another hotel, maybe even a human hotel for now."

Basil stared at me like I'd lost my mind. "The tenants. Where will they go?"

I rubbed my eyes. "No idea. How about you and Raymond work on that? You can use Errol too. He won't have much sneering to do now that most of the guests are gone. See if you can find temporary housing for now."

Hell, that included me too. I didn't think Elsa, Jade, and Julian would be pleased about looking for a new place to live on such short notice. And that left me. But I wasn't going anywhere until I stopped this madness.

"I'll be back to check on you," I told the drunk witch. "I need to do something first."

Basil's head was stuck between a shake and a nod.

I didn't have time to deal with him now. I had something more important to handle.

I was going to confront Valen with what I knew. I was done waiting.

CHAPTER 21

My blood pressure rose as I made my way to the restaurant. I clenched and unclenched my hands, trying to rid them of the tension. This wouldn't be a pleasant encounter with the restaurant owner.

I was nervous. Part of me hated what I was about to do, but I didn't have a choice.

It didn't help that I kept playing and replaying our dancing last night, how close he held me, how he smelled, his dark, mesmerizing eyes, and how he made me feel. I wasn't going to lie. I was hot for the guy. Real hot. Something about him drew me in, and I wanted to know more about him. I wanted more.

I was mainly focused on how he tensed when I asked him about his paranormal side, his race, and how that subject made him nearly physically uncomfortable. And then the part when he'd just left when the demon attacks started.

I didn't know if it was because he wanted to hide

the evidence, though that couldn't be it since I found elements of the ritual and the closed Rift in one of the guest's rooms. Maybe he wanted to be gone so no one suspected him of having a hand in all of this.

With a deep breath, I yanked open the door and marched into Valen's restaurant. Even if it was just after eleven in the morning, the lighting was dim, which kept the ambiance intimate and relaxed. A few customers sat at the tables, eating an early lunch. I glanced at a waiter balancing plates topped with food as he made his way through the maze of tables and chairs.

I walked past the hostess booth and made my way toward the back of the restaurant near the kitchen, which I suspected was where I'd find his office. My heart thumped the whole time, like I'd jogged here.

I didn't think someone like Valen would come voluntarily with me so the Gray Council officers could show up and then take him to one of their holding cells while he awaited his trial. I hated this part of the job the most and knew having a partner would have come in handy. But I'd always worked alone.

Plus, if he wasn't going to come willingly, the fact that it was daytime, my starlight magic was at its most vulnerable. If he was as powerful as I thought he was, I was going to need backup.

Damn. I should have asked my new friends for help. But then I hadn't told them everything I'd discovered about Valen. I hesitated a moment, thinking about leaving right there and then to come back when I had more help with me, but I was already here. I also wasn't sure they'd be so inclined to help me with this mess. And that's precisely what it was—a mess.

The idea that he was behind the Rifts left a bitter taste in my mouth.

I saw a short hallway with two doors on either side. This must be it.

"Can I help you?"

I turned to the sound of the voice and saw the hostess standing behind me with a concerned frown on her pretty face. I recognized her from the many times I'd come to eat here with my friends. She'd told me her name, but for the life of me, I couldn't remember.

"Yes. I'm looking for Valen."

The hostess was still eyeing me suspiciously. "He's not here." She crossed her arms over her chest.

I noticed how she didn't want to volunteer where he was. I was getting a kinda overprotective vibe from her. That or she liked him, and she thought I was competition. "Do you know when he'll be back? It's important that I speak with him."

"What about? Maybe I can help you." The hostess kept staring at me. Yeah, something was definitely going on between the two.

"It's a private matter." I saw her eyes widen at my comment. "Do you have a phone number for him?" I had to try and get him to come to me somehow.

At that, the hostess seemed to brighten a little.

"Sorry. But I don't give out Valen's number to strangers."

I frowned. "I'm not a stranger. You've seen me in here multiple times. And I've spoken to him." I gave her a smile. "You could even say we're friends." Yeah, that was a long shot, and by the narrowing of her eyes, I knew she didn't buy it.

"You can come back later this afternoon and see if he's here." The hostess walked away with nothing else to say.

Maybe Elsa or Jade had his number. I'd even ask Julian for it. Yeah, I'd have to spill the beans about him, but I couldn't wait any longer. Valen was tied to the demons in the Twilight Hotel, and I was going to figure out how.

I stepped out into the sunlight on the sidewalk, maneuvered around a few humans, and headed back to the hotel. The hotel's limestone exterior blazed in the sun. I could see it now. The spell that had rendered it invisible to me only happened once. And then Valen had conveniently showed up. Was he the one behind that too? Possibly.

The thought that maybe the hostess knew where Valen was and wouldn't tell sprang into my head. Yeah, she definitely knew where the man-beast was hiding. And then I realized that maybe he was in his office. On the other hand, perhaps she just wanted me to think he was gone when he was inside the restaurant.

Yeah, she got me. Got me good. But I was onto her.

"You haven't seen the last of me," I muttered.

Making the split-second decision to go back to the restaurant, I made to turn around—

Something hit me on the back of my head. Black spots marred my vision as I fell to my knees. Agony stabbed me in the head as ice picks plunged into both temples. I cringed and doubled over. Oh God. It hurt.

Fingers grabbed the back of my neck, and I was hauled up and dragged. My vision was dancing from black to blurry to dangerously close to passing out. But I couldn't do anything. My body and limbs were hanging down like a lifeless puppet.

After a moment, I was tossed, and I landed on something hard: pavement, I was pretty sure. My head throbbed, like my skull was cracked open from the back, and warm liquid oozed down the back of my neck.

"You fuckin' bitch," said a voice I knew all too well. "Thought I wouldn't find you. Well, I did. I fuckin' did."

I turned my head slowly through the pounding behind my eyes as I strained to focus on my ex-husband, who was only a shape. "Martin?" A wave of nausea hit, and I turned my head and vomited.

The shape loomed over me. "Did you know I needed surgery after that performance? Surgery to fix my dick."

I knew one day I'd pay for my folly. I just didn't realize it would be this soon. And the bastard had cheated on me multiple times over the years. I'd call that a fair exchange.

I spat and then opened my mouth to tell him exactly that, but he kicked me in the stomach. My breath escaped me as I rolled on the hard pavement. My ribs were on fire. Yeah, he'd broken some with that kick. Tears fell down my face, and I looked up at the shape I used to be married to for all those years, not recognizing the person standing over me. I knew he'd become a bastard. Guess I just didn't know how far that bastardry stretched.

"You humiliated me," hissed Martin, though I couldn't see his face clearly, I could imagine the fury. "You're dead. I told you I'd kill you."

He leaned over, but before I could react, his fist made contact with my face. Pain exploded as my head snapped back. I tasted blood and pain. This was not going well.

"I don't care if you're a witch," Martin said over the white noise pounding in my ears. "You're fuckin' dead. And the divorce? You think I'd forget what you did to me because you paid someone to get a divorce? Never. You gonna pay for that. Pay for it good."

I rolled on my side, trying to blink away the double vision, but it didn't work. "I did what you deserved." Okay, probably not the best thing to say to someone who was trying to beat me to death, but I couldn't help it.

Martin's shape pulled his hand back, and I braced myself as he backhanded me. Stars exploded on the backs of my eyelids as darkness slammed into me. The same pain hit—only more intense.

Everything kind of switched off, and darkness settled in.

I didn't know how long I was out, but when I woke from the searing pain around my neck, I couldn't breathe. I blinked into what was a blurred version of Martin's face.

Panic filled me. I hit and pulled at his hand around my neck, trying to pry his fingers apart, but it was like trying to bend steel with my hands. His grip on me was iron tight.

I was going to pass out again. I knew it would be the death of me. I needed to do something, and I needed to do it fast.

The panic was too deep. It clouded my focus. Still, I closed my eyes and drew my will, calling out to the stars. And nothing happened—just the constant throbbing in my head and ribs, along with the realization that Martin was going to kill me.

Over the pounding in my ears, I heard Martin's sharp intake of breath. His hold on me lessened, and I dropped to the pavement.

"What the fuck are you?" came Martin's terrified voice, high-pitched and filled with fear. I'd never heard him speak like that before. Not even when I broke his teeny pee-pee.

Who was he talking to? I raised my head, but all I saw were shapes—a small shape and a massive one. Or was that a tree? I had no idea.

I heard the sudden sound of fists pounding on flesh and then Martin's shape, what I thought was Martin, flew in the air, followed by the horrifying sound of bones crunching as he hit the side of something. Maybe a building… or a car.

Was Martin dead? Who had done that?

A large shape loomed over me, but I was too hurt and nauseated to be scared. If it was going to kill me like it did Martin, well, get on with it. Maybe then the pain would stop.

Something rough slipped under me, and the next thing I knew, I was floating. Then something warm and soft was under me like a duvet made of leather. The scent of perspiration and musk blended with something else filled me. Wait a second. I'd smelled that scent before.

"You're going to be okay. I'm here now. I've got you."

I moved my face toward the sound of the voice. "Valen?"

"Yes. It's me. He can't hurt you anymore. Close your eyes. I'll take care of you."

I tried to see his face, but it was blurry and, like, four times its normal size. Boy, Martin had seriously hit me hard. And Valen's voice was different too. More profound, not like before, but booming, more guttural, and louder, like my head was next to a speaker.

"Sleep," soothed Valen.

And then the darkness took me.

CHAPTER 22

When I opened my eyes again, I had another full-blown panic episode. I was lying on a bed or a couch or something. The room was dark, except for the light of a side lamp. The curtain or blinds or whatever were drawn. It didn't smell familiar, more like spices and a bit of musk. This wasn't my apartment. Where the hell was I?

The day's events came back with a start.

Me going to look for Valen. Martin trying to kill me in an alley. And Valen again. Or who I *thought* was Valen. Martin had struck me hard, so it could have been Santa for all I knew. Possibly Batman.

What I did know for a fact was that this was not my place.

Overwhelmed by the tremors of restless fear, I tried to sit up, cried out, and lay back down. "It hurts."

"Not so fast. I think you have some broken ribs."

My heart slammed in my chest.

Valen came around holding what looked like a steaming cup of tea. He was responsible for the demons, the one I was supposed to bring in to the Gray Council.

"Valen? Where am I?" I pulled myself up slowly, this time to a sitting position. I was aware that I was covered by a lovely, soft, expensive-looking throw blanket, and my head was propped up with soft pillows. It hurt too much to try and wrap it around what I was seeing and experiencing. He was the bad guy. Right?

"My place. Just above the restaurant."

I stared at the ruggedly handsome man, beast, witch, whatever, as he handed me the steaming cup. "It was you? You saved me?" I was a little humiliated that he'd found me in such a state, but I was more shocked that he'd helped me.

"Drink," he ordered, not answering my question.

I doubted he would poison me at this point, so I took the mug. "What is it?" The smell it gave off wasn't unpleasant and could have been citrus, maybe ginger.

"Healing herbs," answered Valen. "It'll help with your concussion and your ribs. You took quite a beating."

I nodded, images of Martin's brutal attack coming back to me. If Valen hadn't intervened, I'd be dead. So why did he?

I took a sip and winced. "It smells better than it tastes." I looked at Valen, and he had a smile on his face. "What happened to Martin? Is he dead?" I hated the bastard, more now after what he did, but I wasn't sure I wanted him dead.

A muscle twitched in his jaw. "Not dead. But he won't hurt you anymore." He sat in the leather chair next to me, leaning forward until his forearms rested on his thighs. "Who is he?"

"My ex-husband," I said, remembering Martin's voice and the pain he inflicted on me. The coward had clobbered me from behind. I reached up and felt some gauze where Martin had struck the first blow.

I met Valen's gaze and held it, aware that his dark eyes were doing all kinds of things to my body.

"Why? Why did you help me?" *Because we all know you're behind the demon attacks.*

Valen looked away from me. "Because a man who beats on a woman is no man. He's a coward. He's weak. He deserved what he got."

I took another gulp and found it more bearable the more I drank. "He was mad at me because I broke his penis when I found him in bed with one of his floosies."

Valen's eyes twinkled, and a grin curled up his face. "That deserves a broken penis."

I smiled, realizing I was suddenly feeling a lot better—a bit drowsy but better. "Yeah, well. He was pissed." I exhaled, tipped the cup to my lips, and drank the rest. "I should have left him a long time ago. It just wasn't healthy for either of us."

Valen took the cup from me. "Relationships are complicated." He moved to the kitchen, which was an ultramodern white kitchen with metal accents.

I took the opportunity to look around. His apartment was maybe three times the size of mine with contemporary manly leather furniture but cozy with large Persian rugs and lots of wood. It was also immaculate, and I wondered if he spent much time here.

I didn't see any pictures of a wife or any other kinds of photos. At least not in the living room.

Valen came back and sat in the same chair. "Should I call someone? A family member? You have a nasty welt at the back of the head. You should be in bed for a day or so."

"I don't have any family," I slurred, my eyes watering at the thought. "My mother died almost sixteen years now. Never knew my father. It's just me."

"I'm sorry to hear that."

"What was in that tea you gave me?" My words were coming out garbled like I was tipsy from four tall glasses of wine.

Valen met my eyes, his dark gaze intense. "A special brew that I make for myself. It'll make you tired, but it'll help. I promise."

"Promises, promises," I said with a laugh. What the hell was wrong with me? I was getting way too comfortable with this guy.

Now that he was here, I needed some questions answered before whatever I'd swallowed wouldn't let me make coherent sentences. Might as well get it over with.

"What were you doing in room nine fifteen?"

There. I'd said it. Well, I think I said it, but the tea was making me doubt if I'd just said it in my head or if actual words had come out of my mouth.

The big man watched me for a moment, his eyes widened for a second, and I knew then that he hadn't realized I was there with Jimmy. Then his eyes went distant, and I couldn't tell if he was trying to come up with a story to give me or if he didn't want to answer at all.

"Are you spying on me?" asked Valen.

Oooh. He's trying to answer my question with a question. "Yes. I'm a Merlin. It's part of my job to spy on everyone." I took a breath, doing my best to focus. "So, why were you there?"

"Someone tipped me off about a possible demon portal," said the man-beast. "I came to check if it was true."

Good answer. But I didn't believe him. "Who whipped—*tipped* you off?" Oh dear. My lips were starting to feel numb.

"A guest in the hotel. Someone I know and trust."

I searched his face. "So, you just came to wee— see? What were you going to do if you faced a demon?" I really wanted him to tell me he was a witch or a wizard.

Valen's brow cocked. "I have ways to deal with demons and other devils from the Netherworld."

I bet you do. "How exactly do you do this?"

He narrowed his eyes. "You can ask your questions, but it doesn't mean I'll answer them."

"So you just came to look and then left without

letting anyone know about the Rift? That doesn't sound like someone who wants to help or cares about the guests in the hotel."

Valen stared at the floor, a smile on his lips. "You think I did this? You think I let the demons in the hotel and killed all those people?"

I tried not to let the humor in his voice bother me. No, it did bother me. "You were seen leaving room nine fifteen and didn't advise management. That's the behavior of someone who's hiding something."

Valen shrugged. "I forgot."

I burst out laughing. Totally unprofessional. "Sure you did."

The big man leaned back in his chair. "I didn't do this, Leana. You have to believe me."

I shook my head. "You're making it really hard to." Maybe he was working for someone else, and he was just the muscle.

Valen surveyed my face. "So what now? You going to arrest me?"

I felt my mouth fall open, and it kept flapping as I tried to close it. "I had thought about it."

"Is that why you came to the restaurant looking for me?" asked Valen.

I narrowed my eyes. "So, you *were* there. I knew it. The hostess. Your girlfriend lied to me." I knew she was hiding something.

Humor sparkled in his eyes. "Simone is not my girlfriend. She was just doing her job."

"What's that? Banging the boss?" Oh shit. Did I just say that? A spark of jealousy crept over me at the thought of that hostess and him going at it in his office. Clearly, I was losing my mind.

Valen laughed. "I asked her not to be disturbed. I needed some time alone."

"Why did you leave last night during the ball?" Okay, I didn't have to ask this question, but it had been burning in the back of my mind since it happened. "You give the impression that you care about the guests. We could have used someone like you to help."

"I needed to check something," said Valen, leaving it like that.

I lay there for a while, not knowing what to make of this man-beast. He was hiding something—more than just one thing. Not only was he hiding his true nature but what he was doing in room 915 and why he'd disappeared last night from the ball. His answers didn't fit. Nothing fit. I wanted to keep pestering until he cracked, but I was in no shape to do so. My head didn't throb anymore, but it was numb, and the sudden urge to giggle became over-whelming as I fought the urge to sleep.

"Is Valen short for Valentine? Like Valentine's Day?" I broke into a fit of chuckles.

Laughter crinkled around his eyes. He had such pretty eyes. "No. Just Valen."

I lifted my hand to point at him, but it kept moving around, so I dropped it back down. "Are you trying to get me drunk? You want to take advantage of me?" At this point, I was all for it. It had been way too long since I'd had some nice assault with a friendly weapon. Hell, it had been years.

Although he shook his head, his smile said otherwise. "No. I would never do that. If I wanted to sleep with you, I wouldn't do it while you were… inebriated."

My eyes rounded. "You *do* want to sleep with me!" Take me, man-beast. Take me. Take me!

Valen leaned forward until his knees were brushing up against the couch. "I think the tea is working. You'll feel a lot better in a few hours. You should get some rest."

I knew I really shouldn't sleep here, not with a possible demon summoner so close to me. He knew I was onto him now. Maybe I'd suffer the same fate as Eddie. I should be scared. I should be terrified and try to plan my escape. But whatever was in that tea made it hard to feel anything other than sleepiness mixed with some horniness.

My eyelids felt like they were made of lead, and it took an enormous amount of effort just to keep them half-open.

I squinted my eyes to try and see only one Valen because right now, there were two of him. I poked a finger in his chest. "You are a bad man. Bad. Bad. Bad."

"Sometimes," came his soft voice. "You really should get some sleep."

"Sleep, sleep, sleep." I giggled and found it hard to stop once the motor started. "I know… let's get naked!" Oh dear. There went my Merlin license. Sleeping with the enemy.

Valen laughed. "You are a strange one, Leana Fairchild."

Just as I felt the weight of sleep rushing over me, I felt a brush of a hand over my cheek, gentle and caring, and then I didn't remember anything more.

CHAPTER 23

I peeled my eyes open and blinked into the darkness. Dread fuzzed the edges of my awareness, and deep breaths helped clear my vision. As my eyes adjusted to the darkness, I recognized the plain white walls, the small room I'd grown accustomed to, and the window that overlooked a neighboring high-rise building. It wasn't much of a view. But it was mine.

I was in my bed in my apartment. But how the hell did I get here? Memories came flooding in. The last thing I remember was being in Valen's place and saying some pretty inappropriate things to him. Heat rushed to my face at the recollection of my words. His tea had something in it all right. It had made me stupid, but he'd been right. The pain in my ribs was a manageable dull ache, and the searing pain from the back of my head where Martin had struck me was a subtle throb.

Still, how the hell did I get here?

I swung my legs over the bed, relieved to find I still had on the same clothes. I spotted my phone on the side table and grabbed it. The clock flashed 9:13 p.m. So I'd slept a good part of the day. It explained why I felt so rested but not how I magically appeared in my bed.

Voices drifted from outside my bedroom door. I smiled. The gang was here. Good. I had work to do, and I needed their help.

But it also told me that Basil hadn't evacuated the tenants—yet.

I stood, feeling surprisingly better than I would have imagined. Following the smell of coffee and the murmurs of voices I suspected were trying not to wake me, I stepped into the kitchen.

Elsa looked up at me, surprise in her eyes. "Oh. Did we wake you? We were trying to keep it low. But you know how Jade gets excited easily, and her voice rises." She sat across from Jade, her fingers wrapped around a coffee mug.

Jade gave her a look. "My voice doesn't rise when I'm excited."

"See?" pointed Elsa. "It just did."

Jimmy rolled his way toward me. "How you feelin'?"

I reached up and felt the bruise at the back of my head. "Better than expected."

Jade jumped up from her chair, grabbed a clean mug, and poured fresh coffee into it. "Here. Have some caffeine. It'll give you a nice boost."

I took the mug. "Thanks." I cast my gaze over my

new friends. "How did I get here?" I had no recollection of entering the hotel, let alone getting to bed. I had a feeling I knew who did, but I wanted to hear it from them.

"Valen," answered Jade, beaming. "He carried you in his arms and everything." A dreamy expression crept over her face. "Such a big, strong man with big, strong arms."

My face felt like I'd stuck it in an oven. "He brought me here? In his arms?" Damn, so everyone had seen Valen carry me back into the hotel? There went my reputation. But more so was the confusion I felt about the man-beast. Why was he being so nice? Especially after I'd accused him of letting the demons out into the hotel.

"And put you to bed," said a grinning Julian, lifting his brows suggestively and leaning back in his chair.

"Urgh." I closed my eyes and slapped my forehead. That was humiliating. A dangling, passed-out witch in the arms of her savior who was also—possibly—the bad guy.

"Don't be embarrassed," said Elsa. "Every single paranormal female in this city wishes it was her."

"And some of the married ones," laughed Jade.

I sighed. Valen was a complicated man-beast. I didn't want to like him. But he was making it extremely difficult not to.

"Who else saw this?" I had to know.

Jade shrugged like it was no big deal. "Not many.

Most of the guests are gone. But Errol, Basil, and most of us on the thirteenth-floor saw."

I sighed. "Great. Wonderful."

"Don't be so down on yourself," said Elsa. "He only carried you. It's not that big of a deal."

"It is when you're a Merlin and unconscious." It made me look like I couldn't do my job. If Basil didn't fire me next, that in itself would be a miracle. Maybe he'd been too drunk to even notice.

I shifted in my seat, remembering some of the things I'd said to Valen. I'd sounded like a horny middle-aged woman. He must have loved seeing me like that.

"How long did he stay?" I asked, wondering what other humiliating aspects of my life he'd been subjected to.

"Not long," said Elsa. "We offered him coffee, and he stayed until he finished his cup."

"What did you talk about? Did you talk about me? What did he say, exactly?" I sounded more inter-ested in what he thought of me than him being my only suspect.

Jade slapped her hands together. "I knew it! I *knew* you liked him."

My lips parted. "I don't like him." Cue in more heat crawling up my face.

"Sure you do." Jade stared at my face. "Why are you turning red, then?"

"Because I have high blood pressure," I told her. "I'm still a bit tense after what happened."

Jade's grin told me she didn't believe a word. "Uh-huh."

"We talked about what had happened to you," said Jimmy, coming to my aid. "When we saw him carrying you like that… well…"

"We all freaked," said Jade.

"We knew something terrible had happened," said Elsa. "I demanded an explanation."

Julian lost his smile, and I saw something dark cross his face. "Apparently, you were attacked by your ex-husband?" Julian's frown told me that he, too, thought men who beat women weren't men at all.

"He told you about that?" I supposed he had to tell someone. It made sense as they were the closest thing I had to a real family. And I felt a warmth in my belly at the fact that they actually cared for me. All of them worried for me, and I had to blink quickly to hide the treacherous tears that threatened to say hello.

"Of course he did." Elsa fondled the locket at her neck. "When we saw him with you in his arms, well, you can imagine the hysterics that followed."

"We made him tell us," said Jimmy, his tail wagging behind him. "Said he left the ex-husband in a bit of a pulp and rightly so." He seemed in much better spirits than when I'd last seen him, and I was glad for it.

"Yeah. He told me." I walked over to the table, grabbed a chair, and let myself fall into it. "It was all a bit blurry. See, Martin, being the asshole that he is, took me by surprise and hit me in the back of the head. I couldn't function or think after that blow. He hit me several times. I blacked out. I think he'd dragged me into an alley, but I'm not sure. And then he was choking me. He meant to kill me. All because I broke his penis." I knew it wasn't the only reason. Martin was unhinged. And it had felt like once he got the taste of beating me, he couldn't stop. He liked it. And I was sure he'd have gone through with it if Valen hadn't shown up when he did.

"You *broke* his penis?" Jade eyed me like she wasn't sure who I was. "Was it a twist?" She gestured with her hands as though she were opening a jar of jam. "Or was it a *break*, break? Like a broken toe?"

I nodded. "A break, break."

Jade's smile widened. "You're my hero."

I laughed, but it was cut short by Julian's growl. He sounded like a werewolf at the moment.

"I would have done the same as Valen," said the male witch. "Worse maybe. Guys like that don't deserve to be walking around the streets."

Jade came to stand next to me. "And Valen saved you. It's like a movie when the strong, dark, silent stranger saves the girl. You have to admit. It's romantic."

I wanted to tell her that being beaten within an inch to my death hadn't been romantic at all, but she was so happy, I decided to keep my mouth shut.

"If Valen hadn't shown up when he did," I said, "Martin would have killed me, and I couldn't do anything to stop him. My magic... well... I couldn't reach it. If he hadn't hit me so hard, I might have gotten away."

"He shouldn't have hit you at all," said Jimmy. "How did he find you?"

I shook my head. "No idea." The fact that Martin had been searching the streets of Manhattan for me gave me the creeps.

"It's my fault." Elsa's face went ashen. "This is all my fault."

I leaned forward. "What are you talking about?"

The witch clasped her locket until her fingers turned white. "I wrote the address of the hotel as your forwarding address on the divorce papers. I saw that you had left it blank. I just… I didn't think."

"Oh." Damn. So the bastard had known where to find me. And had waited for the perfect moment to strike.

"He couldn't find the hotel since he's human," Elsa prattled on. "He couldn't see it. How did he know where to find you? Unless he watched that area for days, hoping to get a glimpse. He shouldn't have been able to find you."

"But he did find me."

Elsa's eyes watered. "I'm so, so sorry, Leana. He could have killed you, which would have been my fault."

I felt my irritation leave as it was replaced with compassion. How could I be angry with a witch who'd only tried to help me get a divorce from this animal? "It's not your fault. I would have told you that Martin was incapable of doing what he did.

Even I would have never guessed the asshole was psychotic."

She nodded, but her eyes kept watering until a tear escaped, and she quickly wiped it away.

At least now I didn't have to worry about how Martin found out where I lived.

"He won't be back," I told Elsa and the others, though I had difficulty believing my own words. "Not after what Valen did. I kinda wish I had seen it." Valen told me that Martin was still alive. I had the horrible feeling he'd come back one day to finish the job, but I'd be ready this time.

"Well, I think Valen likes you," said Elsa, her face stained with red blotches. "I can always tell when a man likes a woman."

Jade chuckled. "Sure you can."

Elsa glared at the other witch. "I can. It's one of my gifts. Anyone with a brain could see how much he cared. He took you to his place, patched you up, gave you some medicine, and then brought you home. That, to me, sounds like a guy who likes you. He didn't need to do all that. He could have called one of us. We would have come to fetch you. But he *wanted* to do this."

I knew what she was implying, but it didn't matter. If they knew what Jimmy and I knew, they might not be so inclined to this fantasy of theirs.

Speaking of Jimmy, the toy dog was staring at me with an expression of "Tell them or I will."

I cleared my throat. "Listen, I have to tell you something about Valen."

"You screwed him already?" Julian clapped his hands together. "I knew it. That's why you're all glowing. You got laid."

More heat rushed to my face. "No. Something you're not going to like."

"What?" said Jade and Elsa together.

"The night I found the first Rift in room nine fifteen, well, Valen was there. He'd been in the room."

Jade shrugged. "And?"

"And, it means he knew about the room. Knew what was in there. It means he could be a witch or a wizard. And that he's been opening portals from the demon realm in the hotel."

Elsa waved her hand dismissively at me. "I don't believe it. Being in a room doesn't prove anything. He could have been there to investigate, just like you."

"Yeah," said Julian. "I'm not sure I'm buying that this guy is hurting people."

"But we saw him," said Jimmy. "We saw him leave the room."

"You knew about this, and you didn't tell us?" Elsa's frown was frightening.

"I told him not to tell you," I began, not wanting Jimmy to suffer any more than he'd already suffered in the last few hours. "Not until I was sure."

"And now you're sure?" asked Jade. "Because you saw him exiting a room?"

"He also took off during the ball when we heard of the attack," I said, losing some of my earlier conviction. "I'll admit. I'm having some serious doubts." I sighed. "I don't know anymore. None of this is making any sense." And now, if I didn't think Valen was behind the Rifts, I was back at square one. I basically had nothing.

Julian shook his head. "Valen's not your guy. He keeps to himself, and yeah, we don't know much about him, but why would he do this? It doesn't make any sense. The guy keeps a nice restaurant and makes sure his customers are happy. Why would he kill the very people who eat in his restaurant?"

He made a valid point, and I shrugged. "Maybe to buy the hotel at a lower price once it's closed?" Okay, that sounded lame now. My earlier theories weren't matching up.

"If it's not Valen, and I never believed it was," Jimmy said, "then who? Who's doing this?"

"Good question." Laughter spilled from the hallway, and I looked up to see the twins running past the doorway. "How many tenants are still here?"

"Only two families have left," said Jimmy, his head angled toward the doorway. "Basil came earlier and tried to evict us. Everyone else refuses to leave."

"Like us," said Jade. "I'm not leaving."

"Me neither," said Julian.

Elsa raised her brows. "The demons will have to try and remove me and see what'll happen."

I pulled my gaze back, thinking. "So, the tenants are refusing to leave, even after being told about the demons. They're not budging." I felt proud that they weren't frightened of what could happen, but I was

216

also afraid for them. I thought about all the guests in the hotel, from the first floor to the very top floor, and how quiet it was going to be now.

And then it hit me like a baseball to the gut. I stood up.

"What?" Elsa was on her feet, rubbing her vintage locket. "Demons?"

"I'll just have to catch them in the act." A smile curled up my lips. "We'll set a trap. I'm hoping you'll help me with this."

"Of course, we'll help," said Elsa. "But how will you set a trap? We don't know where or when another Rift will appear."

My heart thumped with excitement. "But we do." I looked at my friends. "See, I didn't realize until now. It might not be Valen, but whoever is doing this wants all of us out. It makes sense. There's a pattern. The Rifts have been climbing up this whole time. First, the victim was on the second floor, then the fourth floor, and then where Eddie was killed on the sixth floor. The ninth floor, and finally the twelfth floor, the night of the ball. They're going up. Which means…"

"Ours is the last one," said Jade, stealing the words out of my mouth, though she paled. "The demons are going to attack our floor. But there are kids here. Old people," she said and pointed to Elsa.

"Watch it," Elsa growled. "You're only a few years behind me."

I gulped some coffee, almost forgetting I was still

holding the mug. "I know, and you're going to keep them away until we catch these bastards."

"They won't want to leave," said Jimmy.

"Tell them it's not permanent. At least have the children and the elderly moved somewhere else. Somewhere safe."

"My friend Janet will put them up for a few days if I ask her," said Elsa. "She's in Queens."

"Good, thank you," I said. This felt good, solid. "I don't know if they'll strike again tonight, but they'll do it soon since we're all still here." That was if my theory was correct, and they wanted the hotel empty. I still hadn't figured out why exactly they wanted that, but it didn't matter. What mattered was setting up the trap correctly.

"So," said Jimmy as he rolled around and then settled near my feet. "How do we set this trap? How are we going to do this?"

"Easy," I said, smiling. "We use us as bait."

CHAPTER 24

How do you set up a trap for someone when you don't know where they will be in a hotel with too many rooms? No idea, but I was about to find out.

Forget about trying to make the tenants leave, even the families with children and the elderly. No one was moving.

"This is my home," the witch named Barb had said, her nightgown floating around her tall, lean frame. "And I'll be damned if I let something as trivial as a demon force me to leave."

"It's for your own protection," I'd told her.

She glowered at me and said, "Make me."

Okay then.

"So, how do we do this?" Jimmy looked up at me from the ground.

I scratched the back of my head. "No idea. I was hoping to have the thirteenth floor cleared. A stakeout would have been preferable. But now…

well, we'll just have to wing it." My super plan of catching these bastards in the act was slowly getting jumbled.

"Sometimes the best plans are the ones on a whim," said the toy dog.

"Maybe." I watched the twins as they pick-pocketed Julian's wallet and proceeded to run in circles around him as the male witch tried to snatch his wallet back but missed every time. "I'm not even sure they'll attack again tonight." Maybe they wouldn't now that everyone seemed to be having a party instead of taking this seriously.

"Air Supply is the best soft rock band in the world," Jade was saying to another paranormal male as she pulled out the front of her T-shirt with an image of two men on it. "I've got three in different colors."

I cast my gaze around the hallway of the thirteenth floor, seeing it like the first time I'd stepped into the hotel. Every apartment door was open, the tenants wandering in and out of the rooms like the entire floor was one giant house, and every room was an extension of their own.

It was a disaster.

"They're not scared at all," I said, watching as Elsa and Barb laughed at something they were sharing. "They should be scared. Demons are not a laughing matter. This is serious. Some of them could get killed." It was clear they didn't think demons were going to show up. Nope. They were more interested in having a party.

My thoughts wandered over to a sexy man-beast who'd saved me from a deadly beating. I was furious at Martin for doing what he did. Furious and disgusted. Never in a million years did I think the man I was married to for fifteen years would have tried to kill me in a back alley. The fact that he'd been stalking me sent a chill through my body.

And Valen had been my knight in shining armor.

The guy was a mystery. He didn't have to save me, but he did. And if he was truly the one behind the demons, he would have let Martin finish the job. Which only reinforced my feeling that the restaurant owner wasn't the one.

My skin prickled at the memory of being held by him, how easily he had carried me, and how warm and gentle his hold was on me. I'd felt safe in his arms. It had been a lovely feeling. Too bad it hadn't lasted very long.

Yet I couldn't shrug off the sensation something was broken about Valen. He had a sadness in his eyes. His wife's death? Maybe it had something to do with the fact that he was hiding his true identity. His beast or his witch powers. Maybe I'd never know.

And maybe I should stop thinking about him and focus on the task at hand.

I let out a sigh. "I'm going to check all the rooms again."

"You want me to come?" asked Jimmy.

I shook my head. "No. You can keep watch here. Holler if you see anything."

I continued on my rounds by just checking each

room, making sure no one was busy preparing a ritual for a Rift. But the more I walked around and checked the rooms, the more I realized it wouldn't happen. At least, not tonight.

I stepped into room 1307. "Hi, Felix, just me again."

Felix looked up from his chair, and his wrinkled face pulled into a smile. "Do your worst, girl," he said and turned back to whatever he was watching on the television.

I wrinkled my nose at the faint smell of cabbage and poked my head into the bedroom. Nothing. Just the same bed and furniture I'd seen when I checked it out the first time about half an hour ago. I let out a sigh. "This is pointless."

"What do you think you're doing?" shouted a voice from the hallway. "You can't do this!" Elsa. And she didn't sound happy.

I rushed out of Felix's room and came face-to-face with at least a dozen strangers dressed in gray robes —both male and female but primarily male— ushering the tenants from their rooms. Ushering was not the correct word, more like throwing them out forcefully.

I rushed forward, right into the onslaught. "What the hell is going on?"

Elsa's face was red, and I knew her blood pressure was dangerously high. "They're forcing us to leave."

"They're evicting us," said Julian, a dangerous expression on his face as he glared at one of the males in the gray robes hauling a teenager out of his room by his arm.

My insides turned. I was partly responsible for this. I'd told Basil to evacuate the hotel. Just not this way. This was wrong.

"Basil hired these mercenaries?" I'd never seen these types before, and I didn't like how rough they were being with the tenants. They were being treated like convicts.

"I had them come," said a female voice.

I flicked my eyes to a tall woman with a pointed face, her pale skin blending with the white of her robe. Her blonde hair was pulled back into a low bun, exposing her thin face severely and adding more depth to her frown. I recognized her. Adele.

"They didn't listen when hotel management asked them nicely to leave, so here I am, asking *not* so nicely," said Adele as she stepped forward, and I hated the fact that she was taller than me.

I gritted my teeth. "On what authority?"

Adele smiled coldly. "On *my* authority. The Gray Council happily lent me their officers."

"Hired thugs to move families and old people," I seethed. "Nice touch."

I caught a peek at the other witch named Declan as he manhandled Barb and pinned her against the hallway wall. My anger soared.

"You can't just do this. You have to have places for them to stay," said Elsa as she came to stand next to me. So did Jade. So did Julian. "We'll be out on the street! All of us!"

Adele flashed a smile in Elsa's direction. "But I can. That's called power, Elsa. Something you'll never have and can't possibly understand. And I have more than you can imagine. You can sleep in the gutter for all I care. You've been given fair warning."

"Less than a day to look for new lodgings isn't a fair warning," I told her. "You need to give them at least a week." I had no idea if that were true. I wasn't well-informed about our paranormal laws regarding the rights of tenants and landlords.

"But I don't," said Adele, giving me one of her fake smiles. "The hotel is closed as of this moment, and everyone needs to leave. Including you, Leana Fairchild, the Starlight witch. Yes. I've done some inquiries. I know everything. What did they call you back at the Merlin trials? Oh yes—Star*dud*."

Ouch.

"Couldn't even work the simplest of spells." She sidled forward. "And I know about that pathetic human you married." She laughed. "We get what we deserve. Don't we?"

"Not fair," I said, hands on my hips, smiling. "All I know about you is that you're a bitch."

Elsa's intake of breath nearly sent me into a fit of giggles. Yeah, this bitch could revoke my Merlin license, but I couldn't help myself. What she was doing was wrong. Worse was that she knew it and didn't care.

Adele's light eyes darkened. "Careful now, Star-dud, or you'll be out of a Merlin license as well as out of an apartment. Don't think I won't ruin your Merlin career, because I will." She stepped closer until she was practically touching me, and the scent of something acrid like vinegar rushed up my nose. "I can make it so that you will never work again on this continent. You don't want to test me."

But I did. I really, *really* did. It wasn't the right time, though. I needed my license to finish the job. And I'd never, ever, *not* finished a job.

I felt a hand around my arm, and then I was pulled back a step into Elsa. "Don't," she whispered. "This isn't the time."

She was right, of course, but it didn't stop the fury that seemed to spill through my pores. I detested this witch as much as I despised bullies.

"You'll be able to go back to your homes once I apprehend those responsible for the demons," I told the terrified tenants who were all lined up together in the hallway with just a few bags filled with their belongings. Some faces brightened at the news I'd just relayed, and I felt a pang in my heart.

It was hard to watch the tenants being evacuated, but this was only temporary. As soon as I caught the culprit, the threat would be over, and the tenants could return to their homes.

"That won't be necessary," said Adele, staring at me like I was an annoying mosquito she was aiming to smack.

I shook my head. "This is a huge problem. Not to mention irresponsible. Someone's opening Rifts all over the hotel and letting demons out. That's got to be stopped. You can't just let it be. The demons will continue to escape into the hotel. It will never be livable again."

"It won't have to." Adele drew herself up to her full height. Yeah. The bitch was a tall one. "The hotel will be destroyed, so no more demons. Problem solved."

"Destroyed!" yelled Jade.

"But you can't," cried Elsa as she fisted her hands. "It's been around for over a hundred years."

"This is our home," said Barb, her eyes filled with tears. "It will be the death of us. Where are we to go?"

"I don't care," said Adele, the slightest satisfied smile on her lips. "I hate having to repeat myself to simpletons. The hotel is going to be destroyed tomorrow morning. If you are still inside, you will die with it. I don't care."

Every time she opened her mouth, I hated her more. The witch had no conscience. "Don't you think destroying the hotel is a bit overkill? It doesn't need to be destroyed. All you have to do is stop the one who's creating the Rifts, and you've solved the problem."

"The decision has been made." Adele's face spread into an icy grin. "The hotel will be destroyed at eight tomorrow morning. That is all."

That is not all, you tall, skinny bitch.

Then something occurred to me, and I felt all the blood leave my face.

Jimmy!

If they destroyed the hotel, Jimmy would die with it. He couldn't leave because of the curse.

I cast my gaze around the hallway and spotted the toy dog. With his ears low and his tail between his back wheels, he knew what destroying the hotel meant.

Tears burned my eyes. I would not let that happen. I would find a way to stop this.

The problem was I only had a few hours, and I had no idea how.

CHAPTER 25

With a heavy heart I watched the gray-robed officers usher out the last of the tenants. Barb actually gripped the edges of a doorframe until an officer hit her fingers, followed by the twins with their faces streaked with tears, taking turns hugging Julian.

When only the gang and me were left, Adele walked into a waiting elevator with her hired thugs. She turned to give us a last coy smile. Her features were drawn with a cold satisfaction, the kind people with power have when they ordain us little people. Her ugly face was the last thing I saw as the elevator doors slid shut.

It seemed that after she'd declared her intentions of destroying the hotel, she wasn't as adamant about getting everyone out. She didn't care if we stayed and died. She truly was an evil bitch.

But right now, I had more pressing matters.

"How do we stop her from destroying the hotel?"

I asked. I sat on the floor in the hallway with my back to the wall. "We can't let that happen. There's got to be a way." I looked over to Jimmy, who'd been silent this whole time.

Elsa shook her head. "I don't think there is. I mean, we could try to contact the Gray Council. That would be the only way to stop her."

My heart leaped. "That's good. Okay. So let's do that."

"But it'll take a while," said the older witch. "It's not like you can just make an appointment. You know how hard it is just to reach them by phone? They don't take calls from just anyone. And it's past midnight. You need to go through your court."

"I don't belong to any court," I said, knowing full well that in order to belong to one of them, you needed to harness either magic, which I didn't. As a Starlight witch, I didn't fit into any of the factions. It had bothered me a great deal when I was in my twenties and left me feeling like an outsider. Now, I couldn't care less.

"But we do," answered Elsa. "And our court is the White Court, and Her Highness's ass sits on one of the seats. If she gets wind of what we're trying to do, she'll put a stop to it."

"That's a problem." I never had to contact the Gray Council directly. It had always been the Merlin Group or whoever I was working for at the time.

Jade rolled over to us. She'd put on her roller skates in solidarity with Jimmy. "I think I might know someone who knows someone on the Gray Council," she said, slightly out of breath.

"Who?" Elsa and I asked at the same time.

"Margorie Maben," she answered. "We're in the same Eighties Forever group on Facebook. She's married to Oscar Maben. He sits on the Gray Council."

I jerked. "That's great. We wouldn't have to go through the White Council. Can you call her?"

Jade screwed up her face as she yanked out her phone from her back pocket. "I don't have her phone number. We've only just chatted on social media. But I'll try to reach her there. It's late, though. I don't know if she'll answer."

"Keep trying." I watched as she began typing on her phone. This was good. If we could reach her somehow and give her our version of what was happening, we'd have a chance at stopping this ridiculous demolition. It was a small chance, but it was better than nothing.

I rolled to my knees. "Is there a spell or something that could allow Jimmy a temporary leave from the hotel? Just in case?" I stared at the toy dog, but he wouldn't look at me.

"I tried for years to find something just like that for him, a potion," said Julian, sitting on the floor across from me, his long legs nearly touching mine. "I never could find anything. The curse is too strong."

Elsa let out a sigh. "Spells are useless unless you have what was used on him. Polly tried. We all did.

Without knowledge the curse the sorceress used, we never got close."

"It's fine, Elsa," said Jimmy, finally speaking. "I know you tried. But let's face it. It's over. Maybe it's a good thing. One can only survive so long as a toy. It's time for me to go."

I frowned. "Don't talk like that. It's not over."

"But it is," said the toy dog. "You have no idea what's it been like for me. To be this… this toy. Not being able to be with a woman ever. Not being able to have a family of my own. I've suffered enough. I'm done, Leana. I'm tired."

Okay, so I had no idea what it must have been like for him all these years. And I would never know. The pain must have been unbearable, and he was a remarkable creature to have endured it for so long.

But I'd just met Jimmy. He was my friend, and I wasn't ready to let him go.

Both Elsa and Julian sounded defeated, like they'd given up on finding the counter-curse. Good thing I wasn't good at letting things go. I wasn't done yet. Not by a long shot. The best thing for Jimmy now was to stop the hotel demolition, and then I was going to find a way to remove the curse.

The ting from the elevator sounded, and then the doors slid open.

Basil stumbled out, and for a moment I wondered if he was still drunk from this morning. His eyes were wide as he took us in. "Hell's bells, what are you all still doing here? I've asked everyone to leave."

Errol walked behind him, like his taller, skinnier shadow. A happy cruelty lurked behind the calm of his features, a contemptuous grin hiding within the ordinary posture of his body. He was loving this. Why? He was out of a job if they tore down the hotel. Still, I didn't like that hidden smirk of his. Something was definitely up.

Basil stood over me. "You even asked for everyone to leave. Why are you still here? Haven't you heard what they plan on doing to the hotel?"

"I have," I said as I stood. I didn't like to have Errol looking down at me. "And yes. I did ask for you to evacuate the tenants. But not like this. Not without having accommodations for everyone. And why the gray robes? Seriously? You didn't need to do that. These people, your tenants, didn't deserve that."

Basil looked uncomfortable, and he flattened the front of his shirt. "That wasn't my decision. There was nothing I could have done to prevent it."

I could tell he wished it had gone differently, but like us, his power stopped at managing the hotel. He wasn't an owner. Adele held all the power now, granted by the Gray Council, the owners of said hotel. And an icy-cold bitch with that kind of power was a dangerous thing.

Elsa pushed herself slowly to her feet. "You could have warned us, Basil. We've lived here for years. Never caused any trouble."

Basil's face darkened a shade. "You think I don't

know that. I didn't get a warning either. They just showed up."

"And you grabbed your ankles and took it like a man," said Julian, staring at Basil with a scary amount of fury. His long coat hid whatever deadly potions and poisons he had there at the ready. I was reminded not to get on his bad side.

"I had no choice," Basil cried, spit flying out of his mouth. "I have a reputation to think about. They're considering me for another management position in Florida. If I spoke out of turn, I'd be finished."

"Oh, you're finished," threatened Julian, and the hairs on the back of my neck rose at the insinuation in his words. "Those were my friends you threw out on the street. I'm not going to let that go, old man."

Basil pointed a finger at the other witch. "Is that a threat?" he shrieked, and Errol snorted behind him. "Are you threatening me?"

Julian's jaw twitched. "Yeah. You're a fucking coward." With a sweep of his coat, Julian was now standing, very tall, before Basil.

The tiny witch lifted himself onto the tips of his toes. "Take that back! I'm not a coward."

Julian had his hands inside his long coat, gesturing that he was about to toss something evil on Basil.

Basil caught on. "Don't you dare!" He flung his hand at Julian's jacket pocket. "If you poison me, you'll end up in the witch prison. And then what'll you do?"

Julian smiled coldly. "It'll be worth it."

"Stop with the pissing contest." I put myself between the two. "You're acting like idiots. Put your sausage fest back in your pants."

Basil's wide eyes met mine. "He threatened me."

I shrugged. "You sorta asked for it."

Basil's mouth fell open, his lips flapping, but nothing came out.

I turned to Julian. "Keep your temper in check. Right now, we need you calm. We must figure out a way to stop Adele from destroying the hotel and save Jimmy."

"What are you talking about?" Basil looked over at the toy dog, who was now staring at the wall, like he was hoping he could burn a hole through it with his eyes. "What's this about Jimmy?"

"Really?" I pressed my hand on my hip. "You've been the manager here for…"

"Thirty years," answered Basil proudly.

"And you didn't realize that destroying the hotel would also kill him?"

Basil blinked a few times, and his eyes went from me to the toy dog. "But I… I didn't realize…"

"Guess not."

Basil stared at the toy dog as though it was the first time he'd laid eyes on him. "Jimmy, I'm so sorry. I never imagined… I forgot," he added at the end, looking ashamed.

"It's fine," answered the toy dog, still staring at the wall.

"It's *not* fine." I glared at Basil. "You must have

some connections. Who do you know on the Gray Council that could help us?"

Basil was shaking his head. "No one."

I gritted my teeth. "No one? You don't know a single soul on that council? Bull."

The hotel manager narrowed his eyes. "I don't. Okay?" And then his face changed as he'd just remembered something. "But I have a friend who might."

"Good. If you want to save Jimmy's life, you'll find that person and tell them what's happening here."

"Yes, yes, very good." Basil cast his gaze over us. "What will you do?"

I sighed. "Someone is still conjuring up Rifts. And as long as they're out there, it's my job to find them."

At that, Errol clapped his hands and hopped on the spot. He looked like a penguin at the circus.

"Okay." I turned to Errol. "What's with the creepy-ass smile? It's starting to freak me out."

Errol's eyes rounded with glee, and he actually rubbed his hands together like some mad scientist from a cartoon.

"Can I tell her?" he asked Basil. "Oh please, it'll be such fun. I want to look her in the eyes when I tell her."

Okay, now that was even creepier. "What the hell is he talking about?" I couldn't help my heart from hammering inside my chest.

Basil let out a long sigh through his nose. "I came here to tell you something."

"What?" I asked, seeing Jade looking our way with her phone still in her hand. Julian and Elsa were staring. Even Jimmy had stopped watching the wall to look over at me.

Basil pressed his lips into a thin line. "You're fired."

"You're fired!" repeated Errol like an eerie, large parrot.

I glared at him, contemplating kicking him in the throat as a parting gift.

"You can't fire her," said Elsa, coming to my defense. "We need her. If we can manage to keep the hotel from being demolished, who will you have to keep us safe?"

"She's the best defense you've got against the demons," said Julian. "It's a mistake."

A vein on Basil's forehead throbbed. "Well, if she had done her job in the first place and stopped these Rifts, we wouldn't be in this mess."

Ouch. Okay. That stung.

Jade rolled up to Basil and stared him down. "You can't blame her. This isn't her fault."

I grabbed her by the arm and pulled her back. "It's fine. People are always looking to blame someone else."

But the fact remained, what Basil said was true. If I had found those responsible, the hotel would still be open, and we'd all still have places to live.

I stood there like an idiot with shock and anger rippling through me, fighting for first place on the emotion list. I couldn't find the words.

"No hotel, no demons, no need for a Merlin." Basil pulled out an envelope. "Here is what I owe you. Thank you for your services."

The tiny witch turned on his heel and walked away but not before Errol gave me another nasty grin. He'd lost his job, too, but it seemed he was much happier that I'd lost mine.

"Don't forget Jimmy," I called out. I didn't care that I'd lost my job. We were talking about a life. "Please, Basil. Call your contact."

The small witch turned and gave me a nod. It wasn't much, but I knew he'd keep his word. At least now we had two possible ways to reach the Gray Council.

The elevator doors shut, and Basil and Errol were gone.

"I never thought I'd hate Basil so much in my life-time," said Elsa. "He's like a different person."

"Don't blame him," I told her. "He's just following orders."

"Yeah, Adele's orders," said Jade. "Hate her and her snobby friends."

Silence soaked in, but I could almost hear my friends formulating deadly plans in their heads.

My heart beat loudly in the silence. My strong friends looked defeated and angry. Jade clutched her arms around herself, a sad look in her eyes.

This was wrong. All wrong.

"What do we do now? Where do we go?" asked Jade, her voice loud in the sudden silence.

Elsa sighed. "I'm sure my friend Janet can put us

up for a few days until we find somewhere new to live." She looked at me. "That means you, too, Leana."

I gave her a smile. "Thanks. But... I don't know..."

"Why not?" asked Jade. "You don't want to stay with us?"

My insides squeezed at the hurt on her face. "Of course I do. It's just..." My eyes flicked to Jimmy. "This isn't right. I can't just leave Jimmy. Any luck with your Facebook contact?"

Jade stared at her phone. "Not yet."

"Keeping trying—"

A blazing, green-blue light exploded from somewhere outside the window. And then a sonic boom blasted around us, making me jump. The lights went out. Darkness fell, sudden and complete, and I fumbled for the wall as my heart lurched in panic.

Then an invisible force hit us, and we all went hurling violently across the hall. I slammed into the wall and slumped to the carpet. The light subsided, and I blinked rapidly, trying to rid my vision of the white spots as the lights flickered and came back on.

"What the hell was that?" asked Julian as he stood up and went to help Elsa and Jade to their feet. Jimmy seemed fine as he turned to look at me.

I pushed to my feet and stared at the ceiling. "It came from above. Outside. From the roof." I knew it in my gut.

And then I was moving.

My breath came in fast as I rushed to the emergency exit. I pushed it open, climbed a few more steps and, using my weight, shoved the roof door open with a slam of my shoulder to step onto the roof.

Part of me dreaded what I was about to discover. I didn't want it to be Valen here on the roof. So far, his actions were quite the opposite of someone who caused harm to others. But the truth was, I didn't really know him. Not really. And he could very well be the one who was behind all this. He could have played the hero card to throw me off my game.

But when I marched onto the roof, I didn't see Valen standing there. It wasn't anyone I would have guessed.

"Raymond?"

CHAPTER 26

I had a few seconds of a what-the-hell moment, but then I quickly recovered.

"You? You're behind this?"

Raymond, the assistant hotel manager, the average-looking man with the unremarkable face and just plain forgettable altogether, stood on the roof.

His strings of mousy-brown hair lifted around his head in the wind. Even in the semidarkness, I could make out the dark circles under his eyes. His face was gaunt, thinner than I remembered, but then again, I didn't really remember. He could have looked this way before, and I wouldn't have remembered. Like I said, he was forgettable.

Yet I did notice something different. His eyes were sunken but burned too brightly, like he had a fever.

The scent of rot and carrion snapped my attention to a spot in the middle of the roof.

Above a blood-drawn circle, six dead chickens lay

in the middle of the roof floor. The same runes and sigils I'd seen before, painted in blood, marked some areas around the circle's exterior, next to burning candles.

A rippling wave of black waters shimmered in the air, a foot above the blood circle. The Rift was open.

It was huge, at least three times the size of the other ones I'd seen, which explained the thundering boom that shook the hotel.

I had to admit seeing him instead of Valen was a huge relief. It meant I'd been wrong about Valen, but it also meant I was losing my touch if I had totally dismissed Raymond as a suspect. He'd had access to the security cameras. He'd been in my face the whole time, yet I'd never *seen* him.

"You're a witch," I said and carefully stepped forward. "I never got that vibe from you. You hid it well. As well as your forgettable appearance." His unmemorable presence had been his weapon. And he'd milked it.

Raymond's face cracked into a smile, his eyes wide with a madman's gleam. Blood trickled from his nose, and a layer of blood covered his teeth when he spoke next. "Yes. Who would ever suspect poor, little, old, frail Raymond."

The sound of heavy breathing and the tread of many feet had me snap my head back.

Julian rushed forward, followed by Elsa and a rolling Jade.

"Holy shit," cried Julian as he joined. "That's the

assistant manager. What's his name? I can never remember it."

See, totally forgettable.

"Raymond," I told him.

"Him?" said Elsa as she stood beside me on my right. "He's the one? You're kidding!"

I shrugged. "Looks can be deceiving."

"I'll say." Jade rolled to a stop next to Elsa.

"But he's the janitor?" asked Elsa, which was more of a question than a statement.

A growl emitted from Raymond at that. "*Assistant* manager," he spat at us. Yup, he had some serious insecurity issues.

I looked behind again, expecting to see Jimmy, but he wasn't there. Maybe he couldn't go on the roof, which was technically outside the hotel.

My anger twisted in my gut at the thought of all this clusterfuck because of Raymond.

The night sky was clear, and my starlight sang to me, ready and waiting. "You put a spell on me so I couldn't see the hotel?"

Raymond gave a sick, wet laugh. "I did."

I clenched my jaw, my anger redoubling. "You let the demons in and killed all those people. You had Eddie killed because he was onto you. Wasn't he? Why would you do this?" Crazy people did crazy things, but they always had a reason.

With my starlight in tow, I could sense Raymond's magic now, cold and unfamiliar. Most of it was directed at the Rift. For now. He might not look it, but he was a powerful witch. He'd fooled me, but I wasn't going to make that mistake again and underestimate him.

"Why? Why?" Raymond threw back his head and let out an unsettling and creepy laugh. He sounded pleased that he'd orchestrated it all, delighted that he'd brought the demons to the hotel and killed all those people.

The demented witch gave out a wheezing cackle. "All my life, I've been ignored and overlooked for jobs. Women don't even give me the time of day."

"Maybe if you'd clean yourself up a bit," muttered Julian. "Hair plugs can go a long way."

"Nobody ever cared about me," continued Raymond, the words rushing out of him with loads of emotion, like he'd been wanting to tell someone for years, but no one would hear him. "Every time there was a new position in the hotel, I'd be overlooked. I've worked harder, longer than anyone at this hotel. And when Jabbar, the old hotel manager, died thirty years ago, the position was open. But did they offer it to me? No. They gave it to Basil. That job should have been mine. And I had to work beneath him all these years knowing he'd stolen my position."

"Okay," I said. "You didn't get the job. I still don't get it. That was a long time ago. But what does that have to do with anything?"

Raymond's eyes narrowed on me. "Because. Because I knew they'd never offer me the job. The only way I could get rid of Basil was to get him fired. To ruin his reputation." An evil smile contorted over his face. "Only when a hotel manager is fired can the assistant manager fill that position."

"Holy shit," I breathed. "All this? All these deaths because of a goddamn position? You *killed* people because you wanted to be the hotel manager?" Clearly, he was insane.

"The guy is nuts," said Julian.

Nuts and a powerful witch. Dangerous combination.

Raymond lifted his head proudly. "I will be the hotel manager soon." He laughed, his eyes gleaming with a manic glee. "The job was promised to me. With this last demon portal, I'll be rid of you, and then Basil will be fired. And then *I* will be the Twilight Hotel manager!"

Elsa sucked in a breath through her teeth. "He doesn't know."

"What a dick," said Julian.

"They didn't tell him," added Jade.

Raymond's confidence cracked as his gaze swept around us. "Tell me what? What are you talking about?"

My skin prickled at the sudden pull of Raymond's magic, and I felt his fury rippling under the surface.

The Rift wavered, and I heard the hissing and guttural moans of creatures from the other side. A breeze brought forth an odor of blood, and a cloud of foul energies struck me in the face. Better to keep them on the other side of that portal.

I took a breath. "They're going to demolish the

hotel," I said, keeping my voice calm. "They're going to destroy it tomorrow morning at eight."

Fury darkened Raymond's features. "Liar. You're all liars. You're just jealous because you want my job." He pointed at us. "You want to be the manager. But you can't. I'm the manager now. The job is mine."

"A total nutcase," I muttered. "Listen, Raymond, I have a job, and my friends here wouldn't dream about being the next manager. But I am telling you the truth."

"If it were true, why are you not leaving?" asked Raymond, the suspicion in his voice still there, though I could feel the uncertainty in his words.

"Because of Jimmy. We're trying to figure out a way to free him of this curse. You know Jimmy. Right? Of course you do. Then you know if the hotel goes down, so does he."

Jade rolled forward a bit. "It's the truth. Why don't you call Basil? He'll tell you."

Surprisingly, Raymond had a phone on him. He grabbed it, texted something, and waited. We all heard the answering ting of someone messaging him back.

He went still. As he stood there, Raymond's face seemed to take on a different cast, the shadows under his eyes growing to make him look ill.

His phone slipped from his hand and smashed against the hard surface of the roof, breaking into pieces.

"See?" I told him. "You did this all for nothing.

You weren't going to get the position because there would be no position for you." Shit, I realized that was not the right thing to say to an already unstable individual. But it was too late.

Raymond's face rippled grotesquely. *"No!"* he shouted. "No. They can't do that to me. I've worked here for years. Years!"

I felt a pull from the Rift. It was connected to Raymond. All he had to do was give it a push of his magic, and it would open.

Raymond coughed and spat the blood from his mouth, but most of it remained around his lips, dribbling off his chin.

"You're sick, Raymond. Let us help you." I knew whatever dark, Black magic he'd been dabbling in took a chunk of payment from him. He'd been changed, corrupted every time he'd used it. He'd been made insane from it. I didn't know if he was already too far gone for me to help him, but I was going to try.

Raymond thrashed around on the spot, looking more and more like a creature, a beast from the very place he'd been summoning them. "Mine. My job. Mine!"

"The guy's lost it," said Julian. "We need to act now."

I nodded. "You're right. That portal's about to burst open. Can't let that happen. You got something on you to hold him? Like an immobilizing potion?"

"Yes," answered Julian. "It'll take care of him."

"Good." I took a deep breath. "And I'll close the portal."

But it was already too late.

I felt a sudden buzz of energy, a pull of magic; a pop displaced the air.

The hair on the back of my neck rose, and I stood horrified as the Rift shimmered and cracked into existence forty feet from us. Twisting, corrupted masses of demons spilled out in search of their human feast.

The air cracked, and demons of every shape and size let out howls of fury as they surged from the portal, the light of the moon glinting on their teeth, talons, and horrible, hungry, sunken eyes. They rushed out, animal-swift, in a blur of twisted, bulging faces and limbs.

I counted thirty before I lost count.

And they all came for us.

CHAPTER 27

My first thought was, *I'm not even getting paid for this shit.* The second was that I needed to do something if I didn't want to become part of the demon buffet.

Demons spilled out of the rippling portal as though hell itself had vomited them out. At least the sudden reek of rot, bile, and sewage smelled like it.

I channeled my starlight, feeling the power in the stars as they hummed their power through me, and held it just long enough before letting it go.

A brilliant ball of light fired from my outstretched hand and crashed onto the first demon. I didn't even have a chance to see what my starlight had consumed as it illuminated and wrapped itself around the creature like white fire.

"Nice one," said Julian, vials of red liquid in his hands. "Why are there so many at once?"

"Full moon," I answered. "It's always easier for

the crazies to show up and the demons to cross over when the Veil is at its thinnest."

"Good to know." Julian rolled his shoulders. "My turn."

I watched as the tall witch hit one of the demons —some lizard-like thing with a mouth of sharp teeth —with one of his vials. The creature howled in pain and shuffled forward, clumsy and slow. It shivered once and then exploded like a piñata, showering Julian in black oil and strips of its flesh.

But the witch didn't seem to care as he pitched another of his vials at another demon with brown fur and a ratlike skull.

Latin rose around me, and I turned to see Jade, spinning around some giant wormlike demon with rows of black spikes covering most of its body. She was firing orange fireballs at it.

Elsa stood with her legs apart for better balance as she fired bursts of wind at a treelike creature, sending it crashing into the massive air-conditioning unit.

A flash of sensation flickered over me as the witches drew in power—a lot of it. Shock waves of our magic shook the roof like a thunderstorm.

A laugh echoed around me. "You're too late. You're all going to die. You will never laugh at Raymond again," said the crazed witch, speaking about himself in the third person. He started to thrash around the blood circle in some creepy ceremonial dance. Yeah, the guy was seriously disturbed.

The sound of hissing reached me, and I spun with my hands at the ready.

Strings of starlight discharged from my hands and hit a demon in the chest with a burst of light, sending it sprawling to the ground sixty feet away. The demon hissed one last time before disintegrating into a clump of ash.

I'd fought my share of demons over the years but never so many at once and never on a roof of a glamorous paranormal hotel.

Too bad I'd be out of a job in the morning.

My body shook with adrenaline as more demons slipped through the portal. Three more. Six more. Ten more.

The difference between this Rift and the others Raymond had risen was that he'd been careful and closed those off after letting out a few demons. But now, it seemed the witch didn't care how many slipped out or how many people died. If the Rift wasn't closed, thousands of demons would cross over to our world before sunrise.

A collection of four demons that looked like enormous rats, the size of bears, with claws and jaws full of fishlike teeth came at me in a rush.

I called to the stars, pulled on my magic, and thrust out my starlight.

Four shoots of starlight strings volleyed, one in the direction of each demon. The starlight twisted and shifted, moving of its own volition like heatseeking missiles searching for their aircraft targets.

They hit.

The four ratlike beasts lit up with white light. The

demons staggered, cries emitting as they fell on their backs, legs flailing. The light went out, and nothing remained of the creatures but clumps of ashes that blew away in the wind.

I cringed at the scent of burnt flesh, my body pounding with starlight. I didn't have time to take a breather. The roof shook under my feet as more demons spilled out onto it.

"We have to shut down the Rift," I cried.

"I'm on it." Julian rushed over to the rippling black wave. He pulled his right hand from his coat pocket and fired a glass vial into the portal's mouth.

I couldn't see Raymond anywhere. Did the coward leave? Probably. But I'd find him. And then I'd make him pay for what he did.

Like a seasoned baseball pitcher, Julian shot vial after vial into its depths, causing the roof to shudder with each impact. I didn't know what kind of potions he was using, but whatever they were kept the demons inside. However, it wasn't closing the Rift. It was just a temporary fix. And Julian couldn't keep this up for much longer. Soon he'd run out of his vials.

We needed to close it.

Without Raymond's help, it could take hours to decipher the ritual and spells he'd used to conjure up a Rift of this magnitude.

Or you needed a crapload of power to shut it down. Enough to short circuit it in a way.

I looked to the black sky, to the shining white disk

looming over all of us. I didn't draw from the full moon often. More like I tried to avoid it. Too much would kill me. The key was to balance the starlight from the moon, which was more challenging than it sounded. But I needed to try.

"I need you tonight," I whispered.

And then I was sprinting toward the portal. I saw Raymond lying on his back, moving his arms and legs like he was doing snow angels. His eyes were open, staring at the sky above.

The guy was lost, but I didn't have time to worry about him for now.

I got maybe fifteen feet before the pain hit.

I cried out as the scorching agony exploded around my left calf, dragging me down to the ground as sharp claws raked my leg. My focus shattered, and my hold on my starlight collapsed. Instincts kicked in, and I kicked out with my other leg.

My boot made contact with something solid. I heard a small yelp of pain, and then I could move my left leg again. I scrambled to my feet. The wetness that soon followed told me a demon had taken a chunk out of my calf.

Favoring my right leg, I straightened to find a wolflike demon shaking its head, red eyes watching me. It had a scorpion-like tail with a stinger at the end. Nice.

"A little help here," cried Julian as he tossed another vial into the Rift.

"I'm trying!" I shouted back and started limping

forward. I pulled on my starlight once again, straining to focus. I was nearly there—

My breath escaped me as something long and hard slammed into my chest.

I grunted in pain as my back hit the hard rooftop. Hot carrion breath hit my face as its weight pinned me down. In a flash, the wolf-scorpion demon went for my neck. I raised my arm just as teeth clamped around it.

Pain racked me as the demon bit down, harder and deeper. I couldn't move. I couldn't speak. I couldn't breathe. My arm was slick with my own blood. My focus fell, and so did the hold on my magic.

Tears filled my eyes. Using my free hand, I made a fist and smashed it against its head over and over again.

But the wolf-scorpion demon wouldn't let go.

Its tail curled up behind it as it drew near until its stinger hung just above my head. Demon venom was not something you could cure. One sting of its tail, once the demon poison was in me, there was no getting it back out.

I blinked. The stinger moved closer and closer to my head.

"I'm running out!" shouted Julian over the pounding of blood in my ears. I could just make out his silhouette next to the rippling Rift. "I'm out!" He leaped back, and the hissing and grunts sounded from the portal.

Movement caught my eye as Jade limped across

the roof, a roller skate on one foot but the other with just a sock. Blood was smeared on the left side of her face, and she looked tired, done in. Her elemental fire around her palms was faint, like the mild burning of a candle. She was running out of her magic.

Behind her, Elsa was pinned to the air-conditioning unit. A line of demons stood before her, pounding and throwing themselves on a thin, shimmering wall of light blue. She'd managed some sort of shield. But from the look of pure terror and the shifting in her shield, it wouldn't last.

There were too many demons. We weren't strong enough. We weren't going to make it.

Something moved in my peripheral vision. I saw the blur of a body, and then the weight of the wolf-scorpion demon on my chest vanished.

I blinked up to see Valen haul the wolf-scorpion with his bare hands, across the roof.

And then the next thing that happened, I'd never have believed if I hadn't seen it with my own eyes.

Valen, the hot restaurant owner, ripped off his clothes, which I would have really enjoyed if not for what came next.

A flash of light was followed by a tearing sound and the breaking of bones. I stared as his features shifted with a sort of rippling motion just beneath the surface of his skin, causing a widening of his head. His face twisted, enlarging and expanding unnaturally until his head was about five times its normal size.

Valen's body grew in length and width until he

stood at about eighteen feet. Muscles bulged with arms and thighs as large as tree trunks. His face was different, with a stronger brow bone, resembling a Neanderthal, but it was him. It was like staring at a version of the Hulk, but much bigger and taller.

Holy shit. Valen was a *giant*.

CHAPTER 28

I'd never seen an actual giant. Giants were things of myths and legends. I barely remembered reading about them in the thousands of paranormal books I'd read over the years. No one even talked about them because we all knew they didn't exist. And I say *we*, as in the paranormal community, where shifters and vampires and fae were among our people. Giants were not supposed to be real. I mean, unicorns were rare, but I knew they were real. Some had been spotted in Ireland. But giants? Giants weren't real.

Yet I was staring at one.

"You're... you're a giant," I told him. From my vantage point, I could barely see his face.

With my heart in my throat, Valen, the giant, crushed a nearing demon with a slam of his fist. The roof shook like an earthquake.

He turned to me and said, *"I am."*

I winced at the sound of his voice. It was ten

times as deep and loud with a more guttural tone to it.

I couldn't help but stare at this magnificent, yet terrifying, naked giant. The muscles on his chest flexed as he stood protectively in front of me, giving me an excellent view of his giant manhood. What? I had to look. Trust me. You would have too.

In response to a flash of fur and teeth, Valen, the giant, spun around to meet the onslaught of two demons. I heard a cry and the sound of tearing flesh. Valen, the giant, tore at the demons with voracious rapidity.

It was both exciting and terrifying to watch.

And then I realized this was what he'd been hiding. He was hiding the fact that he was a giant. But why?

A growl came from behind me. Valen stepped forward, grabbed a handful of demons, and lifted them as though they weighed nothing at all. Then he crushed their skulls together, like they were nothing more than eggshells, before tossing them.

"Leana! Help!"

I turned to the sound of Julian's terrified voice. He had a metal pole in his hand, swinging it at an oncoming demon that looked like a panther with an eagle's head. He had no magic to defend him.

I struggled to my feet. "Can you protect them? I need to get to the Rift and close it. Can you help my friends?"

Valen stared down at me with those same dark eyes. *"I can. You can close the portal?"*

"I'll do my best."

Valen turned, stepped on a demon in his way, and hurried over to Julian. I wanted to stay and watch this giant beat the crap out of the demons. It wasn't every day you witnessed a mystical creature that wasn't supposed to be real. But I had a Rift to shut down.

Picking myself up again, I limped across the roof, glad that Valen had cleared me a path. I made it to the Rift without being attacked, where Raymond was still lying with his back on the roof, staring up at the sky. He was a deranged sonofabitch.

I let out a breath and then called to my will, to my starlight. I felt the soft tug of its power as it answered, the flow of brilliant white energy churning inside my core. I held it there for just a moment. I planted my feet for better control, as I knew my injuries might make me stumble.

I stood before the demon portal. The air sizzled with cold energy as the scent of death, blood, and evil hit me in the face. It pulsed like a constant humming from a power line. The reek of sulfur and rot was overwhelming, and my ears popped with the pressure shifting. A mighty wind blew around me, lifting my hair off my shoulders and slapping it against my face. It was unnatural, acidic, and poisonous to us mortals. I recognized it. It was the Netherworld's air, coming from inside the portal.

I could see shapes through the gateway. Thousands of forms were rushing toward the opening of our world.

Shit. If they reached us, I wasn't sure even Valen could stop them.

I grabbed all the starlight magic I could to spindle it inside my core, channeling the emanations and harnessing that celestial energy beyond the clouds. I felt a tingling as it answered.

A spool of blinding white light curled up in my palms and wove through my fingers in a slow crawl.

Blazing light soared forth from my outstretched fingers, and I directed it at the Rift. It poured out of me like a never-ending shoot of white energy, illuminating the roof like it was daylight.

Screeches echoed from somewhere deep inside the portal. I couldn't see them anymore, but their voices were near. Too near. I had to hurry.

Again, way harder than it looked, and I kept my magic ready, like a loaded gun. I was ready to blast any sonofabitch who came through the portal while I tried to close it.

And then, as I held on to my starlight, I called to the moon's power.

I reached out my will to the moon, to its energy.

It answered.

Another, larger, blast of white light fired through me and hit the portal.

Pain hit my body, like my insides were liquifying. Dizzy, my balance wobbled as the magic gushed out of me like a fountain, drowning me in a flood of fatigue.

Calling up the power of the moon was not an easy feat. Like I said before, too much and it'd kill me. Fry me right there on the spot, like fried chicken.

But it was working.

The portal shifted, and it started to fold on itself.

"What are you doing!"

I turned to see Raymond on his feet next to me, staring wild-eyed at the portal as it continued to get smaller and smaller.

I didn't have the energy to waste speaking to him. One mishap and I could be finished.

"You can't do this! Stop! Stop it!" he shouted.

Yeah, I was never very good at taking orders.

The starlight kept firing out of me and into the portal. Sweat broke out along my forehead, and I started to feel the beginnings of tiredness along with a bit of nausea. But still, I held on. Only a bit more, and it would be all over.

Distant cries and howls of outrage found me. I squinted into the Rift. Countless shadows appeared in view, getting bigger and closer. I could make out wings and tails and tentacles. Their movements were frantic and desperate. The demons saw what I was doing, and now they were making a run for it.

Hands appeared out of nowhere and wrapped around my neck. I blinked into the mad face of Raymond, his eyes crazed, as he tried to crush my neck with his cold, stiff fingers.

"I'll kill you! Kill you!" he screamed, his spit flying into my eyes as he pressed harder, taking away my ability to breathe.

Again with the choking? Seriously? I wasn't

afraid anymore. I was angry. Pissed. I'd had enough of men trying to choke me to death.

I couldn't let go of my starlight, and I couldn't use my hands.

So I used the only other thing I had at my disposal.

And I kneed him in the balls.

When in doubt, go for balls. And it worked like a charm.

Raymond let go and bent over, hands on his man berries. "Bitch," he wheezed.

Of course, I had to kick him again after that.

Raymond stumbled backward and fell right into the portal, vanishing.

Oops. I hadn't meant to do that, but it was too late. The witch was gone.

Adrenaline flooded me. The moon's energy seemed to shred me into thousands of pieces, held together only by my skin and my will. Searing pain exploded in my head, and blackness flooded my eyes. I couldn't see, but I still held on.

Guttural shrieks rose from the depths of the portal, but it was too late. Their cries of outrage rose, echoed, and then vanished.

With a pop of pressure, the Rift was gone.

CHAPTER 29

I let go of my starlight and the moon's energy and collapsed to the floor. Dizziness hit, and my heart was hammering, like I'd just run around the block ten times for fun. I was burned out but still proud that I'd managed to close it, something I'd never have been able to do without my friends. Without Valen.

The scent of body odor wafted up. I sniffed myself and winced. "Definitely need a shower." I stank!

Worse, I was buck naked, the cool air rolling over my lady bits. All that starlight had once again burned away my clothes. Whoops.

"You did it. You fucking did it," said Julian as he walked over to the spot where the portal had stood. "That was incredible."

"We all did." Speaking of my friends, I turned around on my butt and stared at the jumbled mess of what was left of the demons. Some were stacks of bones and heaps of meat, and some were just piles of ashes. But they were all vanquished. Not one demon remained standing.

Jade came limping our way, still missing one of her roller skates, but otherwise she seemed okay. Elsa was hobbling along behind her. She looked exhausted, but her smile was vibrant as she stared at me.

And Valen? Valen was still huge. Still naked. Still glorious.

"That was quite something," said Elsa as she neared. "It was like watching a star being born."

"Yeah. It was amazing," echoed Jade. "Wish we didn't have to fight off those demons so I could have watched. Pictures would have been nice, too, maybe a few videos."

"Here." Elsa pulled a green shawl from her bag and handed it to me.

"Thanks." I wrapped it around myself, my face burning as I felt Valen's eyes on me.

Elsa turned on the spot. "What happened to the janitor? Did the demons get him? I hope they did. Can't believe he did what he did for a promotion."

"A promotion he'd never get," interjected Jade. "Have you seen my roller skate? I swear I saw it here somewhere?"

I shook my head. "No." I gestured at the space that had held the portal. Only a few streaks of a black, tar-like substance remained. "He fell through the Rift."

"Fell or pushed?" asked Julian, a smile on his face.

"Accidental push?" I told them with a shrug. "He was trying to choke me, so I kicked him, and he fell over and through it. Oopsie."

Julian laughed. "Serves the bastard right. The world's a better and safer place without him."

Probably. But I still wished he hadn't fallen through. Prison would have been a better option. Now, who knew what had happened? All those demons on the other side probably ripped him to pieces—a bad way to go.

"Good riddance," said Jade, yanking the sleeve of her shirt with a long tear in it. "Always gave me the creeps anyway. Oh, the goddess help us." Jade's eyes widened, and I turned to see Valen coming our way in all his naked, giant splendor. Man berries and stem swinging. Yup. It was hard *not* to look.

"That's a big boy," said Julian, giving Valen's junk an approving nod. "A king of kings."

I shook my head. Men and their junk. I'd never understand.

The giant had splatters of dark blood all over him, not his blood. *"You okay?"* he asked in that deep, profound voice.

"I'll live," I told him, still trying to wrap my mind around the fact that I was staring at a giant and wasn't dreaming. Giants were real. Holy shit.

"Here. Take this." Julian tugged off of his coat and handed it to the giant. "You shouldn't be allowed to walk around exposing a thing that big."

Valen stared at him, and for a second, I thought he would refuse. But then he wrapped the coat around his man parts and tucked it in like a pair of makeshift briefs.

Julian raised his brows. "You can keep it."

I laughed. "This has been a strange night."

Elsa had her head back as she took in all of Valen. I could tell she wanted to ask him about being a giant. Hell, we all did, but we stayed silent. Call it respect. It was obvious he wasn't comfortable talking about it. But he'd revealed it to us. Without his help, we would have been toast.

"What time is it?" I asked.

Jade yanked out her phone. "Uh… two a.m."

My heart gave a jolt. We still had time to save the hotel. "Did you reach your friend?"

"Just a second." Jade frowned as she swiped a finger across the screen of her phone. "Oh. I missed a message from her." Her eyes widened as she read whatever her friend had written. And then her mouth fell open.

"What did she write?" My heart pounded, and I felt Valen's eyes on me, which were seriously more intense than before, being in his giant state.

"Oh my God," said Jade after a moment.

"What!" we all chorused together.

Jade looked at us. "She says she told my story to her husband and that he was already contacted by Basil to ask for an extension for the hotel's demolition. Listen to this! Turns out not all of those on the Gray Council were aware of this.

And they weren't happy to find out so last minute."

"That bitch," I said, realizing Adele was abusing her power. She hadn't even told the rest of the council what she was up to. It was also scary to think what else she was doing without proper approval.

"They've canceled the order." Jade smiled, tears filling her eyes. "The hotel stays. It won't be destroyed."

Elsa hid her face in her hands as she sobbed openly, only to get grabbed in a hug by Jade.

My eyes burned at the sight of them crying but also because Jimmy would be okay. Basil had done well, but I wouldn't tell him that. What he should have done was double-check with the council before letting that skinny bitch Adele into the hotel and believing any word that came out of her mouth.

"Ahhhh." Julian took in a deep breath and threw his arms out in a stretch. "Nothing like a good screw to end a battle." He rubbed his hands together. "See you gals later. I've got some ladies waiting for me."

I laughed. "Can you find Jimmy and tell him?" My chest nearly exploded at the news that he'd be okay. I wanted to tell him myself, but I didn't think I could stand at the moment. My legs felt like jelly, and I was still a little bit dizzy from all that starlight and moon power.

"You bet." Julian walked away with a hop in his step.

Hot tears fell down my cheeks as I watched the tall witch exit the roof door. Valen was still watching me when I turned around, and I couldn't tell what he was feeling. And I found I couldn't look away either.

Elsa looked between us. "Come." She grabbed Jade by the hand. "We need to find Basil and tell him what happened. About Raymond. About all of it. And we need to get everyone back into their apartments." She walked away with Jade, throwing me looks over her shoulder as she let the other witch pull her.

I wiped my tears with the back of my hand, waiting for Valen to say something. When it became apparent that he wouldn't, I opened my mouth. "So, a giant? Have you been able to transform like that, for long?"

The giant bent his head to look at me. *"I was born this way."*

"Right. Of course." What a stupid question. I craned my neck. "You think you could… lower yourself? I'm getting whiplash just trying to look at you."

The roof squealed and cracked as the giant settled himself down next to me. *"Better?"*

I stared at his face. "Better." Even sitting down, he was like six feet tall. "How did you find us?"

"Jimmy told me," answered the giant, and I found myself staring at his lips while he talked. *"When I heard about what the council wanted to do with the hotel, I came to help."*

I turned my leg over, where the demon had bitten it. My calf was soaked with blood. So was my arm.

"You're hurt," said the giant, and I heard something like worry in his voice.

"It's not that bad. The wounds aren't deep. I don't need stitches." But I'd need to clean it before it got infected. "Thank you for saving me. Without your help, we would have all died, been eaten away by those demons, or been pulled back into that portal."

A noise erupted from his throat that could have been him agreeing. *"It's my job to keep everyone safe."*

"Your job?"

"I'm a watcher."

"A watcher?" I repeated like an idiot. What the hell was a watcher, and how come I'd never heard of them?

"All giants are watchers. Protectors."

It made sense, being as they were so freaking big and robust. "So how come no one has really seen or heard of you giants? As far as I can remember, giants weren't real. You were just stories parents told their children when they misbehaved."

Valen nodded and looked to the ground. *"There aren't many of us left. Over centuries ago, we were feared because of our size and strength. We were hunted. Killed. Only a few left all over the world."*

"That is sad," I told him. "Is that why you don't want people to know?"

"Partly."

"If you had told me that you were a giant, and weren't so secretive, maybe I wouldn't have thought you were behind the portals."

The giant frowned, which, let me tell you, was a scary sight. I found myself leaning back.

"Would you have believed me if I told you I was a giant?"

"By the skepticism I can hear in your voice, I'm going to go with… no?" I said. "Okay, I probably wouldn't have believed you because, well, giants aren't real." I smiled at him and felt warmth in my belly as he smiled back. "Those are some big-ass teeth."

Valen laughed, sounding like a cross between a roar from a lion and the grinding of rocks.

"I'm sorry I accused you," I said to break the sudden silence.

"I should have told you. We are on the same team."

I twisted my face. "What do you mean?"

"The hotel hired me." Valen was silent for a moment. *"I came here five years ago. To work as a watcher for the hotel and for the surrounding area."*

"Ah." Things were starting to all make sense now. "So when I saw you in room nine fifteen and then before that in Eddie's room…"

"I was asked to be there by the hotel."

"So why did they ask me to work for the Twilight Hotel when they already had you?"

"Not the same." Valen's eyes glimmered in the moonlight. They were so big and beautiful, I felt myself leaning forward. *"You are an investigator. An agent. I'm just the muscle."* He flashed me another one of those big-ass smiles. *"I'm the guy you want with you to bring in the bad guy. I protect."*

I winced on the inside. I can't believe I had ever thought he was the bad guy. *Good one, Leana.*

He'd saved me twice now. Yes, he'd been a brute when we'd first met. But all that was in the past. What did that mean now? And why was he still here with me? Why didn't he leave with the others?

"Tell me," I said, staring at all those ginormous, manly muscles and finding myself wildly attracted to a giant. Did that make me weird or just horny? "What exactly does a watcher do? I get the watching part. The... overseeing and making sure there's no evil lurking in the shadows. But do you work only when you're a giant? Or is it a constant thing? All day... all night. I mean, you do have a restaurant."

"You ask a lot of questions."

He was smiling, so I didn't think he took my pestering as a bad thing. "I've got more. How long are you staying?"

Again, the giant laughed, and my heart skipped a beat.

"I'm always a watcher," answered the giant. *"But I patrol the streets at night in my giant form."*

"Really? You must have a huge invisibility cloak." I laughed. "How can you hide"—I made a gesture with my hand over his body—"all that from human eyes. If you were a pixie, that wouldn't be a problem. But you're like a thousand times bigger than a pixie."

A smile broke over the giant's face. *"Natural glamour. Don't need cloaks."*

My lips parted. "What the hell is that?" I'd never heard of such a thing. Potions and spells that put a glamour on you or objects like the hotel, but never a natural glamour. I began to realize that I knew close to nothing about giants. And I wanted to get a crash course right about now.

"All giants are born with an inherent glamour. No human can see us. Only paranormals, shifters, vampires, witches, like you."

"That's really impressive, and I'm kinda jealous. Walking the streets at night and no one seeing you. Must be nice."

Valen grinned, and then the sounds of police sirens pulled his attention toward the skylight.

"Are you working tonight?" I asked, searching his face. The longer I stared at it, the more I liked it. Yes, it was a larger, more primal face, if I could describe it like that, but it was also soft, and his eyes were the same... but bigger.

The giant looked at me, making my stomach flutter. *"Yes. You want to come with me?"*

A burst of excitement rushed from the top of my head all the way to my toes. "Hell, yeah."

Valen leaped to his feet surprisingly fast for such a big, big man. The roof whined and trembled under his weight, and I bounced along with it.

With effort, I struggled to my feet, feeling tired but also excited. "There's a problem," I told him, my head tilted back so that I could see part of his face. "I'm a bit tired from channeling all that magic. I don't think I can keep up with you." He was probably really fast. He'd take one step, and I'd have to take ten. Yeah, I'd never catch up.

"You won't have to," answered the giant.

"Uhh?"

Before I could protest, Valen's gargantuan hand reached out and grabbed me, not hard, but gently, like he was holding on to an egg that he didn't want to accidentally crush because he could. He really could. One accidental flinch, and I was as flat as a pancake.

I leaned into his hold and then squealed like an idiot as he lifted me up and onto his shoulder. I sat very comfortably there, my legs dangling over his collarbone. The world looked different from this high. Eighteen feet high. I did not want to fall. I reached out and wrapped my hand into his long, dark locks, inhaling their woodsy scent. He did smell good.

My butt was literally on his shoulder, on his skin, and I prayed to the goddess I didn't accidentally let out a nervous fart. That would be embarrassing.

Valen walked across the hotel's roof with me rocking back and forth but finding it pleasantly comfortable. He stood at the edge of the roof.

I looked down. "Wow. That's high. How are we going down? There's no way you can fit inside the elevator." As soon as the words escaped me, I knew. "Fuck me."

"*Hang on,*" said the giant, my stomach finding its way to my throat.

And then he jumped.

CHAPTER 30

I stood on Cherry Street, staring at one of the piers of the Manhattan Bridge. The sky was a dark blue, the sun coming up in a hazy line. It was hinting at the horizon, but I still had about forty minutes left before I would run out of my starlight magic. It would have to be enough.

I'd spent nearly the rest of the night riding on Valen's shoulder as he walked through the streets of a city that never slept. It had been amazing walking among the humans but them never seeing us. Because I was riding on him, touching his skin, I'd guessed that his glamour had also hidden me from human eyes.

He was careful not to touch anyone as he walked, twisting and avoiding them as much as possible. Roofs were his thing, apparently, as he'd showed me by leaping from one to the other. It seemed he was not only gifted with strength but with the power of leaping great distances. I was jealous about that too.

I didn't realize I'd fallen asleep on his shoulder. And when I'd woken up, I was back in his apartment, and he was back in his normal size and fully clothed, unfortunately.

"How long was I out?" I'd asked him, sitting up from his couch.

"About an hour. How you feeling?" He handed me another tea.

I took it and stared at it. "Is this..."

Valen laughed. "It won't make you sleep. This is just regular tea."

I stretched and yawned. "Like a new me. I feel great, actually." It made me wonder if giants had healing abilities or something because I shouldn't feel this rejuvenated. I took a sip of the tea and placed the mug on the side table.

The couch bounced as Valen sat next to me, his thigh brushing against mine. It felt nice, and I didn't move.

I stared at his face. "You must be tired?"

"Not at all," he said, staring at me with such intensity that I felt about to spontaneously combust. "I'm used to it." His eyes moved to my lips, which sent a spike of desire to my core.

"I'm sure you are." He was close. So very close.

"You're very beautiful," he purred, and I think I actually moaned.

"I saw you naked," I said. Why the hell did I say that?

Desire flashed in his dark eyes. And without so much as a warning, he tilted his head and kissed one corner of my mouth. Then the other side, pulling gently on my lips.

I stiffened in surprise. His lips moved against mine, warm and soft, my heart pounding as I kissed him back. When he slipped his tongue in between my lips, my pulse jumped, and heat bloomed over my skin, alluring, spinning a thrill through me from my lips all the way to my toes.

I'd forgotten how good it felt to be kissed like that, with passion and desire, the kind of kissing that set your lady drawers on fire, like this one.

He slid a hand around my back, the other at the back of my neck, edging me closer. I felt myself move my arms around his waist and his back. My breath came fast as he darted his tongue deep into me. He tasted faintly of coffee, and his kisses made me ache for more.

I let out a little moan and wound my fingers at the nape of his neck, pulling him closer.

He made a surprised sound, and his kiss turned more aggressive. His hands tightened around me. I felt his desire and his need in them. It sent a surge of heat through me, my lady bits pounding. A part of me wanted to rip off his clothes, to feel his hard body against my skin.

Damn, he was a good kisser. Did all giants kiss like that?

My breath left me in a moan as I eased against him, one hand wrapped around his neck and the other in his soft, silky hair. I felt his muscles tighten, and it was all I could do to keep from ripping off his clothes.

His hands moved under my shirt, and the roughness of his callouses sent my skin tingling. Sensing my desire, his touch became aggressive, and hot ribbons of pleasure spiraled through my core.

And then he pulled away.

"I'm sorry. I can't," he said, his voice low and full of emotions. His breath came out in a slow exhalation. Not only did he pull away but he walked away, too, like, to the kitchen.

It was hard not to feel hurt or hit with a giant ball of rejection. We were on our way for some bedroom rodeo. I'd felt his hard desire for me, but something held him back. Or someone...

I sat on the couch in silence for as long as I could before it became awkward. "How much did we patrol? How far did we go?" I asked, breaking the uncomfortable silence and looking up at the man who wouldn't meet my eyes.

Valen surprised me when he returned and took the chair next to me. He remained a good distance away from me but close enough I didn't feel rejected again. Yeah, still a little. "All the way to Harlem and then back down to Chinatown and then here."

I raised a brow. "That was a lot of ground you covered. You must know the city pretty well." A thought occurred to me. Being a watcher, Valen had patrolled the streets of Manhattan for years. He knew where all the dark, vile critters lived, renegade demons, outcast werewolves, and vampires. Among others…

"I do," answered the giant, his dark eyes holding me for a moment.

I swallowed. "Do you know of a sorceress named Auria? She'd be old. Past her one-hundredth birthday."

Valen's brows met in the middle as he thought of it. "Not the name. But I do know of an old sorceress who lives under the Manhattan Bridge. She's been there for many years, apparently. Why?"

My heart slammed in my chest as I stood. "I need to go." I really did need to put some distance between the hot giant and my thumping lady regions. I had to do something else, keep my mind from feeling that rejection again. Because it hurt. I wasn't going to lie.

Valen stood up slowly. "Now?"

"Yes. Before sunrise. I still have time."

I wasn't surprised when he didn't offer to come with me. It was obvious Valen had some inner demons to take care of, and I was just making it worse. Yeah, that didn't make me feel a lot better either.

I'd left his apartment with my heart a little sore. But nothing that couldn't be mended. I didn't want another man in my life. Or so I thought until I'd met Valen. But I wouldn't let myself get too attached to someone who wasn't ready, or someone who couldn't let go of the past.

And now here I was. A half hour later and staring at the stone pier.

Part of me had wanted to stay with the giant. I felt a definite pull between us. But I had something more important I needed to do.

Feeling rejuvenated because of Valen's giant magic—though he hadn't confirmed it—I stepped toward the stone pier and looked for the door. At first, I couldn't see a door or doorway. After going around the pier, it was obvious it wouldn't be easy to find.

"There has to be a door. Right?"

Being a powerful sorceress, Auria would have the door glamoured and hidden by a spell. Good thing my starlights could find it.

Looking over my shoulder to make sure no curious humans were around, I pulled on my starlight magic, held it, and then lifted my hand and sent it out.

Hundreds of brilliant white miniature globes shot out of my hand and hit the stone pier, draping it in a curtain of white light. The starlights moved around the stone wall, and I followed them. Then they came together on a spot on the stone. Their inner lights shone brighter. The starlights shimmered and then dissolved to reveal a door carved into the stone.

I smiled and, putting my shoulder into it, pushed it open and stepped through.

CHAPTER 31

I found myself in some sort of hallway with a low ceiling that stank of old rugs, mildew, cat pee, and other fouler things I tried not to think about. Nasty. I wrinkled my nose at the scent of incense and candles as I stepped over the dirt-packed ground chamber that ended in shadow. It was dimly lit by glowing flames from a few wall torches.

It was cold, about ten degrees colder than outside, and I wrapped my arms around myself.

Just as I took three more steps, a sudden, cold tingle of magic energy rippled over my skin, making it riddled in goose bumps. Hard to tell if it was Dark or White magic. But an evil energy definitely pulsed around me, slow and thick like the beating heart of a giant beast.

The sorceress's magic. With something extra in it.

"You put a curse at the entrance," I muttered, feeling the cold thrumming and familiar pulse of a curse.

"Ooh. It's a bad one. Kill-me-on-the-spot kind of baddie." But I'd been prepared for it.

With a burst of strength, I pulled on my starlight. Energy crackled against my skin—the energies from the stars tingling over me.

I gave a burst of my starlight, lighting up the hallway with white light and eating away at the darkness. The pressure in the air drifted and disappeared. With a crack, the cold pricks in the air vanished as though they'd never been there.

The curse was broken.

If she didn't know someone had come through her door before, she would now.

I kept going, following the stench and feel of her cold magic. Cobwebs stretched out along the stone walls. The floor sloped slightly up, where a mound on the cave floor gave rise to a larger space.

The room sported a small kitchen area, where a collection of cauldrons were pushed to the sides, a cot that I guessed was her bed, tall bookcases crammed with books, and a long table covered with melted-down candles, books, and bowls. Shelves and racks lined parts of walls, packed with an assortment of jars with unidentifiable objects, all covered in a thin layer of dust. Candles, animal bones, crystal balls, pendulums, chalk, scrying mirrors, cauldrons, and books were crammed in every corner.

I saw no bathroom, which possibly explained the smell.

And there, staring at me from her chair next to what could only be described as a magical fire with green-blue flames, was a woman with more wrinkles and folds around her face than a Shar-Pei dog.

Even bent with age, she had a powerful quality to her. Wisps of white hair fell loosely around her face, her arms and legs hung weakly, and she was painfully thin.

She looked like she had celebrated her two hundredth birthday recently. But her eyes shone with sharp intelligence.

Auria. The sorceress.

Laughter echoed around the room. The old woman lifted her chin haughtily and pointed a gnarled finger at me. "You are a fool. Only fools venture into my home." Her voice was scratchy, old, and withered, just like her.

"Possibly." I was a fool, but I wasn't stupid. I knew she was powerful. But I wasn't leaving until I got what I came for.

I walked in closer, my skin tingling with the pressure of her magic. I was on her home turf, where her magic was strongest. But I had my magic with me too. The old sorceress didn't scare me.

She watched me, sizing me up. "You broke my curse. You a Dark witch?"

"No." I stood as close as I allowed myself. The old woman gave off a horrible stench of an unwashed body.

Auria made a disapproving sound in her throat. "Who are you? What do you want?"

I clasped my hands behind my back. "My friend wants his life back, and you're gonna give it."

The old sorceress narrowed her eyes at me. "Who's your friend?"

"Jimmy." I knew with the slight arch of her brow and the way her lips pressed tightly, she realized who I was talking about. It also confirmed that she was indeed Auria, the sorceress.

"Why should I care what your friend wants?" said the old woman, a smile in her voice.

"Because you cursed him into a toy dog. I think you made your point. Jimmy suffered enough. It's time you break your curse and let him go."

The sorceress's jaw moved like she was gnawing on food. "Never."

Irritation flared as I took a step closer. "You will. Don't make me hurt an old lady because I will. He's my friend. He's a good person. He doesn't deserve this."

The old sorceress laughed a wet laugh. "He's a fool."

"Why? Because he didn't return your love? It happens. Grow up and move on."

Auria leaned forward in her chair. "You're an insolent creature."

"And you're a bitch. I don't care how old you are. You will tell me how to remove the curse. And I'm not leaving until I do. But I'm hoping it's soon, 'cause... you really stink."

The sorceress snorted. "You think you scare me? You're just a witchling. Your White or Dark magic can't do nothing to me."

"How do I remove the curse?" I asked. "The sooner you tell me, the sooner I can leave you to get back to whatever you were doing." I did not want to know.

"I will never tell you or anyone," said the sorceress. "He deserves what he got. Men are nothing but tools for reproduction. They're weaker than us. And I don't care."

I shrugged. "Sure, some are scumbags like my ex-husband. But not all men are bastards. Just like not all women are bitches."

Auria glowered, which was a scary sight, and she nearly lost her eyes in the folds of her wrinkles. "I don't like you."

"I don't like you either."

She waved a crooked hand at me. The other hand I noticed was over a book on her lap tucked neatly in the creases of her robe. "Leave, or I'll do to you worse than what I did to your friend."

"I told you. I'm not leaving until you tell me how to remove the curse from Jimmy." The old sorceress didn't look like much. She seemed like a gust of wind would blow her to ashes. But we all knew in our paranormal world her frailty might just be a cover. I wasn't going to let her play me.

"Others have tried and failed to get their hands on the curse," she said, her voice proud, and it made me feel sick. "Our curses are an extension of our power, of who we are. We don't give out our secrets. Otherwise, we wouldn't be powerful. We wouldn't be feared. Like you... like *your* secret."

I frowned, not liking that she was trying to guess what kind of magic I wielded.

My blood pressure rose. I knew I didn't have much time left. I had to finish this.

"Give it," I told her and took another regrettable, holding-my-breath step closer to her.

She watched me silently, her eyes gleaming with the promise of pain and death. Her face pulled in a grimace. "Fuck you."

Yikes, that was all kinds of weird coming from an old lady's lips.

I was so shocked by that, I missed that flick of her hand and the word, "Atucei!"

A gust of energy rippled out of her like a wave of death.

My arms snapped to my sides as red misty tendrils wrapped around me like a rope. Searing, white-hot pain exploded around my body as though teeth sank into my flesh and back out again. Yikes. That hurt like a bitch.

"Okay," I wheezed and then laughed. "You got me."

In a blur, I was yanked across the room, the wall acting as my savior when I hit it instead of crashing through the window. I slipped to the floor like a rag doll.

"I'm going to enjoy killing you," said the sorceress, and I lifted my head to see that she was still sitting in that damn chair.

Yup, she was powerful. They were right about that. But so was I.

With my heart hammering, I took a deep breath and tapped into my core, my will, and reached out to the magical energy generated by the power of the stars.

Bright light exploded into existence as my magic mixed with my hatred roared in. It overflowed my will and poured into my body. In a rush, the starlight magic raced all around and through me, like a pounding high-voltage conductor until it consumed me.

Starlight magic blasted out of me, breaking through her spell like breaking through chains.

The blast hit the old woman, and she was thrown out of her chair, landing somewhere behind it.

No. I was not sorry.

I stood, dusted myself off, and walked over, looking for what I had the feeling contained my answers.

A book lay a foot away from the sorceress—the same book she'd been protecting on her lap the whole time I was there. I bent down and grabbed the book.

"That's mine!" She crawled on her hands, pulling herself forward. "Give it. Give it back!"

With my phone's flashlight on, I balanced the book with my right hand and hip and flipped it open. The thin book didn't have a lot of pages in it, which was good. I cringed at the many brown smears and stains on practically every page.

"You take the meaning of dirty witch to a whole other level," I told her.

"No one can break my curses," she spat. "No one. I'm the only one who can."

"But I just did," I said, flipping through the pages.

She looked up at me and started screaming as loudly as a banshee.

It didn't matter. I found what I was looking for. There, on the top of a page, written in scribbly letters, was *Maledicere Alicui Rei*.

My Latin was rusty, to say the least, but I knew *maledicere* meant curse, and the little dog that was drawn next to it gave it away.

My pulse quickened. This was it. I knew it in my gut.

I snapped the book shut. "Nice doing business with you." I stepped over the witch, wanting to put as much distance between me and her horrible body odor as soon as possible.

"What are you?" asked the old sorceress.

I turned and tucked the book under my arm. "A Starlight witch."

And with that, I left a wide-eyed, stinking sorceress on her dirt floor and walked away.

CHAPTER 32

"You think it's going to work?" Jimmy stared at me from my kitchen floor, inside the chalk circle I'd just drawn around him.

"I do." I placed Auria's book back on the table. I was about 90 percent sure, but I wasn't about to tell him that. By the time I'd returned to the Twilight Hotel, the sun was up and bathing the sky in pinks, oranges, and blues.

Echoes of rich voices reached me, and I turned to see Barb, a hand on her hip in a scolding, grandmotherly manner while she pointed at the twins in the hallway. Word of Raymond's defeat and the hotel's reinstatement spread quickly, or Elsa and Jade had been busy waking up the tenants from wherever they had taken up temporary lodgings while I was out and had come back to their homes.

The thirteenth floor was just as vibrant and noisy as it had been the first time I'd set foot on it.

"I can't believe you found her." Jade was on her

knees on the floor, carefully lighting each candle that encircled Jimmy, with a whisper of words. It was truly impressive, something, unfortunately, I would never be able to do, being a Starlight witch.

"We looked everywhere for that horrible sorceress," said Elsa, fiddling with her locket in one hand as she flipped through Auria's book with the other. "We even paid a private werefox investigator. Cost us a fortune, and he never found her."

"How *did* you find her?" Julian stood with his back to the wall, looking refreshed and smelling like soap and aftershave. Next to him on the counter was a bundle of clothes I'd asked him to bring for Jimmy. I had no idea if he'd come back fully clothed or as naked as a newborn.

"Valen helped me," I said. Then, knowing they'd all seen his giant shape, I continued. "He patrols the city at night. Sees a lot of what we don't see. Hears rumors. Anyway, he knew of an old sorceress who lived under the Manhattan Bridge. It was her." The memory of that passionate kiss we'd shared was still very hot in my mind, and my body tingled at its recollection. It had been a kiss of *giant* proportions.

Jade leaned back on her heels. "I wish I could have seen the old hag's face when you took her book."

Elsa picked up Auria's spell book. "I would have enjoyed kicking her in the ass," she said, surprising me.

I laughed. "I doubt she'll be bothering anyone

anytime soon." The sorceress was powerful, but she looked in poor health. She'd probably not left that place she called home in many years, from the smell of it. And if she ever did crawl out of her nest, I'd be ready for her.

"Are we doing this?" Jimmy's eyes flicked from me to the others, his tail swishing behind him in a nervous whip.

"We are." I shifted my weight and looked to the witches in my kitchen for help. My starlight would be of no aid at the moment, and curses and counter-curses weren't exactly my forte. I was going to need their help to make this work.

Elsa came to stand next to me, Auria's curse book in her hands. "I've studied her curse. Sorcerers' and sorceresses' magic is different from ours. The words they use. The way they draw their power. But nothing here is too complicated. We have her exact words, enough to produce a counter-curse. Enough to unmake what she did to Jimmy."

I smiled down at the nervous toy dog. "See? We've got you."

Elsa glanced at us. Her eyes sparked with something hard and determined. "Auria's a powerful sorceress, more powerful than any of us when she made that curse. We'll need to join hands and combine our magic if we want to match it."

I took a breath, excitement rising through me. "Let's do this."

We all took our places in a circle around Jimmy. Then I took Elsa's hand and Julian's as he took Jade's, and she closed the circle with Elsa's. We were all connected physically.

My hand shook with sweat and nerves, and I hoped Elsa and Julian were too focused on the counter-curse to notice. I took a calming breath as a tiny thrill of excitement rushed in, knowing we were about to pool our magic together. I'd never done this before, shared magic with other witches. I had always been a lone gunman—gunwoman. I wasn't sure what to expect. I felt vulnerable. Open. But I'd put aside my fear and insecurities to save a friend.

"Okay," I said, feeling the warmth in my friends' hands. "I'm guessing we have to say the counter-curse together?" I remembered the conversation I'd had earlier with Elsa when she was studying the curse and preparing the counter-curse.

"Yes," answered Elsa. "Do we all remember the words? We've been over it for the last half hour."

I nodded as Julian and Jade both said, "Yes."

Elsa let out a breath. "Together now."

"We call upon the forces of the Dark Mother," we chanted in unison as I reached to the powers of the stars. "Let flesh be flesh and bone be bone; return what was taken, and remade whole. Make right again that we must; reverse the curse that made this mutt. Undo the magic acted here; reverse the spell, so all is clear."

I drew what energy I could from the stars in the middle of the morning, which wasn't much.

But then my pulse quickened at the sudden surge of magic, my friends' magic, sending my skin rippling with goose bumps as magical energy poured into me through our hands.

My hair lifted in a sudden wind, carrying the scent of wildflowers, earth, and pine needles—the scent of White magic. The air hummed with power, and I stared, startled as a visible shimmer of blue, orange, and yellow rushed through me and the others.

With a flash of blinding light, I closed my eyes.

When I opened them, instead of a wooden toy dog, stood a man in the chalk circle. An ethereal shimmer rippled over him like a mist, and then it was gone. He had fair skin and hair, graying at the temples. He was about an inch shorter than me. And yup. He was naked.

"Oh my God! It worked!" cried Jade as she let go of the others and began clapping. "It really worked!"

Jimmy's blue eyes, his *real* eyes, stared at me in wonder. "You did it. I can't believe you did it."

I smiled, happy that his voice was the same as it had been when he'd been a wooden toy. "*We* did it. All of us." Which was true. I'd felt the magic of the other witches pour through and around me. Without them, it wouldn't have worked.

Jimmy raised his hands in front of his face, wiggling his fingers like he was trying them out for the first time. That's probably how it felt after being in a wooden body without fingers for so long.

"Here. Cover your junk before the ladies throw themselves all over you." Julian handed Jimmy a bundle of clothes, and we all turned around as he pulled on a pair of jeans and a shirt.

"You can turn around now," said Jimmy.

I spun around, smiling. "You look good, Snoopy."

Jimmy laughed. "Thanks, Merlie."

"You're going to need to hem those jeans," I told him. His feet were entirely hidden by the jeans' bottom hem. The shirt was also too big. He looked like a kid trying on his dad's clothes. He was so cute.

"It's fine." Jimmy folded back the sleeves of his shirt. "I don't care that the clothes don't fit. It's me. I'm me again." When he met my eyes, his were brimming with tears. "Thank you," he said, freely crying now. "This would never have happened if you hadn't accepted the job at the hotel. You gave me back my life."

"Ah, hell," I said, my eyes and throat burning. "Now you're going to make me cry." Shit. Now I was crying too. Big, thick tears poured out of my eyes, like the emotions of the past weeks just starting to make their appearance.

"I'm already crying," said Elsa as she grabbed Jimmy into a hug, which had his head smacking into her armpit.

"Me too," said Jade as she squeezed herself into their hug. After another squeeze, Jade released her hold and stepped back. "Who wants coffee?"

"Me," I said, suddenly realizing how tired I was.

"I'll have one too," said Jimmy, his eyes round with excitement. "I haven't had a coffee in... more than sixty-eight years."

Damn. The poor man hadn't had food or anything to drink all this time. Damn that Auria. I was pretty sure I hated her even more now.

We all watched in silence as Jimmy accepted a steaming cup of hot coffee and took a sip. When he started to cry, hell, we all started to cry again. Damn, what a day.

"I wish Cedric were here to see Jimmy," said Elsa, rubbing her locket.

"How long were you married?" I asked her, guessing she was talking about her dead husband.

Elsa blinked some tears from her eyes. "Thirty-seven years. He loved Jimmy. He would have been so happy to see him like this. The two were very close."

"What happened to him?"

"He died in his sleep. Healers say it was a heart attack."

I felt a heavy pang in my chest. "I'm sorry, Elsa."

Elsa sniffed as she leaned over and popped open the vintage locket. "He's always with me." And there, resting inside the locket, was a lock of brown hair.

"He had good hair," I told her, my chest squeezing at her smile.

"He did." Elsa snapped the locket shut and kept her hand on it, visibly shaking from a rush of emotions. She cleared her throat. "You hungry, Jimmy?" she called out. "I'll make you anything you want. Just say it."

Jimmy grinned. "Bacon and eggs would be great."

293

Elsa flashed him a smile. "Consider it done."

A few minutes later, rumors of Jimmy's miraculous transformation spread throughout the thirteenth floor, and soon my apartment was filled with every single tenant on that floor.

"It's nice to meet you man to man," said an older paranormal man whose name I couldn't remember.

"You're just as cute as you were when you were that dog," said Barb.

"You're short," chorused the twins.

My heart swelled with emotion again. Just seeing Jimmy's happy human face made everything okay.

And then my heart started to speed up, not because of Jimmy, but because of the big, husky man who just sauntered in.

Valen walked into my apartment, all smiles, as he shook Jimmy's hand and, with the other, gave him a manly pat on the shoulder.

I traced my eyes slowly over the giant—yes, the giant. It was still mind-blowing. I took him in. All in. My eyes grazed over him very, very slowly. I saw the confidence, the strength in those broad shoulders and muscular arms, and that hard chest I'd been lucky enough to feel with my face.

"Oh good. You're still here."

I turned around to see Basil standing behind me. "Yeah. I haven't packed yet." I was so tired. I was hoping they'd let me sleep off some of the exhaustion. But it didn't look like it. "I'll be gone in an hour. If that's why you're here."

Basil shook his head, and I noticed the bags

under his eyes. He hadn't slept yet either. "It's been a rough night." He blinked at me. "I'm told you were the one who found Raymond and defeated him."

"I found him on the roof. But we all defeated him. Well... his demons."

"But you closed the Rift."

I nodded. "I did."

"So Elsa told me," said the hotel manager. "Never imagined Raymond would do this. I thought he liked his job. I thought he liked me."

"Pretty sure he hated you."

"I know that now." The short witch exhaled. "What a disaster."

"At least you were able to stop Adele and her plans to destroy the hotel."

Basil frowned and stroked his beard with his fingers. "Yes. I'm glad *that* is over. Glad I still have a job."

I pursed my lips. "Good for you, I guess." What the hell did he want? A pat on the back?

Basil cleared his throat. "I'm sorry I fired you. It was a bit hasty. I wasn't myself."

"We were all under a lot of pressure," I told him.

The hotel manager sighed. "Well, if you'll reconsider working for us, the hotel would like to extend a permanent position."

My pulse raced. "Really?"

The witch smiled at me. This time it was a true, genuine grin. "We owe you a lot. The owners feel that having you here full-time would put their minds at ease. They want a Merlin assigned to the hotel permanently."

"And Valen?" I asked. "I know the hotel hired him. I don't want to take his job."

Basil waved a hand at me. "No, no, no. Your jobs might be interlinked, but we need you both. You each have different responsibilities. So, what do you say?"

"Yes. I'll take it. Thanks." I shook his hand when he offered it.

Basil gave me a nod and walked away. I watched him make his way around the paranormals to Jimmy.

I stood for a moment, emotions high, as I felt a sense of pride and joy mixing with a sense of relief. Faces blurred as I cast my gaze around them, their voices distant, like hearing them from a radio far away.

I got my job back.

I felt eyes on me and darted my gaze back to where Jimmy was. Valen was watching me from across the apartment and gave me one of his drool-worthy smiles.

My heart sped up as I found myself incapable of looking away. I smiled back as a fluster rushed through me at the memory of our kiss, practically hitting me in the face. Those dark eyes had held both a promise and a desire.

Valen, the rude guy I'd bumped into on the street, turned out not so bad after all. He was a rare race of paranormal—a giant, watcher, and protector, and he'd done just that. He'd saved my ass twice.

We held each other's gaze for a moment, my body prickling and reacting to the heat between us.

Damn. Damn. Damn.

I didn't want to be in a relationship with anyone at the moment, not after the years I'd spent in a bad marriage. I wanted time alone. To be myself. Time for me. I didn't want to get involved with someone who clearly had some serious baggage.

But then… then there was Valen.

Yup, I was definitely in trouble.

After dealing with Rifts and demons, I thought I'd get a few days off. But I was wrong.

Guests avoid The Twilight Hotel like the plague after the teeny-weeny demon invasion. To keep the hotel from financial ruin, management decides to host a Casino Week to get things going again. Sounds great. There's just one problem. People in our paranormal community turn up dead.

So when a new nemesis stirs things up in New York City, it's up to me to settle the score. And I'm ready for them.

Don't miss the next book in the Witches of New York series!

BOOKS BY KIM RICHARDSON

THE WITCHES OF HOLLOW COVE

Shadow Witch

Midnight Spells

Charmed Nights

Magical Mojo

Practical Hexes

Wicked Ways

Witching Whispers

Mystic Madness

Rebel Magic

Cosmic Jinx

Brewing Crazy

WITCHES OF NEW YORK

The Starlight Witch

Game of Witches

Tales of a Witch

THE DARK FILES

Spells & Ashes

Charms & Demons

About the Author

Kim Richardson is a *USA Today* bestselling and award-winning author of urban fantasy, fantasy, and young adult books. She lives in the eastern part of Canada with her husband, two dogs, and a very old cat. Kim's books are available in print editions, and translations are available in over seven languages.

To learn more about the author, please visit:

www.kimrichardsonbooks.com

Printed in Great Britain
by Amazon